THE
ILLEGAL
AND THE
REFUGEE
AN AMERICAN LOVE STORY

THE ILLEGAL AND THE REFUGEE
An American Love Story

Quand on n'a que l'amour
A s'offrir en partage
Au jour du grand voyage
Qu'est notre grand amour
Quand on n'a que l'amour
Mon amour toi et moi
Pour qu'éclatent de joie
Chaque heure et chaque jour
Quand on n'a que l'amour
Pour vivre nos promesses
Sans nul autre richesse
Que d'y croire toujours…

Jacques Brel
From the song : « Quand on n'a que l'amour »

TABLE OF CONTENTS

PART I

PART II

PART III

PART I

ARIZONA

They didn't even know that they were less than a thousand yards from Arizona's Route 86 when they fell and died. One right after the other, not more than a minute apart at the most, on their knees at first and then on their faces and a small puff of Sonoran Desert dust rose above their heads as they impacted the soil. The temperature was close to 100 degrees and it was only 9:30 a.m. In a way, they had made it—to the U.S., that is—so close yet so far, and so cruel and so heartbreaking. That's the way it had ended for them, poor disillusioned souls, desperate enough for a better life to actually try to walk across a boiling desert in the middle of July.

They had travelled a long way, Eduardo Olmeda and his two companions, Arturo and Mauricio, all the way across Mexico from the southeast, to a small northwestern town on the Mexican side of the U.S. border. The town's bars were filled with smugglers and criminals of all kinds, so it hadn't been hard to find someone to help them cross illegally into the U.S.

The guy they found was Vincente Carrillo, and they had met him at the second bar they had gone to. Actually he had approached them—he had seen them walk in, timidly looking about, and he had known right away that they would be easy marks. He had walked over to them and introduced himself, shaking their hands and smiling warmly. He had only one good eye and Eduardo had tried hard not to stare at the other one, the glass one, but he couldn't help but look at it. It was of a dull hazy gray and so cold and unnatural that it gave him a sinister air, scary almost. A cigarette hung loosely from the corner of his mouth as he checked them out, and wisps of smoke curled slowly in front of his unblinking glass eye. He looked them over quickly and they seemed like three university students to him. He was good at that, Vincente, sizing people up rapidly. Where he came from it was the first thing you learned, if you wanted to survive. He was right about them, of course, that's exactly what they were, three young puppies, green and inexperienced and so out of place in that bar, they stuck out like an ugly scab on a swollen lip.

Vincente smiled a lot and quickly engaged in small talk, ordering shots of tequila and trying to make them feel comfortable. Eduardo downed his shot and nervously glanced sideways at his two companions, and then leaned towards Vincente and made their business known to him. Vincente stared at him with his one good eye, his face emotionless, and he nodded his head gravely up and down as if he were pondering what Eduardo had just told him. He slowly put on his dust-covered hat and motioned to them to follow him outside.

He was a mountain of a man, Vincente, at least six foot six and powerfully built. His arms and chest were massive and he could have taken any one of them out with just one arm for sure, or maybe even the three of them all at once, but it was not something Eduardo and his two companions were eager to find out. He wore a faded sleeveless shirt and walked with a swagger, and his worn and smudgy cowboy boots fell heavily on the used and crooked wooden floor of the bar as he made his way out.

Eduardo and his two companions followed him meekly outside, eyes darting from side to side and arms hanging uncomfortably at their sides. He led them into a dirty, garbage-filled alley and that's where the deal was made, the deal that would seal their fate.

At the end of the alley Vincente stopped and turned around to face them.

"So, you want to cross over into the U.S., eh?" He asked with his thick arms crossed and a stern expression on his face. Eduardo answered for the three of them.

"Yes, that's what we want; do you know anybody who can get us across…any *coyotes*?" Eduardo turned his head sideways towards his companions, smiling nervously. He was fidgety and intimidated by Vincente and he hoped it didn't show too much. Vincente pretended not to notice his trepidation.

"Well, I can get you across, no problem, how much money do you have?" His good eye looked straight into Eduardo's, unwavering.

Eduardo was surprised by the question, and he turned towards his two companions again, who had lowered their heads and were shuffling their feet about nervously.

"We have enough, how much does it cost?" He said with a touch of bravado, as he turned to face Vincente.

Vincente remained silent for what seemed like a very

long time, looking him over and shifting his weight from one leg to the other.

"Well," he finally said after clearing his throat, "because you are three and you seem like good guys, I will make you a special deal and instead of the usual two thousand five hundred dollars each, I will only ask you for two thousand dollars each and that's a very good price, believe me, you won't find anybody who will do it for less around here, that's for sure."

Eduardo's heart sank. Even at the reduced price it was more than all the money they had left between them, and he knew that none of them could call home to ask their parents for money. As for turning back, it was simply out of the question. He looked timidly towards Vincente and said,

"We've got four thousand dollars between us, that's all we got and that's all we can pay."

Vincente nodded his head gravely. Eduardo's answer was exactly what he had hoped it would be. He smiled and adopted a friendly posture in an effort to appear warm and sympathetic.

"Ok look, I'll tell you what, even if you don't have enough money to pay for the passage, I have a way that maybe I can help you with that. But you will have to do something for me in exchange." Eduardo looked at him and frowned, wary of what was coming next.

"And what would that be?" He asked hesitantly.

Vincente looked around as if he wanted to make sure no one was listening, and he leaned towards him and lowered his voice,

"Well, it's very simple really, all you have to do is carry a backpack into the desert across the border, each one of you that is—but don't forget that it will be nighttime and it's pitch black out there and no one will be around to spot you. Then all you have to do is walk a few hours, drop off the backpacks under a tree and then walk away. It's as simple as that, nothing to it really. There's a tracker device in one of the backpacks and they'll be picked up by my people the following day. Look, I've done this before, hundreds of times, it's that easy, believe me." Eduardo stared at him intently, in shock at what Vincente was implying. He understood that this meant drugs and he knew how serious that was. He turned towards his companions again. They both had grave expressions on their faces and were obviously as uncomfortable and nervous as he was about what they had just heard. He slowly turned his head in Vincent's direction and there was an uneasy wavering in his voice when he spoke.

"Well, I don't know, Vincente… I'm not sure about this, I mean, this is not something we had thought about doing and we'll have to talk about it, you know, between us." He motioned towards his two companions, who both shook their heads in approval. Vincente raised his hands and put on his warmest and most sincere smile,

"Hey, sure guys, I understand that, no problem. So what I'll do is let you discuss this between yourselves and when you've made up your minds, I'll be in the bar, ok?" He pointed towards the bar and began to walk out of the alley. As he left, he paused beside Eduardo and whispered,

"Just remember, whatever you do, this conversation stays between us, ok?" He was looking down at Eduardo, and the menace in his eye sent a shiver down the younger man's spine.

"Yes, of course, complete silence, I swear—we all do."
Eduardo turned towards his two friends, who both
acquiesced vigorously with their heads even though they
had not heard what Vincente had said to him. They had felt
the vibe and had instinctively known that the only good
answer they could give was an affirmative one.

"Ok, good then," Vincente began to walk away.
Eduardo looked in the direction of his two somber-faced
friends and he took a split-second decision, the worst split-
second decision of his entire life. He called out to Vincente
before he had walked out of the alley.

"Ok, yes, we'll do it." Vincente took a deep breath and
looked up to the sky and smiled, and he slowly turned
around and walked back towards them. He came up to
Eduardo and hovered over him, close enough for Eduardo
to smell his foul breath.

"You sure?" He whispered under his breath.

"Yes, I'm sure," Eduardo answered, looking straight at
him without glancing at either of his companions. He was
too scared that they would contradict him.

"Ok, then," Vincente smiled, and there was a twinkle of
satisfaction in his eye.

So the deal was made. It was agreed they would give
him all of their money, minus fifty dollars each. He would
equip them with food and water and everything else they
needed to cross the desert, and he would arrange for their
pickup in the U.S. and their transportation to L.A. He
warned them not to talk to anybody else about their
arrangement. He came closer to them when he said that.
They formed a circle around him, and he looked about the
alley suspiciously and whispered,

"There are criminals everywhere around here, murderers and robbers and you have to be very careful. Trust no one and especially not the *coyotes;* they are the worst of the worst and all liars. All they want to do is steal your money and leave you to die in the desert. You have to be very careful who you deal with, very careful, there are many bad people around here. Believe me, I know, I have suffered because I wasn't careful." He pointed to his glass eye and looked at them gravely. "But you, my friends, you are the lucky ones, you have found me and I will help you and protect you." He broke out into a smile, and then took each of their hands and shook it vigorously. Eduardo let his hand be shaken as he looked Vincente over in stunned silence. He was not sure what he had just gotten himself and his friends into. He had misgivings about Vincente and was concerned about the whole enterprise, but still he went along, not because Vincente was trustworthy, but because, like his friends, he was young and inexperienced and he wanted to believe what the huge man was saying—and more than anything else, he desperately wanted to get across the border and into the U.S.

They all headed back to the bar and Vincente bought them some beers and a few shots of tequila, and after a while they all relaxed and things lightened up a bit. Eduardo and his friends had a few good laughs about school, and they talked about what they would do once they got to L.A. Vincente just looked at them and smiled knowingly. Tomorrow his business with them would be done.

That's what he did, Vincente, that was his line of work, to find people like Eduardo and his two friends and to give them what they wanted, in exchange for what he needed them to do. It was not an easy job and it took some ability, but he was good at it and he enjoyed the rush when he succeeded. Most of all, though, he enjoyed the deception.

He had not had an easy life, Vincente, and he had learned very young to fend for himself. He had never known who his father was, and his mother had been a junkie and a prostitute. His childhood had been spent waiting outside dirty infested rooms while his mother did a customer, or drugs, and he had more or less raised himself alone. His criminal career had started early, and at thirteen he began to steal and to hang out with the wrong people. He quickly became violent, beating up anybody who looked at him funny or got in his way. Soon he had made a name for himself on the street, and by the time he was eighteen he had become a full-fledged member of a notorious street gang. The gang, which specialized in illegal immigration and drug smuggling, was well known for its excessive violence and acts of cruelty and revenge— Vincente fit right in with them. He felt secure in their vicious company and he appreciated the camaraderie and loyalty that existed among the gang members. To him, the ferociousness and brutality that resided at the heart of the gang's core was confirmation of how the world was and how it should be.

By the time he was twenty he had become a ruthless killer, not just for the gang, but for his own personal pleasure too, and the personal part of it had ended him up in jail. He did fourteen years' hard time in a Mexican jail— fourteen years for three prostitutes he had brutally raped and murdered and whose bodies he had desecrated and defiled. It cost him plenty. He had been beaten, stabbed, and had lost an eye in a fierce prison brawl, but he had survived. Those prostitutes were just the three they had caught him for. There were a lot more of course, but he hadn't told them about the others, even though the cops had beaten him repeatedly and nearly killed him during his interrogations. He hated cops, almost as much as he hated whores.

"Fucking scumbags, they are the real criminals, rotten bastards, one day I'll kill myself a few of them," he used to say to himself in the confines of his cell, even though he had known even at the time that he would never act on that threat. To kill a cop in Mexico was more than trouble and more than jail, it was a bullet in the back of the head somewhere in the desert and an unmarked hole in the sand for a grave. So he had kept his hatred to himself while he was in jail, storing it for later, for when he got out, and for when he would have the chance to get even, on something, or on someone.

When he did get out of jail, the gang set him up in business up north, near the border. His job was to get drugs across the border by any means he could, and he quickly became very good at that. He was very creative, he knew how to get people to do what he needed them to do. There was never a shortage of people showing up who wanted to cross into the U.S. So it was easy for him to find mules for his drugs, mules that he either tricked or cajoled or threatened into doing what he wanted them to do. He was a scary man and his threats were always taken seriously. As for the authorities, well, they were all on the payroll and conspicuously absent from the area most of the time, and

Vincente knew how to take full advantage of that.

All in all, he was content with his life and he had everything that he wanted and lacked for nothing. Whenever he had an urge to kill a prostitute, he would take an overnight trip to Ciudad Juarez. It was the only reason that he went there. He hated whores intensely, and he loved "to do one once in a while." He had become smart and careful about it, though. He always wore gloves and disguised himself, and he always acted under the cover of darkness. He was very meticulous and cautious on how he went about his business. Going back to jail was certainly not something that he wanted to do. He would choose his victims carefully, making sure that the girl had a room where he could be alone with her and that no one saw them together.

Once he got inside the room, he would waste no time in doing what he had come to do, although it was never fast enough or violent enough for his taste. The second the door was closed he would grab the girl by the throat with one of his powerful hands and pin her brutally against a wall, lifting her up slowly with her feet thrashing about wildly, and then he would watch her struggle and turn slowly white as he strangled her with just one hand. The suddenness of his method always knocked the wind out of them, and they never made much noise. Sometimes they would try to hit him with their hands or kick him, but they never did much damage, and he would just apply more pressure and then observe them as they dangled at the end of his arm, fighting frantically and hopelessly for their lives. Sometimes he would finish them off by beating them to death with the closed fist of his other hand, so that the bone-crunching thud of his powerful fist landing in the girl's face was the only sound that filled the room. He loved the sound of crushing bone and the sight of gushing blood as it spurted on all sides, it excited him and augmented his pleasure. Sometimes he would stop his hammering for a second or two and stare sadistically into the terror-stricken eyes of the half-dead girl and flash a depraved smile at her, before resuming his ruthless pounding.

When they were dead, he would lay them down on the floor and proceed to punch hundreds of holes in their bodies with a large, thick-bladed knife. He loved to kill them like that, mean and dirty, and to dishonor their "filthy fucking whore bodies." When he was done, he would wash the blood from his hands and clothes and then take a few minutes to catch his breath and to let the adrenaline and the excitement of the kill leave his body. Then he would discreetly slip back into the night and drive away. The cops were not something he worried about too much. As far as he was concerned, they were too lazy and too incompetent to put two and two together. "And anyway," he would say to himself, "what's the life of a whore worth in Mexico, eh? Nothing, that's what it's worth, nothing at all."

The night following their first meeting, Vincente had driven Eduardo and his two companions up a dirt road in his battered pickup truck with all the lights extinguished, to within a short distance of the fence that separates Mexico from the U.S. border. Eduardo and Mauricio had sat up front with Vincente and he had explained to them as they drove cautiously along why no *coyotes* were crossing with them into the States.

"Well, this is the main reason why I can charge you so

little and also, you don't need anyone, you have the GPS device that I gave you. It will lead you to where you have to drop off the backpacks, and then to my associates the next evening. They will pick you up and bring you to safety in L.A." He had words and explanations for everything. "And don't worry about the backpacks, they are a bit heavy, but you guys are young and in shape, and you'll only be carrying them for a few hours, you'll see, it will be done very quickly." Eduardo looked over his shoulder and saw the three large black backpacks on the floor of the pickup truck. They looked ominous and foreboding to him. Sitting on the floor in the near corner and staring at them was a very concerned and worried Arturo.

They had all been reticent about carrying the drugs, and had argued a lot about it that morning. Arturo was particularly opposed to it, but Eduardo and Mauricio had succeeded in convincing him, certain that it was their only chance at getting across the border quickly. After a heated argument, Arturo had finally relented and had reluctantly gone along with the plan.

"This is the best route, guys," Vincente continued his reassurances. He knew how to fill the void created by the tension of the situation—he had done this often, and was good at it. "The U.S. agents don't patrol in this area and it's an easy walk, you'll see. You don't have to worry about anything, I've done this hundreds of times, there's nothing to it." Eduardo and Mauricio were only half listening; both were lost in their thoughts and scared out of their minds. Eduardo could feel Mauricio's leg shaking involuntarily against his own.

When they reached their destination, Vincente gave

each one of them a ration of food and water, and handed a small compass to Eduardo.

"This is in case you have a problem with the GPS. Just remember to always walk north," he whispered in the darkness to Eduardo, "and don't worry about the food and water, you'll have plenty left when you get to L.A., trust me." The mention of L.A. reassured him. "Also, you have to travel light, you want to be fast out there," he smiled. And Eduardo believed him, what else was there to do at this point?

Vincente was lying, of course, about everything. The real reason he wanted them to travel light was that the backpacks were very heavy. The safe arrival of those backpacks for pick up in the U.S. was more important to him and his partners than the lives of Eduardo and his friends, it was as simple as that. The backpacks, which had a tracking device in them, had to be dropped off under a tree or some bushes after exactly four hours of walking, not more, Vincente had insisted a lot on that. "This is very important, guys, check the GPS regularly, you have to drop these off at the right time and also, you don't want to have them with you when you rest after the first night of walking, now, do you?" They had all nodded yes. "The quicker we get rid of these backpacks, the better," Eduardo had thought.

The last instructions Vincente gave them were about their own pick up.

"Now, once you've dropped off the backpacks, you just keep walking until the sun comes up, and then you stop and find a place to hide and to stay out of sight. You only resume your walk when it gets dark again that evening. At the end of the third night of walking, you find a place to lay low for the day and wait for my people to come and pick you up after sundown. Do not move and do not make a sound during the day, as the border patrol is in that area and they are looking for people like you, understand?" They all nodded their heads and shifted about nervously on their feet, as they were anxious to get on their way. "Ok then, off you go, and good luck." The three companions lifted the heavy backpacks onto their backs and then filed silently past Vincente and onto the trail that led into the desert and towards the border. Vincente watched them disappear into the darkness and smiled, happy with his work.

That first night of walking was excruciatingly difficult, especially during those first four hours when they carried the heavy backpacks. Even though it was nighttime, it was July and it was still very hot out and the air was thick and difficult to breath. They were sweating profusely, and they stumbled along the rugged trail in the darkness and fell a few times, scraping their hands and knees and pricking themselves often on the cholla cactus bushes. There was a lot of cussing and grunting, and they were all relieved when Eduardo finally gave the signal that it was time to drop the backpacks off. It had been four long hours of backbreaking and difficult walking, and they were all out of breath and drenched in their own sweat.

After a short twenty-minute break which barely allowed them to catch their breath, Eduardo got up, and his two companions did the same. Nobody wanted to stay a minute longer than they had to close to the backpacks. They resumed their walk for another grueling five hours, and even though it was a bit easier without the backpacks to carry, it was still very difficult and physically demanding work. When the sun began to rise, they found a good hiding place in a thicket of bushes and let themselves fall to the ground, exhausted and out of breath. It was not very comfortable because of the heat, and they nodded in and out of sleep.

It was the heat that woke them up a few hours later. The day was a scorching hot one, and even though they were in the shade and didn't move or make any kind of effort, it was difficult to breath. The heat was excruciating; it crushed and suffocated them and burned their faces with its blistering presence. It felt like they were in an oven and were being broiled alive. They were in great pain all day, and their sweltering predicament was a lot worse than any one of them could have ever imagined it would be. It sapped at their strength and resolve, and fear entered their hearts. Eduardo even caught himself wondered if they would come out of the desert alive.

Arturo had been the first to go, at the end of the third night of walking. They had just reached the pick up point as indicated by their GPS, and day was breaking. The sun was up on the horizon and the heat was already upon them. They had just stopped, and Eduardo and Mauricio had let themselves drop heavily to the ground at the foot of a large Palo Verde tree, when suddenly and without warning, Arturo had become delirious, foaming at the mouth, eyes turned upside down, shouting and laughing out loud like a mad man. He had lost control of his bowels and fallen dead before they had time to think, do, or say anything.

Eduardo ran over to his friend and fell on his knees in the sand, searched for a pulse, but was unable to find one.

He knew it was hyperthermia, or heat stroke, as people called it. He had read an article about it in a medical magazine at university and he remembered it well, as it had struck him at the time. The article had said that when humans were exposed to extreme heat, the body's cooling system got overstressed and the internal temperature could soar to 107 or more. Blood pressure would plummet, vital organs fail, and then there would be cramps, nausea and exhaustion and very quickly, a sudden and agonizing death. Eduardo turned to look in Mauricio's direction. He was staring at the fallen Arturo with a stunned look on his face, and neither one of them spoke. There was nothing to say. He slowly walked back towards Mauricio and sat down heavily under the tree and let out a long, deep sigh.

The shock of Arturo's death had a devastating effect on them. They were drained, physically and emotionally, they were exhausted from the walking and the heat, and now this had happened. They fully realized as they stared at Arturo's crumpled body that there was a very real possibility that they would be next. They didn't get much sleep on that third day of lying low, because of the heat mostly, but also because of the presence of Arturo's body only a few feet away. It was beginning to decompose because of the heat, and it smelled badly. When they did manage to nod off for short periods of time, the heat and the smell would wake them from their intermittent slumber. As the sun began to set at the end of the day, Eduardo became more and more worried about their predicament. They were out of food and down to a few drops of water, and he began to fear that no one was coming to pick them up.

They waited a long time for their pickup, but as Eduardo had anticipated, none came. Just before midnight, he got up, and Mauricio slowly got up too. Neither of them had to say anything—both of them knew what they had to do, and that was to start walking. Eduardo threw the GPS device into the bushes in disgust, and took out the compass Vincente had given him. He was convinced now that Vincente had sent them out into the desert to deliver his drugs and to die, and he was determined not to let that happen.

They hadn't buried Arturo because they were too weak to dig, but Eduardo had fashioned a makeshift cross and had mumbled a prayer of some kind, partly for the benefit of Arturo, but also for himself and Mauricio, as he was scared that they too would die like him in the desert.

They began to walk north, following the indications of the compass, and as they silently passed Arturo's corpse, Eduardo noticed that the flies had already begun their swirling dance over his inanimate body, the morbid dance that flies have been doing since time immemorial, and the irrefutable indication that a person has passed from this world.

They walked slowly and silently that fourth night, heading north. Eduardo hoped that they would eventually come upon a village or a town or some sign of civilization, and he prayed it would be soon, because without food or water, he knew they wouldn't last long. There was no wind, and the air was immobile and suffocating. Every step they took was more difficult than the one before, and every hour of walking became more and more laborious. They were beyond tired, at the limit of their strength, and they didn't speak much during that last night, even when they stopped every so often to catch their breath and to regain some strength. They pushed on and walked all night, and when the sun began to point itself on the horizon, they kept on walking. They were advancing more and more slowly now, and Eduardo fell to his knees a few times. Each time it was harder to get back up, and he only succeeded in doing so by repeating to himself over and over again, "I have to make it, I have to make it, I just have to make it."

He was surprised by his own stamina and strength; he was not a physical man, and never had been. He had never liked sports or physical activities. It was not his thing. He was more of an intellectual, book-reading type of person. "Who would have guessed that I would last so long in this hellhole?" he asked himself. "Certainly not Vincente Carrillo, that's for sure." He laughed out loud, and even though he knew it was silly to laugh considering his situation, it felt good. He was taken aback by the hoarseness of his own voice. He looked up to the sky where the light of day was beginning to appear, and its brightness hurt his bloodshot eyes. His hair was disheveled and his lips were cracked and dry, and he tried to laugh again, but the only sound that came out of his mouth was short-winded and sounded more like a croak than anything else.

Mauricio had been walking behind Eduardo and he was having difficulties, too. He had fallen on his knees a few times, but had always managed to get up and keep going. Now he fell again, and this time the whole length of his body crashed heavily into the sand. He did not have the strength to get up, and it was with great difficulty that he lifted his sand-caked face in the direction of the slow-moving and vacillating Eduardo who was walking twenty or thirty feet ahead of him. His head felt like it was on fire and about to explode, and he tried to call out to Eduardo, but no sound came out of his parched mouth. He raised his hand in a final attempt to communicate, just as the last bursts of life left his body and his head fell heavily back onto the sand, sending up a small cloud of dust into the air.

A few moments later, Eduardo turned and saw his friend lying face down in the desert. He knew that he was dead—he didn't have to go over to see, he just knew. A tear rolled down his cheek, and he turned around. The sight of Mauricio lying that way was just too much for him to bear. Anger began to build up inside of him, like the foreboding winds and the dark ominous clouds of an approaching storm, and he raised a fist to the sky and shouted,

"Why God, why?" He fell to his knees, and tears made clear paths as they trickled down the cheeks of his dust-covered face. He was beaten and he knew it. The desert had won. "How could I have been so stupid as to believe that bastard Vincente, how could I? Oh Mama, Papa, please forgive me, I love you, I'm so sorry, so sorry." The last image that flooded in his mind as the dizziness took hold of him and he fell toward the desert floor was that of Maria, the love of his life, sweet and tender Maria. He smiled at her just before his face crashed into the desert sand, extending his lips in a final attempt to kiss her one last time, before his eyes closed for eternity.

Eduardo and Mauricio lay where they had fallen, their faces imprinted in the Sonoran Desert sand, saliva slowly leaking from their open mouths. The sun and the heat would soon do its work on their bodies, and then the flies and the maggots would move in and quickly begin their grisly task. Dead bodies deteriorated fast in the desert because of the heat and the sun, and of course there were the coyotes. For them it was a free meal, they didn't mind the smell or the maggots and they would do their business to the corpses as soon as they found them. They were very efficient at that, and generally left only scattered body parts for the U.S. authorities to puzzle over, if they should find anything at all.

That same morning, Vincente was in high spirits as he drove his battered pickup truck down a dusty and empty Mexican country road, his radio blaring out a *corridos*, lamenting the hardships of crossing the border into the U.S.

"Oh I know all about the hardships of crossing the border, ha, ha, yes sir I do, ha, ha," he laughed hoarsely. He had one hand on the wheel and a cigarette hung loosely from the corner of his mouth. He always let his cigarette hang from the left side of his mouth, because the billowing smoke from the lit cigarette didn't bother his artificial eye. Hot ash fell on his chest through his open shirt and it stung a bit, but he paid it no mind. He had received word the night before that the shipment he had sent with the three students had been picked up, and he was glad about that.

"Can you believe those idiots," he shouted, "they actually paid me to have them bring drugs into the U.S., not a lot of money, but still, all the money they had and their reward for their trouble is to probably die in the desert, go figure, eh? Stupid fucking morons, they bloody well deserve to die for being that dumb, ha, ha, ha, ha, ha." He pushed his hat up on his forehead and smiled maliciously, and the sun reflected eerily against his glass eye. He was feeling good about things, he had done well for himself and he hadn't even thought about killing a whore for some time.

"I need a fucking tequila," he shouted over the music, "tequila and pussy, ha, ha… that's what I fucking need." He banged his hand on the dashboard and roared, "…ha, ha, ha, tequila and pussy, yeah," and made a sharp turn on the dirt road and headed towards the town and its bars and whorehouses. His one good eye was filled with an uncommon craziness. Sweat poured down the side of his face, and his large arm, leaning out the truck's open window, was shimmering with perspiration in the brilliant sunlight.

It was an uncanny sight, a shouting, laughing, one-eyed monster of a man, slamming his thick hand violently on the dashboard of his beat-up pickup truck, in rhythm to the fiery music belching from tin-sounding speakers and barreling down a dirt road at full speed, leaving behind him a cloud of dust that plumed skyward. Everything was there, around and all about him, the beauty and the brutality, the vastness and the proximity, the old and the new, the dead and the deadly, the eternal and the finite, and one could almost feel the footprints of the maker and the shadow of the devil as the sun rose swiftly, over the silent and unforgiving desert.

MEXICO CITY

Eduardo Olmeda was from Veracruz City, a southeast port north of the Yucatan. His father, like his own father before him, was a dock worker, and he earned his living unloading ships, ten or twelve hours a day, six days a week in the sweltering heat. It was back-breaking work, but Armando Olmeda never complained—he had no education and it was a good job, all things considered, and plus, he had a family to feed. He had seven children in all, four boys and three girls, and Eduardo was his eldest son. All of them were in school and growing up under the protective and watchful eye of his strict and loving wife, Alicia. There were many rules to abide by in Alicia Olmeda's impeccable house. She taught her children to be polite and well-mannered, to speak when spoken to, to be clean of their person, respectful of others, and silent when they sat down to eat as a family every evening. She was a devout Catholic and never once missed Sunday mass with her brood. In her active involvement with every aspect of family life, she contrasted greatly with her husband. Armando Olmeda was a taciturn and moody man. He did not speak much or often, but when he did, he instilled fear and respect in his children. Should any one of them have the audacity to disobey his wife or to commit some other unpardonable crime that only children can commit, his thick, leathery hand would come down on the culprit's backside, to sharply remind the child of his authority and exhort that son or daughter to never again cross whatever line had been crossed that day.

Armando had realized early on that his son Eduardo had a propensity for books and for knowledge, and he encouraged him in his desire to learn about the world. Being an uneducated man himself, he wanted more than anything for his son to succeed at school and hopefully one day attend university. Eduardo was a shy, soft-spoken, introverted boy, highly intelligent and sensitive, who excelled at his classes. At a very young age he became interested in the sorts of subjects that usually interested only adults. He was brilliant and quick-witted, and his father was very proud of him. One day, when he was fifteen and sitting outside with his father after dinner, he put his book down and said,

"Papa, someday I will be a journalist and I will write about all the things that are happening in our country and tell the true story of what is going on." His father had looked at him and smiled, admiring his youthful enthusiasm. He had often told him that the media was controlled by the ruling political party, and that they distorted the truth and only told the stories the way they wanted them to be heard. He was happy that, even at such a young age, his son understood the importance of his words.

They were a close-knit family, the Olmedas, and proud of their origins, with their dark, intense eyes, high foreheads and thick black hair like that of their Spanish ancestors. Although they were poor, the children carried themselves with panache, and had an innate grace and sense of propriety that had been instilled in them by their strict and loving parents. Alicia and Armando Olmeda's uncompromising sense of right and wrong, and their love for each other and for their children, were the defining characteristics of their household and of Eduardo's childhood.

When Eduardo left for university, it was an emotional and tearful moment. His mother and sisters cried, but his brothers all smiled at him enviously, happy that he was the first of them to get out into the world. His father stood upright and proud as he watched his son, "his own flesh and blood," leaving on his grand adventure. For Armando, it was a dream come true. He took Eduardo in his arms and hugged him.

"Do well, my son, work hard and make us proud," he said with tear-filled eyes. Eduardo had never seen his father get emotional, and it touched him. He felt tears welling up inside of him, too.

"Yes Papa, I will," he blurted out, and then quickly turned and jumped into the waiting cab. He waved for a long time to all of them, standing outside of their humble home as the cab sped away, and then he turned and looked straight ahead, repeating over and over again in his mind,

"Mexico City, here I come, Mexico City, here I come." He smiled as he wiped the tears from his cheeks, so excited that he had to refrain himself from screaming out loud.

Mexico City, the largest city of the Americas! The sheer size of it amazed Eduardo. He had never seen anything like it. He was impressed by its grandeur and intrinsic beauty, by its surrounding mountains and the sprawling, seemingly endless barrios, and the thick, slow-moving traffic, by the pandemonium, the endless flow of people everywhere, and the scorching heat. He had to take deep breaths at first—not only was Mexico City one of the most polluted cities in the world, but it was also very elevated, and the air was thin. The atmosphere was laden with smog and the air seemed almost toxic to him. The taxi he rode in took him passed the *Angel de la Independencia* on *Paseo de la Reforma*, and he marveled at it, sticking his head out the car window and looked up and around with wide open eyes. It seemed to him that everywhere he looked, there was something new to see and to take in, and it sent his senses into overdrive.

When he reached the university, he was impressed by the size and the architecture of the *Ciudad Universitaria* and by its grounds, teaming with students hurriedly scurrying about. He took it all in, feeling the constant tingling in his body that kept him on edge—he was excited like he'd never been before in his life.

He spent the next few days settling in, working on his course schedule, and finding his way around the huge *Ciudad Universitaria*. In the process, he made some new friends. Like him, Arturo and Mauricio were first year students from Veracruz City. He had recognized their accent while standing in a line in front of them, and the three had struck up a conversation. It had felt immediately as if they were old acquaintances; being from the same city and new at the university had made things easy. Arturo was tall and lanky, with a thick black beard that made him look older than his age, and Mauricio was short and stocky, with a beardless baby face and round, pink, flushed cheeks. When Eduardo thought of them later, he referred to them in his mind as the tall, skinny one and the short, chubby one.

They had beers and ate together that evening. Arturo and Mauricio were as excited as Eduardo was, and they chatted incessantly about the things and the people they saw around them and about how amazed they were with Mexico City. All of them were energized by their new surroundings and the seemingly limitless possibilities the city presented.

Not far from where the three young men were sharing a meal and some drinks, Maria Torres, another first year student, was sitting in a student lounge, busy organizing her first semester at the university. She was going through her course choices and schedule and making a list of the supplies she would need. Maria had worked hard to get there and she was determined to make the most of her time at the university. She was an impulsive and passionate young woman, and a committed social activist. She was very involved in her local community and did a lot of volunteer work. Like most young people, Maria was an idealist, and she had signed up for studies in social and environmental sciences. Once she graduated, she hoped to help the disinherited and the disenfranchised and to do her part for the environment. Heavily influenced by her father, a committed union organizer and activist, Maria had vowed that she would do well at university and make her father proud of her.

"Study, study, study, and no boys and no boyfriends as long as I am in school," she had bravely promised herself. "There will be time for all of that after I graduate." She reaffirmed this position whenever the subject came up in her mind, failing to admit to herself that the real reason she had decided on this radical course of action was because she was still reeling from her breakup with Cesar, her boyfriend of the past two years. "That little cheating bastard," she hissed to herself under her breath. The thought of him made her angry and her face turn red.

Maria came from a large family, and was the third of a brood of twelve. She had been born and raised in one of the poorest *colonias populares*, or barrios of Mexico City. Her father, who had had no formal education, was a manual laborer and a community leader, and was appreciated and well respected by his peers. His left-leaning sympathies were well known, and his vocal and constant denunciations of the ruling party's policies had brought much misery upon himself and his family through the years. Yet he had never faltered and had always stayed the course, remaining true to his convictions and to his beliefs. No matter how many beatings he received or how many jobs he lost, or whatever other afflictions the party in power imposed on him, Victor Torres just got more enraged and more committed to denouncing and destroying the corrupt, authoritarian and unfair one-party system which had ruled Mexico for most of the twentieth century. They were his mortal enemy, and his hatred for the political leadership and its cronies knew no bounds.

Maria grew up in that charged environment, and was impressed at a very young age by her father's determination and courage. He was a passionate man with profound convictions, and Maria grew up to believe what he believed and to be certain that only the truth and nothing else ever came out of his mouth. When he hated, she hated, when he was angry, she was angry, and when he spewed out a litany of complaints about the injustice of the system, she drank in his words and her eyes would light up with all the fire and fervor of youth, fascinated by his verbal fluency and eloquence. He was her hero, and she was the child that was dearest to his heart. They were very close. Without a doubt, her father had been and was the determining influence in her life, and his resolve and tenacity in the face of adversity had contributed greatly to the choices Maria had made and to the person that she was and wanted to become.

In her youth, Maria did not have to go very far to witness the injustices that her father so vehemently denounced. Like sixty percent of Mexico City's residents, the Torres family lived in one of the *colonias populares*. In reality, the neighborhood was nothing more than a slum, where sanitation, clean water, public safety and transportation were a constant preoccupation and crime and violence were as much a part of the community as the thick, soiled air that they all breathed. It was human misery and poverty on a large scale, and Maria had been brought up in it from the day she was born. At a very young age, she had promised herself that she would make something of her life and make a difference in the world. Maria was the type of person who kept her promises, especially the ones that she had made to herself. To help those who could not help themselves and to contribute to making people's lives better were her goals and what drove her forward.

She understood that the first thing she had to do was to get an education, and so she had set her sights on that goal from a young age and had toiled hard towards that end. Sometimes the pain of their acute poverty had been difficult to bear. There seemed to be always something that they were in need of, be it clothes, food or medical supplies, and Maria, like all of her siblings, had had to work throughout her childhood in order to help her father feed the family. This was not something that was optional in the Torres family; everybody had to pitch in.

Life itself had been a constant challenge for Maria, but she had made it and had survived the poverty of her youth. That realization suddenly hit her as she looked up from her laptop and outside at the *Ciudad Universitaria.* It was a marvelous feeling, filling her with pure, unbridled joy. She smiled, breathing in deeply and letting the excitement of the moment enter her body.

They had been attending university for about a month when they met. It had been an awkward moment to say the least, and also a comical one in a way, mostly because of Maria's impulsiveness and quick reactions, which had almost ended their relationship before it had even started. Eduardo had taken the habit of going to the university's library every evening to study. The room he rented was small and stuffy, and he loved to sit in the vast and quiet library. One night he arrived a bit later than usual, and the place was packed. There was only one empty chair at a table, and so he quickly went over and sat down. As he took out his things, he noticed that there was a strikingly beautiful girl sitting at the same table directly in front of him. Her head was buried in her books, and she was writing frantically and paying no attention whatsoever to her surroundings. Eduardo opened a book and tried to concentrate on his studies, but he was unable to do so. He had too much adrenaline pumping through his body, distracted by his environment. He looked around at all the students busy studying or writing and at the magnificent library. He was admiring the splendor of the place when, by chance, his gaze met that of the girl sitting opposite him. She was looking directly at him, and he smiled shyly and his face reddened, not realizing that she was only looking in his general direction, not at him. She made a face and curved her eyebrows downwards, then shook her head in a negative gesture and returned her attention to her books. Eduardo quickly lowered his head, a bit embarrassed, and stared blankly at the open book in front of him.

In the brief instant that she had looked his way, Eduardo had been seized by the girl's beauty. She was a remarkably attractive young woman, with long, shimmering black hair, intense, gleaming black eyes, and finely chiseled features. She had very little make-up on, and was wearing a white cotton blouse that exposed her graceful neck, around which hung a delicate silver chain with a sideways heart clasped to it. She was superb, and Eduardo just could not keep his eyes off her. Inevitably, what was bound to happen happened: she looked up and caught him staring at her. It had always been a mystery to Eduardo how women could feel the eyes of a man on them. It was as if the eyes of a man pointed in their direction physically touched them and they instantly knew it. She lifted her eyebrows and put her pen down, then crossed her hands slowly in front of her and tilted her head sideways in an inquisitive gesture which clearly said, "What the hell are you looking at?" Eduardo felt his cheeks get hot again, and he immediately lowered his eyes, lifting a hand in the air and shaking his head in a movement of apology.

After that, he only dared raise his eyes again for a second or two at a time, pretending to look around while furtively trying to catch fleeting glimpses of the girl. In those brief seconds, he saw that she was busy with her studies and oblivious to him and to his growing interest in her—in an attempt to slyly take another peek at her, he moved his elbow sideways and accidently pushed his heavy textbook from the end of the table. It crashed flatly to the floor, with a very sharp, loud, heart-stopping bang. Maria jumped in her chair, her shoulders stiffened, and she looked around for a few seconds, frozen in place like a terrified hare in the headlights of a car. Everybody was looking up and staring in Eduardo's direction and he looked around, unable to move, his face a deep crimson red. He was more embarrassed than he'd ever been in all of his life. He slowly leaned down to pick up the book, and when he came up and looked in Maria's direction, he saw that she was standing. She was tall and slender, and she was scowling at him with her hands on her hips, obviously angry and very displeased with him.

"What's wrong with you? Don't you know this is a library, that people come here to study?" She shouted. "Can't you just sit there and be silent and stop fidgeting and dropping books on the floor, for God's sake? I nearly had a heart attack, you moron." She was speaking rapidly and firing away, as was her habit when she was ticked off, and everyone in the library had stopped what they were doing and was looking their way. Eduardo was frozen in his chair, unable to speak, and he just stared at Maria with wide open eyes, not knowing what to do or say. He felt terrible. He wanted to crawl under the table. The worst part was that the girl shouting at him a few feet away did not seem like she was going to let up any time soon.

"Well, do you speak, what do you have to say? Are you going to be quiet from now on, or am I going to have to get you evicted from this place so we can all study in peace?" She gestured with her arms to the people around her and held her head high, moving it from side to side, soliciting their approval. Her eyes were lit up, defiant and full of fire, and she stared Eduardo down harshly.

"I'm sorry, miss," he stuttered and sweat began to appear on his forehead. "The book... the book, it fell, and I... I..."

"I know the book fell, you idiot, I heard it," she cut him off ferociously. She wasn't done with him yet. "Now, will you just tell everyone here that you will be quiet from now on and that you will not throw any more books on the floor to get attention, or for whatever other reason you did that?"

"I didn't throw the book on the floor!" Eduardo looked around frantically for approval from the other students. He had also raised his voice a notch. He didn't like being accused of something he hadn't done. Just then, a severe-looking library attendant walked up to them and glared at the two belligerents sternly.

"Is there a problem here?" she asked dryly.

"Yes, there is," Maria immediately took the lead. "This person keeps disturbing everyone, and just now he dropped a book on the floor so loudly that I nearly had a heart attack." She was looking at the library attendant in a way which said, *well, don't just stand there, do something about it!* Eduardo got up and quickly began to gather his things.

"Look, I'm sorry about the disturbance," he said to the

library attendant. "I didn't mean to bother anyone, and certainly not you, miss." He turned and looked at Maria. "I will leave now, and once again, I'm very sorry." Without another word, he turned and bolted towards the exit, eyes riveted to the floor. The library attendant watched him walk away and then looked back towards Maria and lifted her eyebrows slightly. Maria gave her an approving smile and sat back down, satisfied with the outcome of things. The attendant turned and walked briskly away.

Maria smiled, content with her victory, and looked around in satisfaction as everyone got back to their business. As she glanced in the direction from which Eduardo had left, she realized that she had felt something when he had stood up. He was tall and handsome and shy, and mysterious, in a way, and so embarrassed that it was actually comical. Maybe it was his eyes, or his soft voice, or his accent—he was obviously not from Mexico City—or maybe it was because he blushed so much when she looked at him, or that he was cute, or that there seemed to be a sincerity about him and a naïveté... Anyway, something about him tickled her and intrigued her, and plus, she told herself, "He didn't even put up a fight, you can't do that, you have to stand up for yourself." The defender of the underdog in her took over, and she made an instantaneous decision. She grabbed her things quickly and ran in the direction of the exit—and in the direction of the very embarrassed and probably very angry, tall and handsome stranger, whom she had just severely scolded in front of a full library of people.

"Hey, you!" Maria had been running in order to catch up to Eduardo. He had been walking at a brisk pace, but finally he turned around and she caught up to him. As she got close, she saw that he had a perplexed look on his face and that his forehead was creased. He obviously didn't understand why she had run after him, and probably thought that she hadn't finished her verbal thrashing of him. Maria put her hand on his forearm, and he looked down at it and then at her with a questioning look. She had her other hand on her chest and was bending slightly forward, trying to catch her breath.

"Hey, look, I'm sorry...that wasn't cool...back there...you didn't deserve that much abuse, ok? I'm sorry." His eyes grew darker. He was still reeling from the scene at the library, and was surprised by her apology. He opened his mouth as if to speak, but no words came out. There was an awkward silence. Maria let go of his arm and straightened herself up. She was still a bit out of breath.

"Well, what's wrong, did someone eat your tongue?" she asked, mocking him a bit, while smiling warmly in his direction and leaning her head a bit to the side in order to make eye contact. "Look, I get it, you're not a very wordy guy and you don't know what to say, and you're probably very angry at me right now, but I know you can speak—I mean, I heard you say a word or two back there." She pointed towards the library behind her. Her smile and warmer tone were having some effect on him, and he half smiled and half grinned at her, lowering his head and shuffling his feet about nervously. He was intimidated by her beauty and by her potency, and he felt uneasy in her presence. He slowly raised his head and looked in her direction.

"Yes...I speak...," he uttered hesitantly and rather

clumsily. She looked at him, perplexed for a second, and then a large smile broke out on her face and on his too, as they both realized how ridiculous what he had just said was. They both broke out laughing, slowly at first, and then they roared, and the laughter eased the tension between them. "Oh my God," she managed to say through her laughter, "I'm glad you do; for a moment there, I thought you might be mute or something," and then their laughter became uncontrollable and Maria held her sides and Eduardo had to turn around and look away to try to make his laughter subside. It took a few minutes for them to regain their composure, but finally Eduardo turned back around to face her. Her confidence and her splendor were new things for him to observe. He had never met a girl like her before. There had been girls back home, of course, but they had been bland, provincial girls, who had no other ambition in life than to get married and raise a family. Nothing serious had ever happened with any of them. But he sensed that Maria was different, very different. He could feel it in her presence and see it in her eyes, like he had felt it that very first second that he had set eyes on her in the library, only it was stronger and more insistent now, and there was a tingling in his body and an excitement like he had never felt before in his life.

Maria wiped some tears from the corner of her eyes. It had been a long time since she had laughed like that, and with a complete stranger, of all things! She extended her hand in his direction.

"Ok, let's start over. My name is Maria, Maria Torres." He took her hand shyly, and shook it lightly and gently, and Maria noticed how soft his skin was. She held onto his hand for a few seconds more than was usual for people who were introducing themselves.

"I'm Eduardo Olmeda, and I am glad to meet you, Maria Torres," he said, and smiled. He was warming up, finally, and Maria pulled her hand away from his and smiled too. Her eyes stared steadily into his and she felt his sweetness and sincerity.

"You are not from here, Eduardo—not from Mexico City, I mean?"

"No, I come from Veracruz City, and this," he pointed with both his arms in all directions, "this is all new to me. I am discovering new things every day."

"Well, I hope today was not too much of a bad day for you, you know, considering how rude I was back there," she pointed towards the library behind her, a flicker of mischief in her eyes.

"No Maria, you were right, I was distracted and distracting. I just couldn't concentrate tonight! It's just that everything is so beautiful and big," he looked around again, smiling, "and then the book, when it fell to the floor I felt like dying, and I was so embarrassed, and..."

"Yes, I know, and then there's me shouting at you like an insane person, I'm so sorry about that, really I am, it's just that it scared me to death, you know, the noise." He turned his gaze to the ground again as the memory of the incident brought fresh embarrassment to his mind.

"Hey, I tell you what; let's go grab a coffee or something. I'll tell you all about Mexico City and you can tell me everything about Veracruz City. What do you say?" Maria, the extrovert and highly social person that she was, couldn't resist inviting him for coffee. After all, he had made her laugh, and he would be a change from her friends from the city. Plus, he was cute, and she was piqued and intrigued by this clumsy, silent stranger. Actually, she was more than just slightly intrigued, and a lot more piqued than she would have admitted to herself at the time, and although all the alarm bells were going off in her head about the promise she had made to herself about no boys during her studies, she just couldn't help it—her desire to know more about Eduardo and to spend a bit more time with him was stronger than her will to abide by her promise.

"I'd love to have a coffee with you, Maria. I'd like that very much. I really would." He smiled at her and she smiled back, and they stood there for a few seconds, eyes locked into each other. And that's when it happened, they would both agree on that later: it was at that precise moment that they had fallen in love.

From that moment on, they became inseparable and were crazily and irretrievably in love, madly so, frenziedly consuming their tenderness and their youth and feverishly drinking from the cup of life. She loved his occasional clumsiness and sincerity and his shyness and timidity and the sensitivity of his silences, and he was dazzled by her ease around people and her eloquence and by her generosity and the richness of her soul. They quickly became very close and intimate, and spent almost every waking and sleeping hour together, grateful to have found each other and convinced that fate had brought them together.

"Don't you understand, Eduardo, Mexico City is in terrible shape, sixty percent of its inhabitants are poor and live in slums, and the air is un-breathable, and prostitution and crime are rampant!" Maria was in one of her agitated states; her face was glued to her laptop and both of her hands were flailing about in all directions. "There is misery and drugs everywhere, and the politicians are corrupt, and the rich live in gated communities and have bodyguards because traveling through the city is too dangerous, and while all this is going on, the drug lords do as they please and act as if they own the country and we still have *bullfighting*, for Christ's sake. Can you believe that, in this day and age?" Something she had read on the Internet had obviously upset her. Maria was a social media junkie, and she was constantly updating her Facebook page and checking out things on YouTube and various other social media sites and blogs. That's how she kept herself abreast of events and how she interacted with people with whom she had shared interests. Maria was very passionate about Mexico and especially Mexico City, the city that she had been born in and the city where her father was now an elected official of the opposition. Ever since his election, Maria had followed municipal politics like some men follow professional sports. She closed her laptop in a gesture of frustration, crossing her arms and scowling. "God, it's frustrating, everything takes forever and nothing ever changes."

Eduardo put his book down and looked in her direction, and then crawled over to her side of the bed and wrapped his arms around her. He kissed the small of her neck and a single tear rolled down her face.

"I'm sorry," she said, throwing herself into his arms, "it's just that everything makes me angry and I want things to happen and nothing ever does, or just too slowly, and it's driving me crazy."

"Hey," he whispered in her ear, "I love you, you know." She turned and buried her face in his chest.

"I love you too," she said in a muffled voice. She lifted her head and looked up into his eyes and he looked into hers. He smiled, and she smiled back, and just like that, the clouds dissipated and the radiance returned.

"Do you think I'm crazy?"

"No, I think you're very passionate about things, and I think that you care deeply about other people and that you hope to make their lives better. That's why you're studying so hard, and that's also why I love you so much." He leaned down and kissed her forehead.

"Thank you, my love, you are so good to me, nobody understands me like you do, nobody." She moved towards him and brushed her lips with his, closing her eyes, and he could smell her sweetness and taste it on his lips. They kissed again, and she took his mouth fully this time. He responded, and they held onto each other tightly, and the youth in their bodies woke up and they began to feel aroused. All their nerve endings came alive, hungering for release, and like a sudden and powerful summer storm, love came to pass, rumbling and shaking and clearing the way for the magical tranquility that follows it. They lay lazily in bed after, and Maria was comfortably tucked into his arms with her eyes closed and the sunlight poured into the room, illuminating their naked bodies with its purity and blessing them with its grace. Eduardo kissed the top of her head and stared in the direction of the silently spinning ceiling fan and said softly,

"You know, Mexico City has the highest number of museums of any city in the world." He looked down at her with a cunning smile at the corner of his mouth. He always did that to her when she was depressed or angry about something. He would fill her head with positive facts about the city, facts and knowledge that he had only recently acquired and that he would bring into the conversation in order to cheer her up. "And...," Eduardo was about to say something else, but before he could say another word, Maria raised her head and put a finger to his lips and said hurriedly, as a child would when she knows what an adult is about to say, "I know, I know, Frida Kahlo and Diego Riviera lived here and just that makes Mexico City beautiful, eh? Isn't that what you were going to say?" There was a mischievous twinkle in her eyes, and he smiled at her.

"Yes, that's exactly what I was going to say. But, I was also going to say that it's important not to forget that the *Basilica de Nuestra Senora Guadalupe* is an extraordinary and unique site of tremendous historical importance and beauty, and that's just one of the things that makes Mexico City beautiful, just one, and there are so many more, my love, so many, many more." He looked at her, eyes smiling, "and... you know what else is beautiful about Mexico City, my love?" He opened his eyes wide, to emphasize how important his question was, and Maria snuggled up closer to his face, smiling. She knew what he was going to say, but she shook her head naughtily to indicate that she didn't.

"You, my love, you were born here, you were created here, and you are part of this magnificent city, yes, you, my love, my one and only, my all and everything, you whom I love more than anything in the world." He had lowered his voice to practically a whisper, and a chill ran down Maria's spine. She reached up and pecked his lips.

"I love you too, Eduardo Olmeda," she whispered back, "and you make me very happy."

"And you me," he said softly, and they fell asleep that way, locked into each other's arms and caressed by the warm rays of the afternoon sun lazily seeping through the open window.

Their first year of school went by quickly. They both worked very hard and got good results, but summer break was fast approaching and Eduardo would have to leave soon to go back home where his father had found him a job at the docks for the summer. It was a good-paying job and it was money that he needed in order to keep studying, and he had no choice but to go. Maria would stay in the city and work in the office of her father's organization and continue to do her volunteer work. It would be a long, lonely summer for the two young lovers, and the perspective of their separation weighed heavily on both of them.

Maria's father and the rest of her family had taken well to Eduardo, and during the school year she had taken the habit of bringing him home every Sunday for the traditional Torres Sunday lunch. The week before school was due to end for the summer break, Maria and Eduardo went to her parents' house for one last Sunday lunch. Her father loved to sit with Eduardo before and after lunch to discuss things with him. They were interesting verbal sparring partners. Eduardo was very much an intellectual, and was mostly interested in literature, poetry and culture, and Maria's father, the tough activist-turned-politician, was more interested in social issues and his constituents' daily preoccupations. They loved to argue, but beneath the bravado and the teasing they enjoyed each other's company a lot, and would talk for long hours sitting in the shade of the backyard. Victor Torres enjoyed taunting Eduardo about being a dreamer and an idealist who was disconnected from the realities of the world.

"You have to get your head out of the clouds, Eduardo! Come down to earth, my friend; join the human race and get your hands dirty a bit."

"But I do, Mr. Torres. I get my hands dirty too, but intellectually speaking, that is. We can't all be laborers, you know, and there have to be some people whose job it is to think about things. I agree that some of the things I bring up are abstract, but they are important things too."

"Yes, Eduardo, you are right about that, but the problem with you is that you think too much and don't do anything about anything! You just think." Eduardo knew Maria's father was mocking him a bit, and answered with a touch of irony,

"But Mr. Torres, I have Maria for that, you know, for the doing something about things part." Mr. Torres smiled; he knew when he was beaten.

"Ha, ha, touché Eduardo, very well put. I have nothing more to say. You have rendered me silent with your wisdom." They both broke out laughing, and Victor Torres lifted his glass in the younger man's direction.

"To you, Eduardo." Their glasses touched, and Eduardo replied,

"To you, sir, and thank you—thank you for having me in your home, and for Maria. I love her very much, you know." Maria's father looked at him, his eyes luminous, and he smiled and said nothing more.

As was her habit on Sundays, Maria was in the kitchen with her mother preparing the family meal. Her mother was mostly a silent and introverted person who kept to herself and who, contrary to her husband, liked to stay in the background. She preferred to listen and to make up her own mind about people and the situations they got into and then, at an appropriate time and only if she deemed it necessary, she would share her opinion with the person whom it directly concerned. She favored one-on-one communication. Victor Torres had always told Maria when she was growing up that listening carefully to what her mother had to say was a very wise thing to do.

"He is the one, you know," her mother said to Maria while stooping over the kitchen sink and working on some vegetables. She did not stop what she was doing or look up.

"What?" Maria feigned not to understand. Her mother stopped what she was doing and lifted her head and looked in her direction.

"I said, he is the one, Maria. Eduardo, he is the one for you." Maria stopped what she was doing and just looked at her mother. For once in her life, she was speechless. Her mother slowly wiped her hands on a cloth and turned to face her. Putting her hands on each side of Maria's face, she looked her in the eyes and very gently said,

"He's the one, Maria, the one for you. You know that, don't you?" She smiled, and Maria looked at her mother and tears began to fill her eyes. She took her mother in her arms and hugged her.

"Oh, I hope so, Mama. I love him so much, you know."

"Of course you do, sweetheart, of course you do." Her mother ran her hand through Maria's hair affectionately and patted her back. Maria pulled back from her mother's arms and wiped the tears from the corners of her eyes.

"How will I know, Mama? How will I know for sure?" Her mother leaned slightly forward and looked into Maria's eyes.

"That he is the one?" Maria nodded her head, and her mother looked at her and smiled.

"You know already, darling. Now come on, let's get back to work, we have some hungry men to feed." Her mother smiled and turned her attention back to the vegetables. Maria came up behind her and, putting her arms around her, kissed the back of her head and rocked her gently.

"I love you, Mama." Her mother turned around and smiled.

"I love you too, sweetheart. Now come on, back to work."

The separation was very difficult for the young lovers when classes ended for the summer. Many tears were shed, and many promises were made before they parted. They kept in touch by texting each other many times a day and making the occasional phone call, but the distance between them made things complicated and as the interminable months of summer ticked by, the pain of being separated from each other for such a long time became harder and harder to bear.

In Veracruz City, when Eduardo was not working or spending time with his family, he was with Mauricio and Arturo. They three of them had become close friends at university, and like him they had part time jobs and were home for the summer. The three friends hung out together every evening after dinner at their favorite local hangout and they liked to challenge each other about everything and about nothing, as young men will sometimes do. They did not always agree on everything, but that was part of the process. Each one would give his opinion, and there were a lot of healthy and lively discussions, about any subject that came up.

There was one subject, however, that they did agree on, and that was how dire their situation was in Mexico and how grim their prospects were to earn a decent living or to have any kind of future in their country. They all believed that even if they graduated from university with the highest honors, they were inevitably condemned to mediocre, lower-middle-class lives, and that perspective depressed them profoundly. It bothered Mauricio in particular. He was the one who came up with the idea of fleeing to the U.S., making a run for it. At least, he was the first one to say it out loud, and he made that case to them every chance he had. He would insist that they should do it right away, while they were young and in their prime. It was his favorite subject, and as the summer moved along it became the only subject that really interested him. He became obsessed with the idea and was relentless in his attempts to persuade his friends to think likewise. As the summer advanced, his arguments slowly began to sink in and to gain some traction with Arturo and Eduardo. Maybe it was out of boredom, or the appeal of an adventure, or just out of daring, but the idea of fleeing to the U.S. and starting a new life began to take hold in their young and restless minds.

"I'm telling you guys, it's not that difficult, I have family living in L.A. and all we have to do is get across the border—which is not too hard, by the way—and then my relatives will help us get jobs and get organized. I mean think about it, we could start our own business. Can you imagine that? In the U.S., everything is possible, guys, and everyone has a chance to make it—everyone." They had been sitting around all evening drinking beers and shots of tequila, and the alcohol was beginning to do its work.

"Yeah ok, but what about school?" Eduardo asked nonchalantly, even though he knew the answer he was going to get.

"Screw school, Eduardo, what are you going to do with your degree in literature anyway, eh? Teach, become a journalist maybe, a writer, who knows, eh? The only thing that is sure is that you will not have an easy life and you will not have any money to buy the things that you want, not in Mexico anyway, that's for sure. You won't be living Eduardo, you'll be existing."

He was right, of course, Eduardo knew that much, and even though he didn't like to admit it to himself, he was attracted by Mauricio's plan. He was tempted by the picture Mauricio painted, more than a little, actually, and the thing that struck the biggest chord with him was that he desperately wanted to offer Maria the kind of life that he believed she deserved. He knew now that he wanted to marry her and to raise a family with her and to offer her and their children everything they desired, and he did not believe that he would ever be able to do that in Mexico.

Arturo remained silent during these discussions, which took place mostly between Mauricio and Eduardo. He was an amiable person who didn't like arguments and who would most probably end up agreeing with whatever they agreed on. Eduardo looked up from staring at the floor and turned towards Mauricio, gazing straight at him.

"Ok Mauricio, let's pretend I'm interested, ok, and just for a minute, let's assume that Arturo and I had decided to go along. Could you just go through your plan one more time for us, but step by step this time and slowly please?" Mauricio moved forward a bit, looking at Eduardo intensely.

"Ok Eduardo, fine, just listen carefully, it's very simple really."

And so that evening, after many more tequilas and a lot of repetition, the three of them agreed to flee to the U.S. in two weeks' time, which would be the last week of July. The next evening they began to plan for their departure. It was agreed that they would not tell anyone about what they were about to do, and certainly not their parents. The only exception was that Eduardo was allowed to tell Maria. They counted the money they had between them and the money they would earn before their departure time arrived, and decided to pool it all together. Eduardo had some misgivings about the plan, but his decision was made, and now all he had to do was convince Maria that it was the right thing to do.

He excitedly told her about their plan over the phone a few days later, putting as much positive spin on it as he could and naively believing that she would be thrilled with the whole thing. He was truly convinced that it was a good idea and that everything would work out as planned. The reaction he got from her was not the one he had expected.

Maria immediately became very upset and shouted at him over the phone that he was crazy, and then hung up. Eduardo was in shock, and he called back right away. He heard her pick up, but she refused to speak to him—the only thing he could hear was her sniffling and some heartbreaking whining sounds she made.

"Speak to me Maria, please, I love you, nothing has changed and I need you to talk to me." She finally relented and emptied her heart out, her voice charged with emotion and laden with bitterness.

"If you loved me you wouldn't want to do this stupid thing. Are you out of your mind? Do you not know how dangerous it is? I can't believe that you have given up on Mexico, you of all people. You know how much it means to me, but you, all you want to do is run away, run away like a little boy who is afraid to fight and to stand up for himself. I'm ashamed of you, Eduardo Olmeda, ashamed of you, do you hear me?" She had raised her voice and was hissing at him, and she was so upset that she gasped for air and could barely finish her sentences. Eduardo was profoundly disturbed and stunned by her reaction.

"Please Maria, please try to understand," he pleaded. He hated to feel her so hurt, and it broke his heart to hear her cry. There was a prolonged silence on the line, and all he could hear was her sobbing. Then she whispered,

"I miss you Eduardo, I miss you so much."

"I miss you too, Maria. Please don't cry, please. I haven't given up on Mexico, darling, and I haven't given up on you, or on us. I want to do this for you and for us. I want us to have a real future together and to be happy. I love you more than anything in the world Maria, you know that? My dream is for both of us, I...," he was cut off and silenced by her loud wails of desperation.

"No, no, please don't do this, Eduardo, please," she implored him, unable and unwilling to hear him out, and begging him again and again not to go ahead with his plan.

"Look, Maria, I need you to be calm for a moment, please. I will be coming to Mexico City soon and we'll talk about this then, ok? I can't do this on the phone, it's killing me. Please can we do it this way?" All he got for an answer were a series of high-pitched sounds that were something between a wail and a whimper. He was exasperated by that, but most of all, it broke his heart.

"Ok, look Maria, please try to calm down, and I'll talk to you tomorrow, ok?"

"Ok," she managed to say through her sobs.

"I love you Maria, I love you very much," he said with a tremor in his voice.

"I love you too," she replied in a tear-filled voice, and then she hung up.

He stood where he was and looked at his phone dumbfounded for a few minutes, unable to move or to think clearly, taking long, deep breaths in an effort to try to ease the pain in his chest. He looked around and his heart was heavy. He hated himself for having wounded her so deeply. His eyes filled up with tears, and he sat down heavily on the ground, put his face in his hands, and just fell apart. He wept uncontrollably, his shoulders convulsing with grief and his whole being overcome by a profound sorrow. What made him feel even worse was the fact that he knew with absolute certainty that he would not change his mind.

Two weeks later, Eduardo, Mauricio, and Arturo

arrived in Mexico City. The three of them were excited about their imminent departure and the secrecy that shrouded the whole thing. They had told their parents that they were going to Mexico City for a few days with Eduardo, who was going to see his girlfriend. They had all the money they owned in the world with them, along with some spare clothes and a few other basic necessities. Mauricio and Arturo were very upbeat about the upcoming trip and talked excitedly about what they would do when they got to the U.S.

For Eduardo, it was different; he was preoccupied and very nervous about facing off with Maria later that day. He was to go to her parents' house at the end of the afternoon to see her, and he knew that it would be a very emotionally charged moment for both of them. They had talked a few times on the phone after that first very disturbing phone call when he had told her his plan, and the mood had changed between them since. Although he had tried to lighten things up and to get Maria to talk about something else, it had been to no avail; she remained furiously opposed to his intentions and she told him so every time they talked and every time he tried to change the subject. It was the only thing she wanted to discuss, and she was in no mood to talk about anything else.

Eduardo stood in front of Maria's parents' door, feeling very tense and very anxious about seeing Maria again. It felt to him like the first time they had met, and there were butterflies in his stomach. Maria's parents and siblings were gone for a few days and she was alone at the house, for which he was very thankful. The thought of having to face her family at the same time as he faced Maria herself didn't really enchant him. Maria opened the door and the sight of her took his breath away. He had forgotten how beautiful she was. She was wearing a delicate pink blouse, some black leggings and her favorite ballerina shoes. Her hair was freshly washed and brushed, and her eyes scintillated in the late afternoon light. There seemed to Eduardo to be something new in her manner and in her demeanor, something that he had not seen or sensed before in her, something impalpable and pure and fragile and strong, and he was overcome by powerful emotions. Suddenly he felt vulnerable in her proximity, and he just stood there looking at her, frozen in place and unable to move or to utter a sound.

She came towards him and wrapped her arms around him, and she held onto him tightly. He could feel a slight tremor run through her body when she did that. Neither of them spoke, but their lips found each other and love took its rightful place. Their long separation had given birth to a longing, a longing that had been forgotten, but that needed to be assuaged. Desire that only instantaneous and incendiary lovemaking could quell ignited their bodies, and they hastily made their way to her bedroom, shedding clothes awkwardly as they went, their lips devouring each other, their bodies taut and reaching desperately for each other and fused together by the immediacy of their need.

After their lovemaking, Maria felt the pain return, and it was stronger than it had been before. It was a constant throbbing sensation that would not leave her. It had been with her since the day he had told her he was leaving, and it pounded at the center of her being and hurt her physically. She could feel her heart beating wildly against her chest, and she took a deep breath and closed her eyes. Eduardo stared at the ceiling and spoke first. His voice was calm, but there was also an undertone of determination in it, and she heard that in his voice and it amplified her pain.

"I am leaving tomorrow, Maria. I know you are against this and I know that it hurts you, but I need to do this, Maria, and I need you to support me." He turned towards her. Her eyes were still closed, and tears began to run down her face. He stroked her hair gently and kissed her forehead lightly.

"Don't you see, my love? I'm doing this for you, for us, for our future." Maria's body became rigid, and she opened her eyes burning with anger and frustration. She violently pulled the sheet off of her and got up suddenly, bolting to the bathroom and slamming the door behind her. Eduardo sat up in the bed. He could hear her sobbing in the bathroom. She came back in the room a few minutes later and sat down on the bed with her back to him. Slowly, she turned her head in his direction, and she looked at him with such a complete expression of sadness that his heart lurched and he suddenly felt like crying, too. He looked at her intently and silently and he felt terrible. Hurting her was the worst thing that he had ever experienced in his life; it felt like someone was cutting him up inside with a knife. Maria took one of his hands in hers.

"You are very stupid, you know, Eduardo Olmeda." Her voice was cracked and faint because of the weeping, and her words were harsh and seething with anger. "How can you listen to that stupid little fat man Mauricio? That asshole! What does he know, eh? Nothing, that's what he knows, nothing, don't you see that he's a loser, Eduardo?

Him and that moron Arturo, who is more than stupid, how can you listen to these people and not to me? I just don't understand." She began to cry again and kissed the palm of his hand. He felt her tears fall in his hand and he began to cry too, unable to hold back his pain any longer. He passed his hand gently along her cheek.

"Oh Maria, Maria, I love you so much, but I have to do this. I…" He choked on his words, unable to continue. She moved towards him and took his face in her hands, kissing him gently, and whispered,

"Please, Eduardo, please don't go, please, I beg you, if you love me, please don't go." He looked at her with tear-filled eyes and pulled her towards him. As he kissed her, the salt of their tears lingered on their lips, and they stayed that way for a long time, crying in each other's arms and rocking each other gently. They spent their last night together like that, making love, crying, arguing, and hanging desperately onto one another. Maria never let up. She argued and pleaded with him all night, and she screamed and cried until exhaustion finally got the better of her, and when she finally fell asleep, it was only for a few hours of agitated slumber. Eduardo was unable to sleep. He held onto her tightly and stared blankly at the ceiling.

The next morning they got up and got dressed in silence and made their way to the kitchen. Maria fixed them a coffee and they drank it with eyes locked onto each other and not a word spoken between them. When he had finished his coffee, Eduardo slowly got up and took her hand and led her to the front door. He opened it, and behind him the sun had begun to rise on the horizon. He turned towards her, taking her in his arms and holding her tightly, kissing the small of her neck and her face and her lips. Tears began to roll down her cheeks and down his too.

"I love you," he whispered in her ear, "I'll always love you." He let out a small cry, tore himself from her arms, and walked away quickly without looking back. Maria just stood there, completely devastated, watching him walk away, and then he turned the street corner and disappeared from her view. It was the last time that she would ever see him alive.

THE TREK

At first Maria was angry with Eduardo for not calling, and then she sulked for a while and thought about the things that she would say to him when he did. "I'll tell him off good," she kept repeating to herself as she tried to push thoughts of him from her mind, but she had difficulty doing that and with every passing day she got more and more worried and only hoped that he would call soon. Two weeks went by like that, and still she had no news. Eventually, she reached a point where she just couldn't take it anymore, and she resigned herself to call his parents, in the hopes that maybe they had heard from him. His mother answered the phone, and as it turned out it was Maria who informed her that Eduardo was not in Mexico City and had fled to the U.S. with his two friends Arturo and Mauricio. Alicia Olmeda was dumfounded—she couldn't believe what she was hearing. She told Maria that neither she nor her husband had known about Eduardo's plans and that they thought he was in Mexico City with her. The worst part of it for Maria was when Mrs. Olmeda told her that they had not heard from their son since he had left for Mexico City. They had called him a week earlier and had left a message but he hadn't called back—which, she added, was unusual for him. Maria filled in the blanks for her, about how Eduardo and his two friends had taken all the money they had saved for school, how they had planned to reach L.A. and start their own business, and how she had been opposed to the whole idea, but that Eduardo hadn't listened to her and had gone anyway.

"He was supposed to call me when he reached L.A., and I don't understand why he hasn't. I thought that maybe because we had a bit of fight about the whole thing before he left that he was punishing me by not calling, and that maybe he had called you?" There was a silence on the other end of the phone.

"No, Maria, we have not heard from him either, nothing at all." Alicia Olmeda's voice had become grave with concern, and Maria tried to be as reassuring as possible, hoping that she hadn't alarmed her too much.

"Oh, I'm sure everything will be all right, Mrs. Olmeda, and that there's nothing to worry about. He'll contact somebody soon, I'm sure. You know, there's probably a very good explanation why he hasn't called," she managed to say, trying to sound calm and cheerful, but all the time her heart was racing furiously and it felt like it would pop out of her chest. Somehow she got through the conversation, and as soon as she hung up, she let herself slide down the wall, put her face in her hands, and began to cry. She sat there a long time on the floor, silently weeping and unable to move, feeling wretched and miserable, with her mind full of bleak and somber thoughts about what might have happened to Eduardo. After a while, she wiped the tears from her cheeks and looked up and out the window at the clear blue sky, imploring the heavens to help her.

"Oh please, God, please let him be ok, please."

She slowly got up and began to pace about her room aimlessly. She continued to pace for a few hours, while going over all the possibilities of what might have happened to Eduardo. The only thing that she knew for certain was that he had called no one, which was completely out of character for him. Suddenly, it dawned on her that maybe he was in a situation where it was impossible for him to make a phone call. She abruptly stopped pacing and her face lit up.

"Yes, of course, that's it. Why did I not think of that before?" She said out loud. "They got caught. They got caught while trying to cross the border into the U.S. and they are being held while awaiting deportation, that's what happened for sure." It seemed to her to be a perfectly plausible explanation for his silence. He was in jail somewhere and she knew that if that were the case, he would be released soon and sent back to Mexico. She smiled, comforted by the thought. "Believe me, Eduardo Olmeda, your ears will burn when I'm finished with you," she spoke out loud again. "I will make you regret this juvenile adventure of yours and I will make sure you never scare me like this again. You just wait, you'll be tired of hearing me remind you of your stupid plan and of your imbecile friends and you'll beg me to stop and leave you alone, but I won't, I won't until I'm sure it's gotten through your thick skull, you stubborn man, you..." Maria stopped in front of the window, suddenly realizing that she was engaged in a dialogue with herself. She starred absentmindedly outside, arms crossed in front of her. Slowly, the emotions of the recent weeks welled up inside of her and the tears started to roll down her cheeks. She turned around and sat down on the edge of her bed, feeling disheartened and depressed all over again.

"Where are you, my love? Where are you?" She wailed out loud as she let herself fall backwards onto the bed and curled up into the fetal position, her body shaken by uncontrollable sobs.

Another two weeks passed with still no news from Eduardo, and Maria became more and more frantic. She walked about in a semi-catatonic state and was unable to concentrate on anything. All she could do was think about Eduardo. She called his parents every week, but they had had no news of him either, nor had the parents of Arturo and Mauricio heard from any of the boys when she contacted them. Everyone was sick with worry, and Maria knew that if she didn't do something soon, it would drive her completely insane. She just couldn't take another day of the uncertainty and the not knowing.

The idea came to her while sipping her coffee one morning. Suddenly, everything became clear, and she knew exactly what she had to do. She stood up, excited about her plan and convinced that it was the right thing to do. The prospect of action energized her and she quickly got dressed. She would go see her father to explain to him her intentions and to solicit his help. Her parents had been very supportive of her since the beginning of her ordeal and that had been very helpful, but Maria knew that what she wanted to do would not go over easy with them, particularly her father. Nevertheless, she was certain that it was what she had to do.

"But Maria, are you out of your mind? My own

daughter who wants to cross the border into the U.S. illegally, it's crazy and I won't allow it, I just won't." Maria's father was very worked up after she had told him her plan to follow in Eduardo's footsteps all the way to Los Angeles, in the hope of finding him. Her father would have nothing to do with it. Maria had to use all of her power of persuasion to convince him that she was going to do this no matter what, and that what she really needed was not his approval, but his help. Maria's mother remained silent, as was her habit on such occasions, but it was obvious by the creases on her forehead that she was very concerned by what she was hearing. Being the reserved woman that she was, she felt that it was not her place to intercede in the heated discussion between her daughter and her husband. She would talk to Maria later, when they were alone, and she would tell her then what was in her heart.

"Please, Papa," Maria pleaded. "I have to do this, don't you understand? I cannot live like this, I'm sick with worry, this is not like Eduardo, he would not do this and I have to find out what's happened to him." Her father's face was red and he was sweating profusely. Maria was his favorite daughter and the one in whom he had the highest hopes. He was scared and angry and adamant that she change her mind, so he argued.

"How do you know that he is not in jail? That is a possibility, you know, and if that is the case, then you will have gone to all this trouble and put yourself in all this danger for nothing. While you are out there looking for him, he will be here waiting for you. What do you think of that, eh?" He turned towards her, his eyes bulging out of his head, obviously very concerned. Maria went over to where he was standing and looked straight at him, and there was fervor and passion in her eyes.

"Papa, I'm an adult now. I don't need your permission; I just need your help." The look in her eyes said it all. Her father knew that look; it was his look, his firmness and his determination when he believed in something more than anything and nothing and no one was going to get in his way or stop him. Maria ran her hands up and down his forearms and he looked to the side, trying to avoid her gaze.

"Please, Papa, please try to understand?"

After a few hours, he finally relented—grudgingly and not happy at all, but still he relented. He knew his daughter and he knew that there was nothing that would make her change her mind. She would do this with or without him, and so even if it was against his better judgment, he agreed to help her. He loved her dearly and if, God forbid, anything should happen to her and he had not tried to help her, his wife would never forgive him and he would never forgive himself.

"Ok, Maria, I will help you, but on one condition." Maria got up and wrapped her arms around him and hugged him.

"Thank you, Papa, thank you, this means so much to me."

"I said on one condition." Maria pulled back and looked up at him.

"The condition is that you keep your mother and I informed of where you are and where you are going at all times. Is that understood?" Maria smiled.

"Yes, Papa, understood."

"Good. So tomorrow, I will pull some strings and try to find out if Eduardo is in the system, you know, if he is in jail somewhere." He didn't say *or if he is dead*, but the thought passed through his mind. "This will take a few days. Until then, just sit tight, ok?"

"Ok, thank you Papa! I love you." She hugged him, and his eyes locked onto his wife's, who was sitting silent across the room and looking at him fiercely. They would be speaking about this later—he could see that in her eyes.

Over the next few days, Maria's father contacted his connections and friends in the government and started inquiring about Eduardo, trying to find out if his name was in the system somewhere. The search came up empty. Then, reluctantly and with a heavy heart, he did something that he absolutely did not want to do, but that he knew he had no choice about. He contacted some relatives in Los Angeles, and through them he obtained the name of a *coyotes,* as they called the smugglers who helped people cross illegally into the United States. They did this for money, of course, and it was a booming business. Maria would need such a smuggler to get her into the U.S., and he wanted it to be someone who was at least recommended by somebody in the family.

Maria was very much in a hurry to get going. She had decided to go by the same route Eduardo had told her he was taking, across the border by the desert into Arizona. She didn't know the precise place he had attempted to cross, but she had an approximate idea. She contacted the *coyotes* by phone and made arrangements to meet up with him in a few days in a small town near the U.S border. Her father had been assured by his relatives in L.A. that this man was totally dependable, and that he would take good care of Maria and see her safely across the border. Her father lent her the money she needed for the trip and to pay for her passage across the border.

On the afternoon of her departure, Maria quickly packed a few things and headed towards her parents' house. She would eat dinner with her family that evening and sleep there, and then her father would drive her to the bus terminal the next morning.

The tension during dinner that evening was palpable. Her mother spoke very little, and a few times, Maria caught her hastily wiping tears from the corners of her eyes. Her father was unusually silent and had a very somber and apprehensive look about him.

"Please, Papa," she pleaded with him after dinner, "please don't worry about me too much. I'll be ok. I'm a big girl now and I can take care of myself." Her father just stared absently into space and did not answer. They were in the living room, sitting across from each other. The unusually loud clanging of pots and pans announced Maria's mother's presence in the kitchen. When her mother was unhappy about something, she made a ruckus; it was one of her ways of expressing her dissatisfaction to her husband or to anybody else in the family who had crossed her. Maria's father was in his favorite armchair and she was sitting on a low cushion at his feet.

"She will kill me, you know," he said to her gravely. "She will kill me if anything happens to you." Maria put a hand on one of his knees.

"Nothing will happen to me, Papa, I promise. I'll call every chance I get and I'll be very careful." She leaned forward and looked up into his dark and very worried eyes.

"There is nothing I can say that will make you change your mind, is there?" His eyes lighted up when he asked her that, as if he were expecting a positive answer.

"No, Papa, there is nothing you can say that will make me change my mind." She fixed him with a steady gaze, and after a moment, he said,

"Ok then, go and comfort your mother now, she needs it more than I do." He pointed towards the kitchen with his eyes. Maria got up and leaned towards him, kissing his forehead.

"Thank you, Papa, thank you for understanding and being on my side." He looked up at her and smiled,

"I will always be on your side, sweetheart, always."

Maria spent the next few hours in the kitchen with her mother. She helped with the dishes and said everything she could to try to reassure her, but it was to no avail. Her mother was inconsolable, and there was nothing Maria could do but cry with her, hold her in her arms, and tell her that she loved her. When they were all cried out, her mother got up, shoulders drooping, and with a resigned look on her face, she shuffled slowly and silently towards her bedroom. Maria wiped the tears from her cheeks, put out the lights, and headed towards her room. There was a light still on in the living room, and she saw that her father was sitting in his chair with a drink in his hands staring blankly into space.

The next day, Maria was up early, and her father accompanied her to the bus terminal. She bought a ticket for Altar, a small town in Sonora State very close to the U.S. border. It was there that she would meet the *coyotes* who would take her across the border. Her father walked her to the door of the bus, and they hugged each other for a long time.

"I love you," he said, holding back his tears.

"I love you too, Daddy." Maria could not hold back her tears, and she felt her eyes welling. She tore herself from his arms and quickly boarded the bus. She found an empty window seat and waved to him as the bus began to move forward, and it broke her heart to see the sad expression on his face.

Maria arrived in Altar late at night after a few days on a very hot and uncomfortable bus ride. Altar was a rugged and dusty town, and one of the busiest staging grounds for illegal immigration into the United States. The square at the center of the town was where the *coyotes* and illegal immigrants met to do their business. The bus let them off near the town square, and Maria was tired and hungry after the grueling trip. She desperately needed a good bed and a warm bath. The bus driver told her where she could find a boarding house with cheap rooms, and she made her way in the direction he had indicated. Although it was nighttime, it was still hot out, and the heat made her clothes stick to her body as she walked. Even at this late hour, there were still many people about and many groups of men standing in small circles, smoking cigarettes and conversing in low, inaudible tones. Nobody paid any attention to her. It seemed to Maria that there was a lot of activity for such a small town this late at night.

She arrived at the door of the boarding house and a large, friendly woman let her in. There was one available bed left, and a bath, and Maria was relieved to hear it. She paid for her bed for the night, and the woman gave her a towel and indicated to Maria to follow her through a door behind her. The room where the beds were was hot and stuffy, and all the beds were occupied. The women who were not asleep were either reading or chatting amongst themselves, and some of them acknowledged her presence by nodding their heads in a friendly way. Maria flipped her bag onto the top bunk that the boarding house women had indicated was hers. There was a thirty-something woman on the bed below. She was heavy-set in a strong, wholesome kind of way, and she had a good honest face about her. Her hair was long and black and her eyes were bright and vivacious. She was resting on her side, leaning on one of her elbows, and she looked up when Maria arrived. She sat up on the edge of the bed.

"Hi, I'm Teresa," she said, smiling, and extended her hand in Maria's direction.

"Oh hi, I'm Maria," Maria took her hand timidly, and smiled back.

"Come, sit down." Teresa indicated to Maria to sit down beside her on the bed. "It's too hot to sleep right now anyway, so we could talk, if you want?" She had a warm smile and a melodious voice, and Maria immediately felt that she was someone that she could trust.

"Yeah, sure, thanks." Maria pushed aside her hesitancy and slowly sat down besides the older woman. She looked around, a bit disoriented, and obviously not completely at ease with her new surroundings.

"First time, hey?" Teresa asked, looking at Maria.

"Yes, first time," Maria said while bobbing her head up and down. She was so out of her element that it did not even cross her mind to ask Teresa how come she knew what Maria was doing in Altar. Teresa took one of her hands gently. Maria felt the thickness and the toughness of her skin, and she knew it was the toughness that came from hard labor; she looked into Teresa's eyes and she saw a tenderness in them, and she knew it was the tenderness that came from a large heart.

"Hey, it's my third time, ok? So relax, it's not that bad, you'll see." Teresa's laid back attitude relaxed her a bit.

"You mean..." Maria began to say, but Teresa cut her off.

"Yes, exactly." She opened her eyes wide and nodded her head up and down to stress the point she was making. "This is the third time I've crossed into the U.S. through the desert." She nodded in the direction of the other women in the room. "That's what we're all here for." Some of the women close by looked up and smiled, and others nodded their heads approvingly.

Maria smiled, feeling reassured. She had been a bit nervous about the whole adventure and a lot of questions had come up in her mind when she had been on the bus, but now she had a feeling that Teresa would be able to help her with most of them.

"Thank you," she said timidly, and she clung to Teresa's hands a bit too tightly. Teresa understood what she was going through, and she stroked Maria's hand and forearm gently.

"It'll be ok, don't worry, dear. Just stay close to me and I'll help you out, ok?"

"Yes ok..., and thank you. I'm just a bit...."

"Scared," Teresa finished her sentence for her.

"Yes," she smiled, "scared."

"It's normal, Maria, we're all scared," she whispered. "Now, why don't you go get washed up, and then we'll go out for a walk? It's cooler outside, and we can talk. What do you say?"

"Yeah, sure, that would be great, thanks. Do you think I can find something to eat at this hour?"

"Yeah, sure, we'll find you something." Maria got up and took the towel the boarding house woman had given her.

"Ok, good, I'll be right back," she smiled, and Teresa smiled back.

"Ok, I'll be right here."

After Maria had washed up, the two of them went outside. Teresa was right, the air was cooler and it felt good to be out of the stuffy overcrowded dormitory. They walked towards the town square, where Maria bought something to eat from a street vendor. They found a place to sit and while Maria ate, Teresa talked about herself and about her life.

She told Maria that she had five children who were staying with her parents back home, and that her husband was dead. "He was killed by those bastard *narcos*." She had lowered her voice when she said that, and had looked around. It was not something one said out loud with impunity in Mexico, especially this close to the U.S. border, where the *narcos* were everywhere and in control of everything. Teresa laughed when she talked about her dead husband, and Maria looked at her perplexed.

"Hey, don't worry, he was a rotten bastard, a *cabron,* all he wanted to do was to drink from morning 'til night and to fuck any woman he could get his hands on, so in the end, he got what he deserved." There was an awkward silence and then she added, "It's hard on the children though, you know, they miss their father." Teresa fell silent, and Maria looked at her but did not comment. She had heard many similar stories from the people she had met as a volunteer worker in the *colonias populares* in Mexico City. She understood that Teresa's story was an accurate reflection of a certain Mexican reality.

"I have a good job in L.A., you know," Teresa continued. "I work as a live-in maid for a well-to-do family, and they pay me well and in cash, you know, because I don't have any papers or anything. Anyway, I can't complain really, I have it pretty good and the money allows me to buy my children the things they need and also medicine for my parents. My dream is that one of my kids will get to go to university one day. It would make me very proud if that happened. You see, we were a large family and very poor, and I never had the chance to go to school. I had to go to work in the fields when I was very young, to help out my parents and brothers and sisters. That was the way things were and I had no choice in the matter." Maria smiled. She liked Teresa, and the simple and touching way that she expressed herself. She was an open book, holding nothing back.

"Well, Teresa, everything is possible you know. I mean, look at me, my family was poor and my father worked very hard all his life and he helped me get to where I...," Maria stopped mid-sentence, suddenly realizing where she was and who she was talking to, and how out of sync what she was going to say was with what Teresa had just told her.

Maria, a university student, from a good family and with a wonderful future in front of her, was getting ready to cross illegally into the U.S. with some migrant workers. It certainly wasn't something that would have made much sense to Teresa, so she decided to tell her the truth about what she was doing there. Maria opened up to her new friend, and told her the story of her and Eduardo, and even though it was not a long story, she stretched out the good parts—especially the bits about how they were madly in love and happy beyond words—and her eyes lit up when she talked about those moments. She felt like she was reliving her past, and she became enflamed when she talked about their love for each other and about their plans for the future.

"He's a bit silly sometimes, you know, with his books and ideas, he's like a little boy who's never grown up. He's a dreamer, too. He likes to imagine things and then he believes they're real, he's so silly." Maria lowered her head, her voice trailed off, and she stared in front of her, creasing her forehead. It felt good to talk about Eduardo, but it hurt also, and she took a long deep breath and sighed deeply, trying to hold back her tears.

"You love him very much, don't you?" Teresa whispered, putting an arm around Maria's shoulder. Maria turned towards her, and her eyes began to fill up with tears.

"Yes I do, I love him so much it hurts here," she replied, pointing to her heart, "and I miss him and I don't know what's happened to him and it's killing me. I have to find him, Teresa, I just have to." Maria's voice had become strained, and Teresa took her in her arms and stroked her hair gently. She rocked the younger woman tenderly, and

Maria began to sob against her chest, her body heaving up and down. They stayed that way until she calmed down. Once things became quiet again, they got up and slowly made their way back to the boarding house.

Maria got up early the next morning. It was already a bright, hot day when she stepped outside the boarding house. She could see that the town was alive with activity and that the small shops and food vendors were all open for business. There was a lot of hustle and bustle about, and many more people around than there had been the night before. There were also many mini-vans that were moving about or parked on the streets near the town square. Maria surveyed the scene and felt optimistic about things. A good night's sleep and a good cry while bonding with her new friend Teresa had given her the boost she had needed. She went back inside to get Teresa, who had promised to bring her shopping, "for all the things you will need when walking in the desert," she had said. Maria trusted her completely, and she had asked her to come with her to meet the *coyotes* at her one o'clock appointment with him.

"Sure, no problem," had been her answer. "I know them all, Maria. I'll tell you if he's ok." Even though the *coyotes* had been recommended by a friend of her father's, Maria had felt uneasy about putting her life in the hands of a complete stranger. Teresa's offer to check things out for her had been more than welcome.

The two women spent the rest of the morning exploring the small town and shopping and haggling with shop owners and street vendors. Teresa did most of the haggling, and Maria just watched; she was impressed by how street savvy Teresa was and how she always got what she wanted. She found out that underneath that warm smile and soothing voice was a pretty tough woman. Teresa bought some canned food and water for both of them, and helped Maria buy a small backpack, some sturdy shoes, and everything else she insisted Maria have, in preparation for their walk in the desert.

"Trust me, Maria; you'll need all of these things. The desert is a very dangerous and merciless place. You will want to have everything you need right with you once you get going. Always remember, the desert does not give, it only takes." Maria was grateful for Teresa's advice and was more than glad to abide by it.

At noon they sat at a small outdoors terrace and had a light lunch, and at one o'clock they strolled over to the town square and Maria quickly found the *coyotes* she had talked to on the phone. He was a small, wiry man in his forties whose brown skin was creased from too much sun exposure. As agreed to on the phone, he wore a red bandana around his neck and was standing near his mini-van on the north side of the square. His name was Rosario, and he politely tipped his hat to the two women and shook their hands. He was courteous, spoke in a low voice, and was respectful in his manner. Teresa and he had a rapid exchange about the route he was taking, the price he charged, and when and at what time he was leaving. She also asked him if there had been any unusual activity by the American authorities. He answered all of her questions quickly and politely, and his answers seemed to satisfy her. She turned towards Maria,

"He's fine; let's go with him. Are you ok with that?" Maria was a bit surprised because Teresa had said, "we."

"You're coming with me? I thought you were already organized?" Maria asked, eyes wide open.

"No, I'm not. I always pick my *coyotes* at the last minute. So what do you say, we go with Rosario here? I think his price is fair and he's a good man." She turned towards him and smiled, and he smiled back and tipped his hat in her direction again.

"Yes, I agree, I'm just surprised that you're coming with me—I mean, surprised and glad, of course." Teresa smiled at her and turned back to Rosario. She settled the last details with him, and the money changed hands. He was leaving that very evening. They agreed to meet up with him at the same place a little after dark. Teresa shook his hand and turned towards Maria.

"Ok, it's done. Come on now, there is something we need to do before we are ready to leave." She began to walk away.

"Oh yeah, what?" Maria asked, as she picked up her backpack and hurriedly followed her friend.

"You'll see," Teresa shouted over her shoulder.

Teresa led her to a shrine dedicated to the Virgin of Guadalupe. Maria was not religiously inclined, but she liked to believe that she was a spiritual person, and she waited respectfully as Teresa prayed and lit some candles. When she was done, Teresa rejoined Maria. Pointing towards the statue behind her with her head, she said,

"She will protect us on our journey. The Virgin has always protected me on my journeys." Maria gazed at the statue for a moment, but remained silent. Teresa turned around, put a knee to the ground, and did a sign of the cross. Maria quickly did a sign of the cross too, not out of religious conviction, but more out of respect for her friend and for her mother, who was also a very religious person.

They spent the rest of the day moping about town, and an hour after darkness fell they headed in the direction of the town square. There were a lot more mini-vans and people around now, and everything was a flurry of activity. People were being loaded into some mini-vans, and others were already leaving. When they found Rosario near his van, there were people already sitting in it, and others standing outside talking or smoking cigarettes. Half an hour later, Rosario gave the signal and everybody got in. It was a tight fit inside the van and once the doors were closed, it became hot and stuffy very quickly. Maria counted fourteen people in all, including Rosario and the driver. The air was fast becoming hard to breath, and everyone was starting to sweat profusely. Teresa looked over at Maria and smiled at her, and Maria bravely smiled back, although she was feeling a bit queasy. As the van got going, a bit of air came in from the open front windows, which was a relief to the tightly seated passengers. No one spoke, and there was an enormous amount of tension inside the van as they slowly made their way out of town. They picked up speed and travelled for a while on a paved road before the van veered unto a rough and bumpy dirt road and extinguished its headlights. It was dark outside, and their speed was reduced to a crawl. They very slowly made their way along the dirt road, the van continuously lurching from side to side, and the passengers continually bumping shoulders with each other.

Finally, after what appeared to Maria to be an interminable amount of time, the van came to a halt, and

Rosario got out and opened the door for them. Some fresh air rushed in, and Maria breathed in deeply, relieved to be at last out of the suffocating van. Rosario signaled to them with his hand to come out and with a finger over his mouth to be silent. They filed out noiselessly, and Maria saw the fear and apprehension on everyone's faces as they stepped out of the mini-van and into the darkness. It was a clear, star-studded night. As she looked up at the sky and into the shadows all around her, she could sense the desert's presence, ominous and foreboding. The mini-van turned around, all lights extinguished, and left in the direction that it had come, quickly disappearing into the shadows.

They were alone now, in the obscurity and the wilderness, and Maria was humbled by the innate power of her vast surroundings. Rosario made them get into a single file and they began to walk, with him in the lead. Maria walked behind Teresa with her eyes glued to the ground, stepping carefully, as she could not see very far in front of her. The silence was eerie, and Maria could feel the remnants of the day's heat that still hung in the air. They walked for about thirty minutes and then stopped. Teresa turned towards her and whispered,

"It's the border." The line moved again, and Maria saw Rosario crouched on his knees, letting people pass through a hole in a barbed wire fence. As Maria bent down to pass through the hole, he whispered,

"*El otro lado*," he smiled at her—*the other side!*—and Maria smiled back. It was the first time she had heard someone call the U.S. by that name, and it seemed quite appropriate, all things considered.

Rosario was the last to pass through, and he went back

to take his place at the front of the line. They began to move again. Maria was nervous. She knew it was real now, and that from this moment on, anything could happen. Teresa had told her that it was a three-to-four day walk, and that the travelling was done only at night. Maria realized that it would be a long and grueling haul to get to their objective, which was the highway on the U.S. side of the border where their pick-up had been arranged. She also understood that they were on U.S. soil now and in an illegal situation, which meant that they could be arrested at any time. She had been pretty freaked out the night before when Teresa had described to her all the things the U.S. border patrol did to try to catch the people who crossed the border illegally.

"They have motion sensors, helicopters, night-vision goggles and a lot of agents that patrol the border area all the time. Once we are across, we have to be very careful and very silent—and lucky too," she had added, smiling. "Nobody wants to lose the money it costs them to get across and then to have to start over." They had laughed nervously about that at the time, but now the reality of her words resonated loudly in Maria's mind. She understood why the fear of being caught and losing their hard-earned or borrowed money was a major preoccupation for these people. They all knew, of course, that they would never do any serious jail time if they got caught, and that the worst that would happen was that they would be sent back to Mexico. But losing the money it had cost them to get across the border was a source of major concern.

They walked most of that first night along a rough and winding trail with only the light of the stars to guide them.

Occasionally Maria felt the sharp stab of a cholla cactus or was clawed by some thorny shrub. She winced when that happened, but was too frightened to utter a sound. It was an exhausting and silent walk. Every once in a while, Rosario would stop for a few minutes and come to the back of the line to make sure everyone was ok and to allow them time to catch their breath or to drink some water, and then he would press on.

With day break came the heat, and it very quickly became oppressive. As first light meekly ignited the sky, they came upon some human remains. They had smelled the cadaver long before they saw it, and it had been a shock to Maria when she saw the decomposing body of a woman, only a few feet from where she was walking. The smell was overwhelming, and everyone covered their faces with something as they passed. The dead woman lay on her back under a Palo Verde tree, her mouth open and her stomach and face bloated and deformed. Her body was stiff from rigor mortis and hundreds of flies were swarming over and around her. There was a makeshift cross made of dead mesquite branches a few feet from where she lay, and a pink plastic rosary was hanging from it. The sand directly underneath the crude cross was freshly tossed and it was obvious by the size of the tossed sand that a child had probably been buried there in a hurry. Maria was stunned and in shock as she passed near the corpse of the woman— she couldn't believe what she was seeing. It was mind boggling to her that a person could die like that in the desert and that nobody who had passed by her corpse would have taken the time to bury her. She looked at the line of people ahead of her, but no one was looking back and everyone was pressing on. Maria understood in that moment that the world she had just stepped into was based in harsh reality and that the only rule that applied was survival. Sometimes even basic humanity was unavailable or unnecessary. It was survival of the fittest and this was the price that some of them were willing to pay in order to make their dreams come true. It took a long time for the image of the dead, decaying woman to get out of her mind, and it haunted her for a long time afterwards.

They walked on and the heat quickly became intense, almost suffocating, and it made the walking much more difficult. To Maria, it felt like every step was extracting something from her, and she moved forward with great difficulty. When the sun finally became too hot to bear, Rosario stopped and told everyone to find a place in the shade. They would resume their walk at the end of the day when the sun was lower in the sky.

Everyone got under some Palo Verde trees and felt relief for the shade they provided. All were sweating profusely and out of breath. Maria let herself fall heavily to the ground, placing her elbows on her knees and her head between her hands. She stayed that way a while, unable to move, and took in long, deep breaths. The going was a lot more difficult than she had imagined. She lifted her head and drank some water, and then opened up a can of tuna and ate it in silence. Rosario had told them to remain as silent as possible in order to avoid detection, but that seemed superfluous to Maria, as no one had the strength to engage in conversation and all of them were either busy eating or drinking, or resting in the shade, or trying to sleep.

"So, you didn't think it would be this tough, eh?" Teresa whispered, as she sat down on the ground beside Maria. She was soaked in sweat and her cheeks were flushed.

"No I didn't, this is a lot harder than I thought," Maria whispered back. Teresa patted her hand gently

"Hey, it'll be over before you know it, it's the first day that's the hardest," she said, keeping her voice low. Maria smiled at her.

"Thank you, Teresa—thank you for everything you've done for me," she whispered, squeezing Teresa's hand gently.

"Hey, it's nothing, just promise me you'll do the same for someone else one day, ok?"

"Yes, ok, I will, I promise." They fell silent, and soon, despite the heat, both of them had dozed off.

When the sun started to get lower in the sky, Rosario went around and told everyone that it was time to go. Their first day of waiting in hiding was over and their second night of walking was about to begin. Although daylight was falling fast, the heat that the day had created was overpowering. It made breathing difficult and their progress very laborious. To Maria, it felt like she was walking inside an oven, being cooked alive. There was also the new and constant fear of the U.S. border patrols. Everyone knew they could appear at any moment and put an abrupt end to their journey. It was an unfamiliar fear for Maria, and it hung over all of them like a shadow. Like the countless illegal immigrants that had passed there before them, it was that fear, and the oppressing heat, which defined the purgatory they were in.

* * *

The next day at noon, on the U.S. side of the border and not very far from where Maria, Teresa and their group were hiding and resting after their second night of walking, Roy Morris and his sidekick Al pulled up to their favorite diner off the main highway that passed through the desert. A cloud of dust blew up around the surrounding cacti as Roy slammed on the brakes of his battered pickup truck. The midday heat was crushing and there were no other vehicles in the parking spaces in front of the beat-up old diner. The diner was owned and operated by Mr. and Mrs. Kelly, an elderly couple who had been running the place for over thirty years. The Kellys were a quiet and hard-working couple who minded their own business and lived in a small apartment in the back portion of the run-down building. Their diner had been steadily losing its customers to the fast food outlets in the new mall which had been built close to town recently. Roy Morris was not one of the ones who had moved his business elsewhere. He was set in his ways, and ever since he had been released from the state penitentiary, he had considered the diner as practically his home and Mr. and Mrs. Kelly as part of his extended family. Although that feeling was certainly not mutually shared, Roy's feelings about the Kellys persisted, and he had become, by consequence, their most faithful customer.

Roy and Al ate lunch at the diner every day, and most of the time they were the only customers who showed up. It made Roy very angry that the local people had abandoned the Kellys and their diner, and he would get very upset whenever the subject popped up in his troubled mind.

"Fuck them fancy places over at the mall and all them fuck-faced, double-crossing bastards that go there. How could they do that to these decent hard working Americans, eh? How could they, Al?" he would ask, while pointing a menacing finger in Al's direction, and Al's eyes would fill up with fear at Roy's growing wrath. He would keep his lips sealed tight, though; he knew better than to try to answer Roy's questions. Roy always answered his own questions.

"You know what kind of people would do something like that, Al? Scumbags, that's who, low life scumbags, every single one of them." There was always a lot of bitterness and harshness in Roy's voice when he talked about the diner's erstwhile customers. He would become flushed and angry, and Al could sense the hatred that was simmering up inside him. It was never far from the surface, the hatred in Roy. He hated everybody and everything, but some things and some people, he hated more than others. The people whom he considered had done wrong by the Kellys were damn near the top of his list, right up there with Mexicans. Roy hated Mexicans more than anything in the world—he had a special place in his hatred for them. Al never argued with Roy about things like that, the Kellys or the Mexicans. As a matter of fact, he never argued with Roy about anything, he mostly just listened and nodded in terror or in grave approval. He was smart in that way, Al, he knew better than to cross a man like Roy Morris, even in the smallest of ways.

The two men got out of the pickup truck and took off their cowboy hats, using them to brush off the dust from their soiled and tattered clothes, and entered the diner. They saluted Mr. and Mrs. Kelly by tipping their hats in their direction and went to sit in the booth at the farthest extremity of the diner. It was Roy's favorite seat. He liked it because he had his back to the wall and from where he sat, he could see the whole diner and still have a clear view of the highway outside. The road was straight except for a sharp ninety-degree turn right in front of the diner, and it stretched both ways into the desert as far as the eye could see. From where he was sitting, Roy could see if someone was approaching from either side. Cops were what made him the most nervous. He hated cops, all of them and without exception. They made his blood turn, and he became very unsettled around them. Luckily for him, they rarely showed up at the diner, and if they did, it was usually just to get some coffee to go.

Roy slipped into the booth and slid his broad-shouldered body towards the window. He put an elbow on the table, rested his head in the palm of one of his thick hands, and stared idly at the desert and the highway outside.

He was a tall and muscular man, Roy Morris—prison muscular, that is. His eyes were a cold, threatening azure grey, more like metal than sky, and his hair was grimy and brush cut in an uneven and disheveled kind of way. He had a long, vicious scar that ran across his skull from left to right, a reminder of a violent prison brawl that he had been in. His hair had never grown back around the ugly scar, and the whiteness of the skin in that area stuck out when he didn't have his hat on. It was unpleasant to look at and it made people uncomfortable. His arms and hands were thick and solid and he loved to wear shirts with cut-off sleeves in order to show off the rock-hard biceps that he had developed in prison. His face was permanently covered with a three-to-four day old stubble and was pot-holed and scarred from his unhealthy childhood. His whole facial demeanor was malicious and unsettling. He was a rough man, Roy Morris, rough and dangerous and angry inside, the result of a troubled childhood and a violent coming of age.

He had never known his parents, and had been moved from foster home to foster home all through his younger years. All the foster parents he had ever had had either beat up on him or abused him, and it had made him violent and vindictive. The only real education he had gotten had been on the street, and that's where he had learned to fend for himself. Nothing and no one scared him, and at a very young age, crime had become his *raison d'être*.

When he was eighteen, his violent streak got the better of him, and he had brutally stabbed and killed a guy in a bar fight over some silly wager. He had been sent to the state penitentiary for that murder and had spent twenty-seven years there. In the first week of his incarceration, he had been severely beaten and raped by three older Mexican gang members, lifers, whom he had unknowingly challenged by staring at them directly. They had punished him severely for that grave error, abusing him in the worst possible way and nearly killing him in the process. The beating and the rape had pushed his already fragile mind over the edge, and he had never been the same again. It was on that same day that his hatred of Mexicans was born. He hated them intensely just like he hated anything and everything Mexican. Every day of the twenty-seven years that he spent in the penitentiary, that hatred grew inside of him like a malignant cancer, and like a cancer, its size and toxicity augmented with time, and its venom flowed in his system, patiently waiting for his release.

Roy came out of prison a different man. Not good different; bad different, and angry too, angry and fired up, like a bomb ready to explode. The shrinks in the penitentiary had always considered him to be a borderline psychopath, but they'd had no choice but to sign off on his release, even though they feared that he was unprepared for exposure to the world. His time was up, and there was nothing they or the authorities could do to keep him in jail. When Roy walked out of prison that day, he was filled to the brim with the poison he had cultivated during his incarceration: a visceral loathing of humanity and of life itself. His goal when he got out was not to reintegrate into society. His goal was to get even.

After his release, Roy lived in an abandoned, rundown shack in an isolated part of the desert. He pretty much kept to himself, and since he minded his own business, people left him alone. The only person he had any real contact with was Al. His full name was Albert, but Roy started calling him Al the very first time they met, and Al it had been ever since. Al had one leg that was shorter than the other and he limped awkwardly when he walked. His face was always contorted as if he was in pain and he never knew where to put his arms, which were always flailing about in uncoordinated movements. He was a simple-minded man, as he would tell people whenever he met them, always fidgeting about uncomfortably and apologetically when he spoke, blushing and staring at the ground with a twisted grin on his face and moving dirt about nervously with his old and ragged cowboy boots. People had always made him feel nervous, and he had never much liked interacting with them or being around them. They made him feel as if his very existence was superfluous and required justification—like he wasn't good enough for any of them. He knew that they all made fun of him behind his back, but it didn't bother him anymore, now that he hung out with Roy. He was convinced that Roy was the only person in his whole life that had ever treated him right, and he was grateful for that.

"He treats me ok, you know, normal and such," he would say if anyone asked him why he was around Roy so much. He appreciated what he perceived as Roy's kindness, and it had earned Roy his unfailing loyalty, even though Roy had never asked for it, or was even interested in having it. After a stint together as temporary laborers on a ranch in the area not long after Roy's release, they had become inseparable. It was a good combination; Roy dragged Al along as an obedient pet, a living thing that he could talk to at will and who never talked back. Al actually listened to what he had to say and agreed with him on everything. This helped Roy vent some of his anger and temporarily forget his violent urges. Al was so taken by Roy, and so certain that he was his best friend, that he didn't even realize how little consideration Roy really had for him, or how close Roy was to being completely insane. To Al, Roy appeared normal enough, and he was just happy to have someone that he believed to be his friend and who allowed him to spend time with him.

As was their habit, Roy and Al sat silently in the empty diner as they waited for their food to be served. They never ordered anything specific—they ate whatever Mrs. Kelly had prepared and Mr. Kelly placed in front of them, on the diner's thick, white ceramic plates. There were never any questions asked, or any negative comments made about the food; Roy wouldn't have allowed that, and anyway, neither of them really knew the difference. For them it was food, and nothing more.

Mr. Kelly came up to them and placed two hot plates on the table, then walked back silently in the direction of the kitchen. The two men immediately began to eat, heads low and utensils ringing as they hit the plates with every downward stroke, busy as bees and silently slurping like sows in a pig pen. They gulped down the day's offerings without any form of decorum or grace, neither of them having any use for eating rituals, table manners, or any other form of gastronomic propriety. The spectacle of them feeding themselves had a stronger resemblance to force feeding than to any form of civilized activity.

Roy greedily pushed down the last two forkfuls of Mrs. Kelly's meatloaf, and a large dollop of gravy rolled down the side of his distended mouth and fell onto his shirt. He didn't bother wiping any of it off, but turned his head and stared absentmindedly out the window. His thick forearms lay flat on the table and he held his knife and fork in his hands pointing upwards. Suddenly his brow grew creased, and his mind seemed to be abruptly troubled by something. Al didn't like it when Roy got that way, "all twisted and turned up inside," it was never good, and he tried to distract him. He turned his head nervously to one side, towards the open television that was mounted on the wall behind the counter at an angle from where they were sitting, and then back in Roy's direction.

"Will you look at that, Roy," he pointed towards the

television, hoping to get Roy's mind off whatever had made him become so somber all of a sudden. The midday news was on and they were airing a story about a suicide bomber somewhere in the Middle East who had blown himself up, killing many people, amongst them many women and children. There were some very grisly images that accompanied the story. Roy did not move or answer; he just kept staring outside, his gaze fixed on the highway, observing the endless waves of heat that rose up from the blacktop.

"It's a bloody shame, don't you think, Roy?" Al kept turning his head from the jumping images on the screen to Roy. "What do all them A-rabs want anyway, eh Roy?" Al pronounced the "A" of Arabs as one pronounces the first letter of the alphabet. "I mean, look at what they do to innocent people, it ain't right. Don't you think, Roy?" Al was becoming a little bit frantic and fidgety, and his eyes kept moving from the screen to Roy and then back to the screen. He was twitching in his seat nervously, in dire need of some kind of response or approval from his friend. Conversations with Roy, when they were initiated by him, made him anxious, and his voice had become slightly high pitched. He cautiously risked another question.

"What do you think them A-rabs are so angry about, eh Roy?" His eyes were bulging out of their sockets, and sweat had begun to roll down his temples. After what appeared to him to be a long time, Roy finally responded, without turning in his direction,

"Who gives a fuck what they're angry about Al, they're just a bunch of ignorant camel fuckers. That's what they are. They can all blow themselves up as far as I'm concerned. It's just good riddance, that's all." Al smiled, happy that Roy had broken the silence and shed some light on the subject.

"You sure are right about that, Roy, you sure are."

Roy turned in Al's direction, staring at him intently for few seconds. His nostrils were flared up a bit and his eyes had a familiar ferocity in them.

"You know what's wrong with this country, Al?" Roy hissed under his breath, his eyes darting from side to side. He was still holding his knife and fork tightly pointing upwards, and Al could see the whiteness of his knuckles because of the pressure he was exerting on them. "It's all those fucking immigrants that we let in, Al, that's what's wrong with this country—and nobody's doin' nothing about it, nobody." Al did not move, but sat looking at Roy with wide open eyes and his mouth slightly ajar. "And you know what the worst of it is, Al?" Al knew the answer to that question, because Roy had asked and answered it many times before, but there was no way that he was going to deny Roy the pleasure of repeating it one more time, so he shook his head sideways a few times to indicate that he didn't. "It's those fucking Mexicans pouring across our border like god-dammed cockroaches, that's the worst of it, Al, and right here under our fucking noses. Can you believe that?" He had raised his voice a bit, and his eyes had an unnatural glimmer in them. He threw his knife and fork onto his plate in disgust. Mr. Kelly lifted his head and looked in their direction when he heard the clanging of the utensils, and Roy turned towards him and motioned with his hands that everything was all right. The old man resumed his business. Roy leaned closer to Al and whispered,

"All I'm saying, Al, is that it ain't right, that's all, and it shouldn't be. I tell you, Al, it shouldn't be." His voice was gritty and sounded like the low guttural growl of a wild animal ready to pounce, and his eyes were popping out of their sockets and were filled with the folly that dwelled within him. Al shook his head gravely, swallowing hard, and pushed back into the booth behind him as hard as he could. He was scared of Roy when he got this way, and so he did the only thing that he knew was safe for him to do in such circumstances. He agreed with him.

"You sure are right about that Roy, it shouldn't be." His voice shook a little, and so he repeated himself with a little more forcefulness, for good measure. "You sure are right about that Roy, it shouldn't be."

* * *

Maria and her group had resumed their third night of walking when the sun started to slip below the horizon. After a few hours, Rosario ordered a thirty minute break, and everybody stopped and looked for a place to sit. Maria and Teresa sat down heavily beneath a Palo Verde tree, both sweating profusely and covered in desert dust. Darkness was falling quickly around them. They did not speak for a while, as they were both struggling to catch their breath. The trek through the desert was turning out to be the most difficult thing Maria had ever attempted to do in her life, and luckily for her, she was in good health. She was stressed out, though, and had a constant knot in her stomach. She felt queasy at times, and she kept having recurrent flashes of the dead woman she had seen decomposing in the desert. When that happened, she would shake her head sideways in a futile effort to chase the images from her mind. They were terrifying images and they made her panic a little. She had to keep reminding herself to stay calm and to breathe.

"Hey, are you ok?" Teresa asked.

"Yeah, but I don't think there's a part of my body that doesn't hurt."

"Shhhhh," Rosario hissed in their direction, signaling with his finger over his lips for them to keep their voices down. Teresa leaned closer to Maria.

"Yeah, me too," she whispered, taking Maria's hand and patting it affectionately. They were silent for a moment, looking out at the darkening desert.

"Do you miss them?" Maria asked, keeping her voice down. "You know, when you're gone like this?" Teresa turned towards Maria and her eyes lit up. The very mention of her children always sent blood rushing through every cell of her body and unleashed a flow of unconditional love.

"Oh my God, yes," she whispered, "I miss them so much, especially the little one, Roberto, he has beautiful eyes and he is so full of life, he laughs and smiles all the time and he is so happy." A tear rolled down her cheek and she wiped it with the back of her hand. "I don't know what he's so happy about, but he is—it's silly, eh?" She turned towards Maria, who smiled and put her arm around her friend's shoulders and pulled her gently in her direction.

"No, it's not silly, Teresa," she whispered. "It's beautiful."

"I wish I was with them tonight, you know, to make them dinner and to listen to their conversations and to their endless questions about everything and to put them to bed and hug them and kiss them good night." She looked up to the sky and smiled. "God, they smell so good, I could hug them for such a long time." Maria looked at her and whispered in her ear,

"I'm sure you're the best mother in the world, Teresa, the very best." Tears rolled down Teresa's cheeks as she fixed the skies with an intent stare.

"It's not right, you know, Maria, it's not right for a mother to be away from her children that way. It shouldn't be."

"No, Teresa, your right about that, it shouldn't be." Maria looked up to the heavens too, shook her head gravely, and repeated, "It shouldn't be." Teresa leaned her head on Maria's shoulder and wrapped an arm around her waist.

"Thank you, Maria, thank you for understanding." Maria patted her hand affectionately, closed her eyes, and inhaled deeply.

"For me, it's Eduardo, you know," she whispered. "I feel like that for him, like you do for your children in a way, but different of course. Still, I love him so much it hurts me in my body sometimes and I feel like I can't breathe. God, I hope nothing has happened to him. I'm so scared Teresa; so scared." Tears began to flow down her face, and Teresa said nothing, but gave her a gentle squeeze.

The thirty minutes passed very quickly, and Maria was dismayed when Rosario signaled to them that it was time to start walking again. That third night of walking was by far the most grueling, and it took every ounce of energy she had left. Her feet were sore and felt heavy, and each step she took hurt her physically and required an effort. The walk across the desert was turning out to be a cruel form of punishment and she did not know where she got the strength to keep on going. Sometimes, she had doubts about whether she would make it out of the desert alive. When the sun became too hot in the early morning, Rosario found a good spot in the shade for them to rest and they all collapsed on the ground, exhausted and out of breath.

The long daytime wait brought no reprieve whatsoever. They had to remain very quiet, because they were close to civilization and there were certain to be border patrols nearby. The heat was extremely oppressive even in the shade, and many times Maria felt like she was suffocating. She had to fight hard to push back the panic that was building up inside of her. To get her mind on something else, she thought about her parents and about her brothers and sisters, and about Eduardo, of course, and thinking about them gave her the strength she needed. Also, knowing that she was close to her goal made her more determined than ever to succeed. Every once in a while, to build up her courage, she would lift her head up and stare straight in front of her, take in long, deep breaths, and repeat to herself over and over again, "Just a little bit more, Maria, just a little more."

It was a short time before sundown that evening when they started moving again and disaster struck. They had been walking for about half an hour, and the last crimson rays of the sun were leaking over the top of the higher cacti, when a bullet from Roy Morris's high-powered rifle shot out of the barrel of his gun and hit Teresa in the forehead. Only milliseconds later, with a sickening thud, she fell over backwards onto the desert floor at Maria's feet. Maria looked at her in disbelief and saw that she had a hole in the middle of her forehead and that blood was oozing from it onto the pristine desert sand, forming a circle around her head. Teresa just lay there motionless, her eyes open. Maria didn't fully understand what was going on. The line had stopped in front of her and everyone seemed frozen in place. For a second or two they all just stood there, in complete incomprehension. It felt to Maria like time had stopped, and she had the distinct impression that she was unable to move her feet. That's when Roy Morris fired his second shot, and she saw the man directly in the front of her in the line go down exactly like Teresa.

The second shot struck home and she sprung into action, as did everyone else. She finally comprehended what was going on, and she dashed to one side, throwing herself under some bushes and scratching her hands badly on some thorns as she dove. Her heart was beating at a thousand miles an hour and she was shaking violently from head to foot. She strained her eyes and ears, searching for any sound or movement in the growing obscurity. Nothing moved. Everything was eerily quiet around her.

Roy observed his "work" from his vantage point on top of a hill nearby. He lowered his binoculars and chuckled to himself.

"Ha, ha, got me two more Mexican critters tonight, good job Roy, good job." He slung his high-powered rifle over his shoulder and turned in the direction of his beat-up pickup truck, which was parked about half a mile away. He started to make his way towards it, his burly silhouette quickly disappearing into the murky shadows.

Maria did not move for what seemed to her like a very long time. Once it was completely dark out, however, she decided to chance it. She cautiously crawled out of her hiding place and looked around for any sign of movement. From where she crouched, she could make out the outline of Teresa's body in the darkness, and she got down on all fours and stealthily crawled over to where she lay. She checked to see if she could detect a pulse, and although she was already sure of the outcome of her query, the lifelessness of Teresa's body startled her. She jumped back a little and let out a short, high-pitched, involuntary cry.

"Pssst." Maria heard a voice not far from where she was and she stepped back a bit, straining her eyes through the darkness in the direction that the voice had come from. For a second she thought it might be the killer, and she was about to get up and run for her life when she recognized Rosario's voice.

"Pssst, come over here, we are here."

She cautiously made her way on all fours towards his voice, and as she came up to some bushes, she could make out the outline of Rosario and the others. Even in the darkness, she could see the fear and terror in everyone's eyes.

"Quick, come over here," Rosario whispered, and he took her firmly by the arm to pull her into their hiding place. He put a finger to her mouth to indicate silence and whispered in her ear, "It's the vigilantes; they're gone now, but we'll wait here a while and then move." Maria nodded that she understood, even though her brain was in total turmoil and was unable to process clearly the harsh reality of what she had just witnessed. She was in a state of complete shock and disorientation. Rosario put his hand affectionately on her shoulder and whispered in her ear, "I'm sorry about your friend." Maria nodded absentmindedly, unable to utter a sound. "We're close to the highway. We'll be in L.A. soon," he added, hoping that his words would be of some comfort to her.

For the rest of the journey Maria was in a daze, her heart and mind in complete chaos. The brutal murder of Teresa had struck a blow deep within her being, and it was a profound and wicked wound, inflicted with an uncommon viciousness and savagery, the likes of which she hadn't even known existed. She would later say that she didn't remember those last few hours in the desert, or their pick up on the highway, or how she got to Los Angeles and finally to her aunt and uncle's house. But somehow she made it, lost and hurt and gravely troubled by her experience, emotionally and physically drained, and broken by the randomness and the absurdity of what she had been through. Nevertheless, there she was, alive and in one piece, one of the lucky ones, who had been allowed by resilience or by chance to live for another day and to stand on the threshold of a new life.

PART II

AMERICA

Yaneti could see some very faint lights at a great distance, barely visible and throbbing discreetly on the horizon. It was a dark, cloudy night, and only a few stars were visible in the murky sky. The ocean was deadly silent, and not a wisp of wind disturbed the hot and heavy summer air. *It must be America,* she thought. *Yes, America for sure,* she kept repeating to herself with tear-filled eyes, and that thought only made her pain more poignant. It was quiet now, after the fighting and the screaming that had happened when the crew had overtaken them and bound and gagged them. Only the irregular pitter-patter of the wavelets breaking against the side of the boat disturbed the eerie silence.

Pedro flicked his cigarette overboard, and they all heard the finality of its hiss at it hit the surface of the water. He slowly turned around to face them, staring intensely into their terror-filled eyes, and smiled. He loved to see them this way, with their hands and feet solidly tied up and with duct tape over their mouths, each one of them scared out of their wits and at his mercy. He was excited to the extreme, and he struggled to contain himself as a river of adrenaline rushed through his body. This was, by far, his favorite moment.

He glanced towards the band of misfits who acted as his crew. They were standing by in silence, waiting for his orders. He smiled cunningly in their direction, and his smile exposed two shining gold teeth at each extremity of his mouth. Pedro was not a pretty sight to behold—his thick, black, permanently disheveled hair was cut in an uneven brush cut, and he had an overgrown black mustache which was in bad need of some trimming. His face was scarred and ravaged, and his facial muscles became slightly twisted when he spoke, as if he were making a physical effort every time he attempted to say something. He arms and chest were thick and covered with scars and tattoos, and he was tall and broad shouldered. Every movement he made seemed dangerous and threatening. His eyes were dark and fleeting, permanently inhabited by a sinister shadow, and his entire demeanor oozed primitive lethality.

"You see these idiots," he hissed savagely under his breath, his face contorted and his voice raspy from smoking too many cheap Cuban cigars. His heavily accented Cuban Spanish was laced with the brutal intonations of one who has lived and survived in the entrails of hell. His crew listened in silence, heads slightly bowed. They were terrified of him. Everyone was terrified of Pedro. No one knew for sure if Pedro was his real name, or what his family name was. All they knew was that he had spent many years in *Combinado del Este*, Cuba's most violent and notorious prison, and that he had come out of there alive, which was in itself a feat. He had the reputation of being a ruthless killer, and he had friends high up in the Castro regime. So when Pedro spoke, they listened, and they listened religiously, and they kept their mouths shut.

"Do you see them?" He asked again, gesticulating violently in the direction of Yaneti and her fellow Cuban passengers: four women, seven men, and two children who, like her, had been trying to flee the island. "Do you?" He insisted, raising his voice, and droplets of his foul spit flew into the thick, humid air. He moved closer to his crew, and they could smell his greasy, soiled hair and rank body odor, and they could see that his eyes were wild from the adrenaline and his innate fury.

"You know what they think, these morons?" He continued his tirade, "they think that over there is where they were going, that over there is America, huh," he pointed towards the faint flickering lights on the distant shoreline, "but, what these idiots don't know, is that it's still Cuba, *si Cuba,*" he repeated, while turning and looking mockingly at his petrified passengers. He scoffed and grunted derisively, and his crew chuckled under their breaths and shuffled their feet nervously about on the deck.

Yaneti was in shock. She couldn't believe what she had just heard—that all they had done in their two-hour boat ride was to go out to sea in a long circle and then come back in Cuba's direction. The realization enraged her and made her sick to her stomach.

"You know what else they think, these idiots?" Pedro continued, and his voice rose with his excitement. He pointed an accusing finger in Yaneti's and the other passengers' direction. "They think that there is no misery in America, and that no one cheats or steals and that all is perfect there and that everyone is rich and eats three times a day. That's what they think, these morons, and that's why they wanted to go there." He paused, and the sudden silence filled the air with an uneasy discomfort. He moved closer to his men, putting his face within inches of theirs and speaking deliberately slowly, his low, guttural voice grating his throat with every word he pronounced. Tiny particles of his putrid spit sprayed them in the face, but not one of them blinked an eyelid, or twitched a single muscle.

"But us, us, we know better than that. Don't we? We live in the real world and we know how things work and how things are done and by whom, don't we, my friends?"

"*Si, si,*" his crew all grunted and nodded their heads in unison.

"But, putting that aside, there is a problem here, my friends. The problem is that I have made a promise to these people, and as you know, I always keep my promises. I promised them that I would bring them to a place where they would have a better life. So I will do that, I will bring them to a place where they will have a better life. As a matter of fact, I guarantee it. " An understanding sneer broke out on the faces of his crew, and they nodded their heads in agreement and fidgeted about, anxious to get on with it. But Pedro wasn't done yet; this was his moment of supreme enjoyment, and he liked to take his time and to make it last. His excitement was obvious now, and he even seemed to find pleasure in the sound of his own voice.

"After all my friends, this is what they paid us for. Is it not?" He broke out laughing hysterically. His laughter was strange and hollow, almost demented, and his eyes were bulging from their sockets and seemed ready to pop out of his head. His coterie of grubby and repulsive miscreants all broke out laughing too, but their laughter was more a reflex of self-preservation than anything really genuine—none of them wanted to displease Pedro, and certainly not for something as silly as not laughing at one of his lame jokes, or appearing not to appreciate his unsavory humor.

Pedro's crew consisted of four men, each one whom held a handgun or an assault rifle. All of them were frightening, even without guns. The scariest was the large black man with huge arms and biceps bigger than most men's thighs. His head was clean-shaven and his eyes held the coldness and emptiness of a cruising shark. The other three were a strange array of Cuba's ethnic diversity. There was a short, stocky, white man with a round protruding belly, who wore soiled clothes and was always muttering obscenities under his breath, which the others either didn't hear, or didn't bother to acknowledge. Then there was a tall lanky mulatto, who was slick and silent and always on edge, and whose eyes were constantly darting from side to side, like those of a wild animal scanning the deep shadows of the forest. Finally, there was a short wiry *Indio*, a descendent of Cuba's first inhabitants, whose skin was creased and browned from too much exposure to the sun and who chain smoked and had eyes that were wild and troubling. He acted like something was burning him up from the inside, and only spoke in one-word sentences. Pedro loved his crew of ex-convicts and derelicts. He had chosen each one of them individually because he knew that they would do anything that he ordered without a second of hesitation.

Yaneti couldn't stop trembling, and tears poured freely

down her face. Pedro's sick laughter and the horror of what was about to happen was hitting her hard. The lies, the deceptions, and the inherent violence and vileness of Pedro and his men, it was all so clear to her now, and so she did the only thing that was left for her to do: she began to pray.

Pedro stopped laughing as suddenly as he had started, and his crew immediately became silent too. They did not move; they had been through this drill before, and they knew the signal would be coming soon, but not until Pedro had finished enjoying the moment. He was sadistic in that way, Pedro, they all knew that, but none of them cared. All they wanted to do was to get on with the business at hand.

Pedro turned towards Yaneti and the other passengers and flashed them a wicked smile. Then he turned his back on them, staring out to the open sea. He lit himself another cigarette, and the stench of cheap Cuban tobacco invaded the hot, humid air.

His mind wandered off to a time when he was a boy and had worked on a fishing boat. That a long time ago now, before all the killing, and before he had been sent to jail by that bastard, Castro. He was a brutal man, Pedro, brutal and savage, and in prison he had been feared by all. Behind his back, men would say horrible things about him. Some of them said that he had not been born the natural way, "but that he had come out of the wrong hole." It was a pretty ugly thing to say about a human being, and of course no one had ever dared to say that to his face. Anybody who had would have been a dead man for sure. Pedro would have "ripped his head off and shit in his body," as he liked to say when he joked about killing someone he despised— or maybe not joking so much.

Pedro loved to kill; it was in his DNA. Life had done that to him, it had forged him that way. He had been orphaned very young and had been raised on violence and neglect by a brutal and alcoholic uncle. Already at a very young age, he had tasted the sourness and bitterness of abuse, and all the worst forms of human indecency that existed had been visited upon him before he was even a man. By the time he was seventeen, he was already severely deranged, and he had killed twice—once a deck hand on a fishing boat, whom he had pushed overboard during a storm because the guy had made fun of his humble upbringing, and then a girl from the country, whose name he couldn't remember, but whose face he couldn't forget. He had killed her because he wanted to know what it felt like to choke someone and to watch them die.

At nineteen, he had enrolled into the army. Castro's army was an opportunity for a brute like him, at least he had thought so at the time, and he had been right about that. The army recognized the cold-blooded killer that was sleeping in him and they woke it up. They used that part of him and they used it often. Then, one day, for no apparent reason, they arrested him and accused him of having committed crimes against the state, and he was thrown in jail. The charges were totally made up; they never told him why he had been arrested and sent to prison. As far as he was concerned, it was probably because he had done too much of their dirty work. He was good at it, maybe too good, or maybe he just knew too much. Whatever it was, he never found out. He kept his mouth shut in prison about what he had done and for whom, and even though he didn't know why he had been sent there, he had shrugged it off and concentrated on the more pressing problem of his own survival.

In jail, everyone quickly found out what he was about. In the first two years he was there, he killed two men. They were men who had rubbed him the wrong way, or had looks about them that he didn't like—to Pedro it really didn't matter the reason, he was willing to break any man's neck if he thought that he deserved it. The guards didn't care either way, for them it was just one less prick that they would have to deal with, and if a guy was stupid enough to get in Pedro's way, well then too bad for him, he probably got what was coming to him. Cuba, after all, was the kingdom of one man, whose army and police ruled supreme over everything and everyone. Prisoners were nobodies who nobody gave a shit about. If you were unlucky enough to have ended up in one of Castro's prisons, you would probably end up dead, forgotten, or both, and that's just the way things were. Pedro had always understood how things worked, and he had always respected whoever was holding the big end of the stick, so he kept clear of the guards in jail and they kept clear of him. They had a silent understanding in that way. His objectives in jail were simple: to survive, and to be left alone. Then, as suddenly as they had arrested him, and without any explanation, they let him out.

A few days after his release, a high-level bureaucrat named Oscar Leon had sought him out and made him an offer to work on "a highly sensitive government mission." He had accepted without even knowing what the work was; he was smart enough to know that it was not an offer that he could have said no to, because if he had, they probably would have killed him or sent him back to jail. So he had accepted, and had gotten into this sordid business. They paid him well for what he did, and as an added bonus, it turned out that it allowed him to do the two things that he liked best: being at sea and killing.

Pedro turned slowly around to face his crew, and he nodded his head. It was the signal that they had been waiting for and they sprung into action. Two of them went below deck and brought up some heavy chains and cement blocks. They proceeded to lock the chains onto the cement blocks and around the bound and gagged passengers' ankles.

The passengers became very agitated and panic-stricken, and some of them squirmed and tried desperately to move or to free themselves, but the restraints were too secure. Others tried to shout or scream, but with the tape covering their mouths, all they could produce was a pathetic, muffled wheezing sound. Mucus came out of their noses and their faces turned red from the effort. Yaneti looked at her fellow passengers through her tears, and she saw the same bone-chilling terror in their eyes that she was feeling in her heart.

She tried to scream as the large black man fixed a chain solidly around her ankles, but she could produce no sound. Sweat ran down her forehead and got into her eyes, blurring her vision. The large black man stooped down and looked straight at her. His eyes were blank and empty, and it made her angry that he seemed to be feeling nothing. She wondered how a human being could get that way, so unfeeling and so callous. She twisted and writhed, but she was soon out of breath and had to stop moving because of the sharp pain in her chest. The chains were about six feet long, and at the end of each one were two large concrete blocks. There was no doubt in Yaneti's mind about what was going to happen next.

All fourteen passengers were frozen in fear as the inevitability of their predicament hit them full force. A last burst of energy suddenly animated them, and they all began to squirm and wiggle at the same time. Their faces became bloated and their eyes bulged out of their sockets and tears flowed freely down their cheeks. Some of them pissed and shit themselves, and the stench of urine and feces quickly filled the hot and humid air.

"Ah ha, my favorite moment at last!" Pedro squealed with excitement and appeared almost jubilant. The crew was all looking in his direction expectantly. There was an ominous silence for a second or two, and then he slowly lifted his arm and pointed towards the ocean.

"Now, get rid of these dogs," he barked, and very quickly, one at a time, two of the men grabbed the helpless, writhing passengers by the feet and shoulders, while the other two picked up the chains and the concrete blocks and unceremoniously heaved them overboard.

The bodies hit the water with a loud splash, and every splash sent an electric shock through Yaneti's heart. She was the last to go, and she prayed in those last few milliseconds, "oh please, God, please, no," and she thought of her mother and father and Ernesto, the love of her life, and how heartbroken they would all be. The last thing she saw before sinking into the deep, dark, peaceful ocean, were the lights, the scintillating lights on the distant horizon that she had thought were the lights of America.

HAVANA

They had met on the night of January 2nd, near the *Plaza de la Revolution*, at a show that the authorities were putting on there as part of the events celebrating the anniversary of the Cuban revolution. By the time Yaneti and her cousin Marisol had reached the *Plaza* the crowd was already thick and the place was filling up quickly. The girls had had a few shots of rum beforehand at a friend's house, and the rum had energized them and made them giddy. They had started dancing the minute the first band began to play, swaying happily to the rhythm of the fiery salsa music.

The crowd was huge, "at least a million people celebrating the revolution," they would say for sure the next day on state television. Who knows, this time it might even be true. You never knew for sure with them, the government people that is, those who defined what was said and what was repeated and by whom. Of course the reality of it was that Yaneti and Marisol were not there to celebrate the revolution. Like most of the young *Habaneros* who were there, they came because it was a free show, and for the great bands and the fireworks and the dancing. It was also one of the rare times when young people could actually get out and enjoy life a little, which was not a common occurrence in an army- and police-controlled state. Cuba was a drab and dreary place to be if you were young and full of life and needed things to move and shake a little in order to convince yourself that you were actually alive.

As the evening progressed, the crowd moved as one, as illuminated as the stage. There were fireworks overhead and bodies pressed close together, and everyone was clapping their hands and swinging to the contagious rhythm of the music. It was during one of the bursts of light from the fireworks that she saw him for the first time, looking straight at her, six or seven people away. He was smiling at her, and spontaneously she smiled back, and then turned her attention back to the stage and to the band. A few minutes later she turned in his direction again, and he was still looking her way, but this time he waved at her and smiled. She waved back and leaned over to her cousin, shouting in her ear to look towards the tall, good-looking guy who was flirting with her a few people over. Marisol looked in his direction and he smiled and waved to her too. She waved back.

"He's cute,' she shouted to Yaneti.

"Yeah, he is." Yaneti let her eyes linger in the stranger's direction, smiling and swaying. The alcohol had made her bold. She turned her attention towards the stage again, and a few minutes later she felt a presence behind her. She turned, and it was him, and he smiled at her. He had an incredibly endearing smile and an inviting glimmer in his eyes, and she was instantaneously drawn to him.

"Hi, my name is Ernesto, Ernesto Rodriguez," he had leaned over near her ear so she could hear him above the music. He extended his hand in her direction and she noticed the multicolored cloth-and-silver bracelets that hung loosely from his wrist. When she took his hand, his skin was soft and warm. He was a good head taller than her, and well dressed, in a cool and laid-back kind of way. His skin was slightly tanned, and he was good looking and sure of himself. She immediately felt that there was an innate kindness and a quiet decency about him.

"Hi, I'm Yaneti," she shouted, "and this is my cousin Marisol."

"Hi Marisol, pleased to meet you," he waved in her direction. "May I join in your celebration?" he added, even though he was already moving to the music and clapping his hands.

"Aren't you with some people?" Yaneti shouted, pointing in the direction where he had been standing.

"No, I'm alone, I'm not with anybody," he shouted back, without missing a beat of the music. Yaneti smiled at him mischievously.

"Ok, you can join us, but on one condition."

"Ok, what's the condition?"

"If you stop dancing, then you have to go away, ok?" He looked at her and smiled.

"Ok, I swear I will dance till the sun rises, so long as it is beside you, Yaneti. And you, too," he added, looking towards Marisol. The girls burst out laughing, and he jumped in between them, gyrating wildly to the explosive music. They joined him, and soon the three of them were moving in sync, hands clapping, hips bouncing, laughing and smiling, happy to be alive, happy to have the music— and in the case of Ernesto and Yaneti, happy to have met each other.

Their instantaneous *joie de vivre* was typical of Cubans. It was something intrinsic to them, the dancing and the joy, and it was something that Castro's regime had not been able to stifle, even after fifty years of revolutionary privations and institutionalized drabness.

Two days after that first encounter, Yaneti and Ernesto saw each other again, and fell madly in love. From that moment on, they became inseparable. Ernesto would later joke about how they were "children of the revolution. After all," he would say sarcastically, "it is because of the revolution that we met, is it not?"

Yaneti quickly learned that Ernesto's dislike of Cuba's communist system was intense, and that his loathing of it was never far from the surface. He did not concede to it any accomplishment; he cursed its very existence and despised it for everything that it was and everything it was not. Even though he was careful about whom he expressed his views to, and even though she agreed with him on most of the things he said, she was worried that his opinions would get him into trouble one day, and she did everything she could to try to make him keep his thoughts to himself.

Life was not easy in Castro's Cuba if you were young, talented, ambitious, and full of hopes and dreams. Not only was it a whirlwind of small dead ends, but the whole country was one big dead end, the epitome of state control and the world capital of redundant rhetoric and bureaucratic insipidity. It was the living proof that even the most inept of governments will always find a way to glorify and perpetuate itself. The Cuban governing elite seemed convinced that only they, because of their infinite and limitless wisdom, "knew what was best for the people of Cuba." They believed that their way was the way of the past, the present and the future, but the reality was that the past had become ancient history, they barely controlled the present, and the future did not belong to them.

It was indeed a curse to be young and full of life in Cuba these days, to want a different life than that of the millions of disheartened and disenchanted people who stood in line for hours every day, waiting to board a moribund and overcrowded bus on the way to a redundant job which paid a pittance, or standing in interminable lines for food or basic necessities. Cuba's citizens had been deprived of their dignity and cut off from the modern world, without dreams or even hopes of dreams, with nowhere to go and nothing to do but wait for the tedium of their dreary existence to take its toll. They had no genuine opportunities, but were condemned to be prisoners in their own country, minds and bodies intact, but spirits broken and to be the helpless witnesses of the accelerated decay of their capital city, Havana, once the country's pride and joy, now eviscerated by years of neglect and abandoned to the forces of nature, a national shame, ugly and decrepit, it's past splendor and grandeur forgotten and buried under years of accumulated disregard and bureaucratic ineptitude.

It was not surprising, therefore, that the main preoccupation of a lot of Cuba's people was to flee the island by any means possible. But fleeing was difficult, and even dangerous, and there was a downside to the exodus, as there always is in such unnatural movements of population: all those who choose to flee were forced to leave their friends and families behind, abandoning their roots and the country of their birth and the love and warmth of mother Cuba, *La Patria*. It was a pain that was practically unendurable for most true-hearted Cubans, and so what most of them did was nothing at all, and they remained on the island, frozen in time, unhappy and chained to their despair, hanging onto the hope that the regime would someday expire from acute insignificance or from geriatric fatigue. They prayed that a better life was waiting for them, somewhere in the not-so-distant future.

This was the world in which Yaneti and Ernesto had met and fallen in love; it was not the best of worlds, but it was their world—the only one that they knew, and the one that they were forced to live in, day in and day out. The only thing that comforted them and appeased their gloom was that they had each other to love and to cherish. No one could take that away from them, no matter what.

Two years had passed since they had met at the Plaza de la Revolution, and in that time, Yaneti had graduated from university, finishing first in her class and obtaining two degrees, one in history and another in education. She had been given a job as a teacher by the state, and although she loved the kids and teaching, she was unhappy with her measly state salary which did not permit her to live decently. At twenty-five, she felt that she was leading a miserable existence. Thank God for the relatives her parents had in Miami who managed to get a few hundred dollars to them every month, permitting them to invite her to lunch every Sunday and to share a decent meal with them.

But eating a decent meal wasn't Yaneti's greatest source of concern—Ernesto was. He was strong and proud, and the blood of his Spanish ancestors still flowed freely through his veins. He could be hotheaded and act unpredictably sometimes. He was a year older than Yaneti, and athletic. He had been a good swimmer when he was younger—good enough that he had almost made it to the Olympics. But he was a bit of a rebel, and she felt that he lived dangerously and attracted too much attention to himself. He had quit school and did not officially work, which was a risky thing to do in Cuba. He earned money by renting out the apartment his parents had given him and by buying stolen cigars from the factory workers and reselling them to tourists and airline crews. Ernesto's parents were retired bureaucrats and they lived fairly well, considering the living conditions of most of the population. They had two apartments which had been theirs before the revolution, one they lived in and another they had given to Ernesto. Ernesto pretended to live in it, but he rented it out most of the time to tourists for cash. He and Yaneti used it as their love nest when it wasn't rented out. It was a good business, and even if he had to declare part of what he earned to the authorities, it still left him with more money in his pockets every month than most Cubans earned in a year. He was always well-dressed, and had a car and a cell phone, and all those visible signs of unexplainable luxury made Yaneti nervous. She was scared that the authorities would pick him up one day and put him in jail and throw away the key. This was the way things were done in Cuba; everybody knew that, and it worried her.

There was one thing, however, that Yaneti was certain about, and that was Ernesto's love for her. He would tell her that he loved her every time he had the chance to do so, many times a day, and she liked that about him. Having him in her life made her feel safe and secure.

"It is forever me and you," he would say, and his eyes would light up when he said it. "Imagine, my love—we have found each other! Do you realize how lucky we are and how wonderful that is?" Yaneti felt the same way about him, and it was because she loved him so much that she was so worried about him. It was not their future together that she worried about, but his plan, the secret one, the one he saved all his money for: his plan to escape Cuba forever and to flee with her to the United States. They would talk about it often, but only late at night in the darkness of their room, and always in whispers, because Yaneti was afraid to talk about it anywhere else. Everybody knew that in Cuba, even the walls had ears.

"I've heard about this guy who will help us get across, I'm meeting him tomorrow," he whispered to her one night when they were lying in bed. Yaneti turned towards him, alarmed.

"Oh Ernesto, please be careful, please, I'm so scared." She began to tremble slightly, and he took her in his arms and hugged her.

"Don't be afraid, my love. I'll be very careful, nothing will happen. I promise." Yaneti nodded her head nervously. "Look, it's Raphael who told me about this guy, and you know we can trust him. Anyway, Raphael heard about this guy from someone whose brother is in Miami. It is a good solid contact and apparently this guy is well-connected. Raphael set me up, and tomorrow I'll go check him out." They fell silent as both of them thought about what would happen if he got caught talking about or planning an escape from Cuba. This was considered a very grave crime. He would be thrown in jail for a long time and his family would be sanctioned—that was the way of the Cuban regime. All was based on fear and retribution, and the retribution was always a lot more severe than the offense. It was meant to be a message for anybody else who was thinking about doing the same thing.

"What if something goes wrong, Ernesto? What if they arrest you? I will die if you end up in jail. Please don't go, please don't do this. I'm scared." Yaneti began to tremble again, and she pressed herself against his chest.

"Now, now, my love," he rocked her gently, kissing the top of her head, "we've talked about this before, remember? And you know I'd rather die than live here, you know that? I just want you to have a better life, my love, you and our future children. You have to trust me on this, and you have to have faith. I promise you everything will be ok, I promise." He kissed the top of her head again in the darkness and she held onto him tightly, her body tense with apprehension.

The following day, Ernesto met Oscar Leon for the first time. It would be one of many long and nerve-racking meetings with him. The only information he had been given about Oscar was that he was connected to the right people. They met in the kitchen of a small house on a quiet street in the Vedado district of Havana. Oscar Leon never met people in public.

He was a diminutive man, not more than five feet tall and adorned with a thick and well-trimmed black mustache. His eyes were small and black and fleeting, darting from side to side when he spoke, and Ernesto immediately sensed that he reveled in his own authority and importance. He wore the traditional Cuban guayabera shirt, and he thrust his chest forward when he rose to shake Ernesto's hand, as if to give himself more stature and physical importance. His hand, when Ernesto took it, was moist and limp and tiny, like that of a child. It surprised Ernesto, and made him a bit wary. He had always feared small men in positions of authority, and he felt that Oscar's undersized build did not make him less dangerous—perhaps even more so.

There had been a man behind Oscar Leon when Ernesto walked in. He was the second man he had seen in the house. The other one had been the man who opened the door; he was a very large and tall black man, whose head was shaven and whose arms were enormous and thick, rippling with muscles and power. He had not smiled when Ernesto had smiled at him, and had only indicated the way to the kitchen with a nod of his head. Ernesto had felt the man's cold, expressionless eyes on his back when he walked in the direction he pointed.

The other man standing behind Oscar Leon was even less reassuring. He stood with his arms crossed, observing the scene. He was also tall and broad-shouldered, and was wearing a sleeveless shirt. His large arms and chest were covered in scars and tattoos, and his grimy hair was cut in an uneven brush cut. He looked directly and intently at Ernesto, his face ravaged and potholed. His eyes were somber and disquieting, and there was a disturbing darkness within them. The presence of the two men there with Oscar Leon was a clear message that he meant business and was not to be toyed with. None of the three were reassuring sights to behold, and Ernesto began to sweat, wondering if the whole thing had not a bad idea after all, as Yaneti had so often told him.

"Please, sit down." Oscar Leon smiled and pointed towards the empty chair in front of him as he sat down himself. Ernesto looked at him. He knew that smile and that manner, it was the smile and the manner of the bureaucrats and those who worked for the government. It was the smile of people who believed that they were constantly being watched and monitored and who spoke and acted accordingly. Such folks were always afflicted by a chronic and idiosyncratic insincerity that was usually laughable— but this was not one of those times. Ernesto was very nervous and a terrible thought entered his mind. *What if this is a trap?* The thought terrified him, and he suddenly felt dizzy. He sat down in a quick movement, afraid he would pass out if he didn't.

Oscar Leon was very poised. He had the awkward elegance of the fallaciously important about him; he held his back rigid and his head high. His tiny, rapid eyes moved cunningly in their sockets as he looked haughtily in Ernesto's direction, as if he were examining some lower form of life.

"So Ernesto, how are things with you, everything good?" Oscar Leon sensed the other's nervousness and was trying to put him at ease. Ernesto's mouth was dry and he felt sick to his stomach, but he knew that he was too far into this now to just get up and leave, so he forced himself to smile and said as calmly as he could,

"Good, Mr. Leon, everything is good, thank you very much."

"I'm glad to hear that, but please, call me Oscar. First names will be ok between us."

"Yes, of course, sir, I mean Oscar."

"Good. So tell me, how is your family? Is everyone fine? All is well with them I hope?" The mention of his family sent a cold chill down Ernesto's spine and he prayed Oscar Leon was only making small talk.

"Yes, they are all well, thank you for asking." Ernesto bowed his head forward slightly in a sign of deference to the other man. He could feel his heart pounding furiously against his temples.

"Well, good then, I'm glad to hear that." There was an awkward silence as Oscar Leon looked at him intently while tapping a small finger on the table. To Ernesto, it seemed like an eternity, although it couldn't have lasted more than seven or eight seconds. Finally Oscar broke the silence.

"Very well, then, let us get down to business, shall we?"

"Yes, of course," Ernesto answered, trying hard to appear calm.

"Ok. There are a few things I need to establish beforehand, Ernesto. The first thing is that this meeting never took place and that I do not know you and you do not know me and we have never spoken, understood?" He paused and Ernesto answered with as much assurance as he could muster.

"Yes of course... understood."

"Good. Now, the second thing you must understand is that I love Cuba dearly and our great leader and everything wonderful he has done for all of us." Ernesto stiffened. He had not expected to hear this, at this time and in this place, and it instantly magnified his fear of the little man.

"But...," Oscar Leon raised his hand in a pacifying gesture, having noticed that Ernesto had seized up at his words. "...I also love my mother, who is very ill and in the U.S.A. That is a very long story, though, and I don't intend to share it with you at this time. Anyway, to make a long story short, I must send her money, lots of money, to pay for her medical bills. Do you know how rotten and capitalistic the U.S. medical system is? It is only for the rich and for those who have money, and the ones who don't—well. They are simply not treated, and left to die on the street, like dogs. Did you know that?" He had raised his voice slightly. Ernesto shook his head to indicate that he didn't, while trying to look as incredulous and as outraged as he could. "Of course you don't. Well, anyway, that is the reason why I am here today, do you understand? I am not a traitor!" He had raised his voice again. "I am just a man." He leaned forward and lowered his voice. "A man who desperately wants to help his sick mother." He leaned back in his chair, bowed his head, and made a movement with his hand as if he were wiping a tear from one of his eyes. A deadly silence hung over the room. Ernesto did not dare move or speak. Oscar Leon raised his head, and it seemed to Ernesto that there was genuine sadness in his eyes.

"You do understand me, don't you?" He asked softly.

"Yes I do, I understand you, Mr. Leon, I mean Oscar, and I'm sorry about your mother." A wave of relief went through Ernesto's body as he realized that there was a chance that this guy might be for real, and that things might work out as he had hoped. Oscar Leon smiled at him. He was happy. He loved to tell his story about his sick mother in America. It always went over well and it helped to soften up the people who came to him to get out of Cuba. They loved that story; every one of them fell for it. That's all it was, though, of course—a story. Ernesto smiled back politely, but he was still tense, and completely unprepared for what was coming next.

"Good, then, now let me tell you a few facts about Cuba and the wonderful work that has been done here since the revolution." Oscar Leon then went on for over an hour and a half explaining in great detail all the benefits of the revolution and how much the Cuban people had gained in dignity and prestige in the world because of it. Ernesto nodded and acquiesced in silence. He would never have dared contradict him, although his own thoughts on the subject were radically different. When it came to the subject of Fidel Castro, Oscar Leon did not even dare pronounce the leader's name, so taken was he by Castro and by his aura and accomplishments. To the apolitical and astounded Ernesto, it was like sitting for an hour and a half in a dentist's chair. Then, suddenly, the lecture was over. Oscar Leon got up and he motioned to Ernesto to do the same.

"Ok, I have to go now Ernesto. I will see you here next week at the same time. Be very discreet, talk to no one about this, and do not be late." He extended his hand in Ernesto's direction, and a stunned Ernesto got up and shook his small limp hand again. Seeing the expression on his face, Oscar Leon smiled,

"Do not worry; today I wanted to see you and to see if I could trust you. You know, to get to know you." Ernesto smiled sheepishly back.

"Yes, of course, I understand, Mr.Le…, I mean, Oscar."

"Good, next time we will get down to the business which concerns you, ok?"

"Yes, ok, next time then, thank you."

Ernesto was shaken and confused when he left the house. He did not know what to think of Oscar Leon and his communist bullshit. Was he for real? Was it a set up? Was it a government trap to take his money and throw him in jail? Many questions were swirling in his mind, and he decided not to share his thoughts and apprehensions with Yaneti. When he saw her that evening he told her that the meeting had gone well and that he would have more information the following week.

There were four more meetings between Ernesto and Oscar Leon over the course of the next two months, and at each meeting Oscar would speak endlessly about the beauty and the benefits of Castro's Cuba. These lectures were like torture to Ernesto, but he put up with them in silence, so desperate was he to leave Cuba. Despite the rhetoric, Ernesto believed that Oscar Leon could actually deliver and get him and Yaneti to the U.S. After all, he had not had Ernesto arrested or thrown in jail so far—he took that as proof of the man's good intentions.

Of course, there was a lot about Oscar Leon that Ernesto didn't know. He did not know that Oscar had failed to rise in the Cuban bureaucracy because he was gay, even though he was a fervent pro-Castro, pro-communist zealot, and he did not know that Oscar's family had been one of the richest families in Cuba before the revolution, strong supporters of the Batista regime, and had fled to the U.S. precipitously on New Year's Eve, the night that Batista had been overthrown. Oscar Leon had only been a baby at the time and was at an aunt's house that evening, a good two hours' drive from Havana. In the haste and the chaos of his family's hurried departure, Oscar had been left behind.

All through his youth he had been stigmatized for his homosexuality, but despite it all, he had become an ardent party activist and had thrown himself wholeheartedly into the construction of Castro's Cuba. As a young man, he had joined the communist bureaucracy and had worked as a low level bureaucrat for a number of years. Things had remained on that low rung for him for some time, until he became the secret lover of an important general who helped and protected him. It was because of his relationship with the general that he had become such a powerful and dangerous man. It was the general who had asked him to recruit ex-convicts to patrol the coasts of Cuba. Officially, they were searching for drug smugglers. Of course, it was clearly understood between them from the get-go that his real job was to 'take care' of the people that the general's cronies recruited who were willing to pay to leave Cuba by boat for the U.S. This was one of the general's businesses and for him, it was strictly about the money. It was also implicit in their arrangement that no one would ever actually reach the U.S., and Oscar Leon was quite content with that; as far as he was concerned, the people that were recruited were traitors and deserved to die. The general didn't care either way, so long as things were kept quiet and he got paid. Ernesto, of course, was unaware of all this as he played along with Oscar Leon, not knowing what he was getting into or who he was dealing with. He had no inkling how dangerous the situation really was.

He did get a bit concerned though—at every meeting he had with Oscar Leon, things kept changing, and it made him nervous. The only thing that never changed was the price: ten thousand dollars per person. It was an enormous amount of money; Ernesto only had seven thousand dollars stashed away. He had to find another three thousand dollars before even one of them would be able to leave, and he had decided that that person would be Yaneti. He was afraid that she would not have the courage to go if he left her behind, and that she would be unable to endure what he had been through with Oscar Leon. No matter how often he turned it over in his mind, Ernesto was sure that Yaneti would have to go first. There was no other way.

He got the three thousand dollars he was missing delivered by an Italian tourist to whom he rented his apartment for a month every year. The money had been wired to the guy in Italy by Yaneti's relatives in Miami, and now the only thing he had left to do was to convince her that she had to go first and without him. That would not be an easy task, and Ernesto knew it. He had decided that he would insist on the positive aspect of things when discussing it with her, like the fact that she had relatives in Miami who were well off and who could help her find a job quickly and get the money together to pay for his passage. Then, hopefully, he would be joining her in Miami in six months to a year at the most. It felt like a good plan to him, and he succeeded in convincing himself that it was. It was also the only plan that he had.

"I'm scared, Ernesto, there are so many things that can go wrong. I will die if I don't see you again, I swear I'll die," she argued through her tears.

"Please, my love, please, you have to trust me, I know what I'm doing. I know this will work out, you have to do this for me, for us." Ernesto was convincing, even though privately he had certain misgivings about Oscar Leon. He also knew how illegal and dangerous the thing they were planning was, but he kept those somber thoughts to himself.

"Let's just call this whole thing off Ernesto, please, it's not too late. Let's not do it, I have a bad feeling about this—I know something is not right, I can feel it."

"Yaneti please, I beg you, I need you to be strong and I need you to do this, please." Ernesto put everything he had into convincing her; he pleaded, he yelled, he cajoled, he cried, he made promises and he reassured her in every possible way that he could think of. Finally she relented and said,

"Ok, Ernesto, I will do it, because I love you and because you will never be happy if I don't. I will go for you and for us and for our future together." Ernesto had hugged her tightly and they had cried in each others' arms and he had thanked her for her love and her trust in him.

There were many more heated discussions between them while they waited on Oscar Leon to give them a departure date, when the doubts and the questions rose to the surface in Yaneti's mind. Almost every night when they lay in bed, she would whisper her fears to him and he would reassure her and tell her that everything would be ok. Many hours were spent this way and it only ever ended when she fell asleep, with the doubts and the questions still lingering in her mind, and in his, too.

They both became extremely nervous and tense during

this period, and every time someone knocked on the door or looked at them on the street, they felt the strain of their situation.

Finally, a last meeting was set up with Oscar Leon. It would be at the same house as all their earlier meetings, but late at night this time. All their previous meetings had taken place during the day. Ernesto was very nervous. He had brought all the money with him, as he had been told to do. It was the money that had taken him eight years to save, together with the money from Yaneti's relatives, and he knew that if things didn't work out, he would be back to zero. He might even be thrown in jail, and then it would be the end of his life as he knew it.

A man let him in the house, but he could not see his face because of the darkness and the way that he stood behind the door to let him in. He heard the sound of the door being locked behind him, and then the man pointed towards the flickering light that came from the kitchen. There was a small oil lamp burning on the kitchen table, and Oscar Leon was sitting at the table with a bottle of rum and two empty tumblers in front of him. The same two men who had been in the house the first time Ernesto visited, and every other time since then, were standing behind him. They were leaning against the kitchen counter, arms crossed, immobile and silent. They followed Ernesto intently with their eyes as he walked in.

"Come on in, Ernesto, sit down," Oscar Leon smiled and motioned to him to have a seat. Ernesto sat down while looking at the two standing men nervously. After a short silence, Oscar Leon asked,

"So, have you brought the money?"

"Yes... yes, I have," was Ernesto's hesitant answer.

"Good... well, come on now, let's have it." Ernesto slowly retrieved the envelope with the money from the front of his pants and placed it on the table. Oscar Leon took the envelope, took a quick look inside, and then put it in the small attaché case at his feet.

"I will count this later, but I trust the full amount is there?"

"Yes, the full amount is there."

"Good, now this is what you will do. You will bring the girl to this house tomorrow night an hour after dark. She must not carry anything heavy such as a suitcase, or anything else that would make her conspicuous. You will drop her off and leave immediately, and please, please, no long goodbyes in the car in front of the house; this is very important, Ernesto. Are we clear about this?" Ernesto saw beads of sweat forming on his tiny forehead.

"Yes, very clear."

"Good, so again, bring her here tomorrow night an hour after dark and we will take it from there, ok?"

"Yes, ok."

Oscar Leon picked up the rum bottle and poured some rum into the two tumblers, indicating to Ernesto to take one. He then picked up the other one and raised it in his direction.

"To you, my friend," he said, smiling, and Ernesto picked up the other tumbler.

"To you, Señor Leon." Ernesto could not bring himself to call him Oscar. They both downed their glasses and stared into each other's eyes for a few moments. Oscar Leon briskly got up and picked up the briefcase at his feet and, without saying another word, he turned around and swiftly left by the back door, with the two men in tow. Ernesto heard a click as they locked the door behind them from the outside. He sat there for a minute or two, stunned and in silence. *What has just happened here?* He wondered. The house was eerily quiet, and his body felt like it weighed a ton. He slowly got up and made his way along the darkened passage towards the front door, and the quiet man in the shadows discreetly let him out. He was acutely aware as he walked towards his car that from now on, his life and Yaneti's were in someone else's hands.

That night, neither he nor Yaneti slept much. They kissed and cried a lot, and they made love, and laughed, and told each other stories about when they were young and how life would be in America and about the children they would have and about their future together. Ernesto spent a lot of time reassuring her and telling her how much he loved her and that everything would be alright.

They got up early the next morning, and Yaneti packed a small backpack with some basic things. They drank their coffee in silence, eyes locked on one another across the breakfast table. It was not necessary to speak any words— they both knew what the other was feeling and thinking. That evening, they went to a dinner at Yaneti's parents' apartment that had been planned a few weeks earlier. They had both agreed that it was better that they go, even though it would be difficult for both of them to try to act normally in her parents' presence. They had agreed not to tell either his or her parents about what they were planning to do. Ernesto would go see Yaneti's parents only after she had safely arrived in Miami.

"It is better that they don't know," Ernesto had said when they discussed it. "That way, if you get caught before you leave Cuban waters, they will be able to deny that they knew what you were going to do and it will be the truth." Yaneti had reluctantly agreed with him because she knew that her mother was incapable of telling a lie.

The dinner was also a perfect occasion for Yaneti to see her parents one last time before she left. It meant she wouldn't have to casually drop by in the afternoon and risk losing her cool and breaking down in their presence. She was glad that they already had a dinner planned, and that Ernesto was coming with her.

They both found it to be a long dinner, and couldn't wait for it to be over. It was particularly difficult on Yaneti, who embraced her parents much longer than she normally would have before she left.

It was dark out when they got into the car and headed in the direction of the house where Ernesto was to drop her off. Both were staring straight ahead, each trying to contain the extreme anxiety and emotions that were tearing them up inside. Yaneti turned towards Ernesto.

"You will call me often, every day, if you can?" She knew that there was only so much he could do and that communication with someone in the U.S. could sometimes be difficult, but she asked anyway.

"Yes, my love," Ernesto took one of her hands. "I will call you every day, two times a day if I can, I promise, as soon as you send me a number to call you, ok? Now stop worrying, everything will be ok, I promise." Yaneti squeezed his hand and bit her lower lip. She tried to hold back her tears, but it didn't work; the tsunami of emotions that had been building up inside her chest all day was more powerful than her will to contain it.

"Ok," she mumbled, and she began to cry softly and then to sob. Her shoulders shook slightly as she was swept by a sudden wave of sadness.

"Please Yaneti, please, you have to be strong, you have to control yourself, please, stop crying. We will be there soon and there can be no scenes in front of the house, nothing, do you understand?" Ernesto was scared she would lose it, and he had raised his voice slightly. She stopped crying and wiped the tears off her cheeks with the back of her hands and stared out the window.

"I'm sorry," she said through her sniffles, "I'm scared, that's all, and I won't be with you for a long time, and that makes me sad. I miss you already."

"I understand, my love, I'm scared too, but I know I'll be with you soon and that makes me feel better." Yaneti did not answer, but continued to stare out the car window. They were silent for the next few minutes and the tension in the car weighed heavily on both of them. They turned onto the street that the rendezvous house was on and slowly made their way towards it.

"Ok, it's here," Ernesto pointed to the house up ahead. "Now remember, just a small kiss goodbye, no scenes, not here, this is very important." His voice betrayed his high level of stress. He stopped the car in front of the house and she turned towards him, locking her tear-filled eyes on his.

"I love you Ernesto, I'll always love you."

"I love you too, my love, and I promise, I'll love you for longer than forever, but please, you have to go now," he leaned over and opened the door for her, kissing her gently on the lips. Yaneti got out of the car and slowly turned towards him.

"Goodbye, my love," she whispered, tears rolling down her cheeks. She noticed that his eyes had started to fill up with tears too, and she closed the car door and turned and walked towards the house without looking back.

Ernesto put the car into gear and it began to slowly move up the street and tears were pouring down his cheeks now and he made no effort to wipe them off. In his rear view mirror, he saw her knock on the door and then disappear into the house. It was the last time he would ever see her alive.

THE CROSSING

Ernesto became sick with worry. He couldn't eat or sleep, or move or think straight. He was petrified, frozen in place by fear and the anguish of not knowing. Yaneti seemed to have disappeared from the face of the earth. One month had passed and still he had had no news. It had been a month of torment and tortured nights for him, and eventually his worry had begun to turn into despair. A week after Yaneti's departure, he had gone to see her parents and explained to them why they had not heard from their daughter in so many days. It had been a very difficult moment for him, and he had broken down and cried like a baby, but Yaneti's parents had quickly brushed aside the fact that they had hidden their plans from them. Their immediate concern was for their daughter's whereabouts and safety. When word came from their relatives in Miami that they had not heard from her either, they, too, became gravely concerned.

It was a very dismal time in Ernesto's life. He was so worried that he developed stomach problems, and the doctor he consulted told him that it was the beginning of a stomach ulcer and that he should be careful of what he ate. But it wasn't bad food that was chewing away at Ernesto's gut, it was the realization that something had to be terribly wrong for Yaneti not to have given news to anyone about her whereabouts, or let them know she was ok.

He spent his days and nights pacing about his apartment and talking out loud to himself. Many times he had wanted to get in touch with Oscar Leon to ask him if he could help, but he remembered the very stern warning he had been given by him about doing just that, and his words still resonated in his mind.

"You cannot contact me before six months have passed, and only when you are ready to go yourself. Also, you must never try to contact me about the current matter once it is done; it will be out of my hands and there is nothing I can do about whatever might happen at sea or in American waters. Do you understand me, Ernesto?" His voice had always been high strung when he mentioned this. He had been very insistent and had brought it up at every one of their meetings.

"Yes, of course, I understand," had always been Ernesto's reply, and Oscar Leon would always add.

"As you know, many things can happen at sea. This is not a cruise ship they are going on and there are no guarantees. No matter what the outcome, you are never to seek me out about this again, this has to be very clear between us." He had repeated the warning so many times that Ernesto understood that to call him out on this would be a grave mistake.

Ernesto now wondered what he had meant by, "…whatever the outcome." It was as if Oscar Leon had known that something would happen. "No, that can't be," he said out loud, shaking his head from side to side, trying to clear his mind of the thoughts he didn't want to have. In his wildest dreams he never imagined that Oscar Leon could have had anything to do with whatever had or had not happened to Yaneti. He was naïve, and convinced that Oscar Leon was a man of honor who respected his word. As far as Ernesto was concerned, there were only two possibilities as to what might have happened to her. Their boat could have had mechanical problems and drifted out to sea. He had heard of this happening to fishermen who had been found at great distances out to sea, after months of drifting. The second possibility he envisioned was that she had been picked up by the American or the Cuban authorities and was being detained somewhere with no way of communicating with anyone. In his mind this was the most plausible explanation. From where he was in Cuba, a country with limited communication to the outside world and with no credible news source, where people disappeared and were never seen or heard from again, or reappeared suddenly after years of absence, it made complete sense.

Once in a while another thought crept into his mind, a dark and frightening thought that he had nightmares about and would put him in a state of complete panic. Although Oscar Leon had told him that the boat Yaneti had gotten on could resist a storm and was well stocked in food and water, he knew there was a possibility that the boat had sunk in a fierce storm. Yaneti didn't know how to swim, and she wouldn't have lasted more than a few minutes in a violent and tumultuous sea. He had horrible visions of her thrashing about in the water and sinking below the surface, her hand reaching out to him and calling out his name. He would wake up in the middle of the night, screaming and sweating, and he could never go back to sleep. When that happened, he would get up and go sit on the small balcony of his apartment and stare aimlessly out to the ocean for hours. When day broke, and only then, would he go back inside and try to get some sleep.

After five weeks, Ernesto couldn't take it anymore. He was exhausted from torturing himself and his mind and health were falling apart. He went to his parents to obtain his father's help and his blessing for what he had decided he was going to do. His father had been an exemplary civil servant all his life and was a good, honest man. He was not a fervent communist believer, but he had "played the game," as he liked to say, and had not made a wave or a mistake in his entire existence. For him, this was the sacrifice that he had had to make in order to give his wife and son the best life possible under the circumstances. It was important to Ernesto to obtain his father's approval for what he was about to do, but what he needed more than anything else, was his help.

Like Yaneti, in an effort to protect them, he had not told his parents anything about what he and Yaneti had planned and done. After he had gone a week without news from her, fearing that she might have been picked up by the Cuban authorities and that he was next, he had showed up at his parents' door in complete panic and had told them everything. It had been an emotional scene, and his mother had tried very hard to reassure him about Yaneti. When he had finished telling them the story, she had gotten up and had come to sit beside him on the sofa. She took his hand and brushed it lightly against her cheek, looking tenderly into his eyes.

"I'm sure everything will be ok, sweetheart," she had said softly, "she's probably been picked up by the authorities and you will hear from her soon." Ernesto had looked into his mother's eyes, wanting desperately to believe her words.

"You think so, Mama?" She had passed her hand through his hair and smiled.

"Yes, my love, I think so." She reached out towards him and took him in her arms, and he sobbed quietly as she stroked his back.

His father had remained stoically in his chair, observing the scene in silence with an expression of profound sadness on his face.

But now, five weeks later, Ernesto was very determined when he came over to his parents' apartment to solicit his father's help and blessing. His mother felt right away that something was different about him and that he had something on his mind. He sat down in the living room facing them, nervously cracking his fingers, and he started to explain to them what he had decided to do. He broke down the minute he pronounced Yaneti's name. It was like that every time he tried to say her name out loud, his emotions got the better of him and he would break down and cry. His mother came over to sit beside him and comfort him, kissing his forehead and hugging him.

When Ernesto had regained his composure, he sat up straight, his eyes red from the tears, and he took his mother's hand in his. Looking at his father, he said,

"I need to find out what's happened to her, Papa; I cannot live like this one more day. I need to know and so what I have decided to do is to retrace her footsteps." His father understood immediately what Ernesto was talking about and also what he was implicitly asking him. His mother looked from Ernesto to her husband, alarmed, suddenly realizing what Ernesto was saying.

"No Ernesto, this is madness, it's too dangerous! Please Julio, speak to him, do not let him do this." She turned to Ernesto and squeezed both of his hands, and her eyes were filled with fear. The thought of losing her son, her only child, terrified her.

"I beg you, Ernesto. Do not do this, please." He looked at her tenderly and put an arm around her and drew her to him, kissing her forehead tenderly.

"I love you, Mama, but I need to do this. I have to, so please try to understand." He looked into her frightened eyes and spoke softly and gently. "I cannot live without Yaneti, Mama, she is the love of my life. We will have children together, your grandchildren." Tears rolled down his mother's cheeks.

"No, Ernesto, please don't do this, I will die if I lose you." She looked desperately from Ernesto to her husband in the hope that one of them would give her a sign that the conversation they were having was not happening. Ernesto turned and looked directly into his father's eyes, and said,

"Papa, I beg you, will you help me?" There was a long silence. His father looked at him intently, and said only one word, but it was the word Ernesto wanted so desperately to hear.

"Yes," he said and nothing more, his eyes locked onto Ernesto's and oblivious to his wife's supplications.

The next day, knowing that his father would help him get the money he needed from his relatives in Miami,

Ernesto got in touch with Raphael, who had set up his first meeting with Oscar Leon. He asked him to try to organize a meeting as soon as possible, and to pass the message on that he had an urgent business proposition to make which just couldn't wait. Ernesto was nervous; he knew he was breaking the rules and that this could turn out very badly for him. Oscar Leon might think that he wanted to question him about what had happened to Yaneti, and he might panic and act before Ernesto had time to talk to him and explain what he wanted. But he had thought it out very carefully and had decided to take his chances. He just couldn't wait any longer, and this was the only lead he had to try to find Yaneti. He was willing to risk everything for that, even his own life.

It took two weeks before a meeting was confirmed. Two weeks of pure hell for Ernesto. He was always checking over his shoulder to see if he was being followed, and he was afraid to go in dark or secluded places, convinced that one of Oscar Leon's men was lurking around every corner, behind every door, and even under his own bed. The confirmation of the meeting was a relief to him, and he concluded that since they hadn't tried to intimidate or kill him, the meeting was his chance. He intended to make the best of it.

The meeting was set for ten at night and Ernesto had trouble finding the place. He wasn't reassured when he stood in front of a run down apartment building in Old Havana. The dark, narrow street had no street lights and was eerily quiet, which didn't help to put him at ease. He climbed the pitch black staircase to the fourth floor landing and heard muffled voices behind the discolored and beat-up wooden door of the apartment where the meeting was to take place. He stood there for a moment, listening and catching his breath, trying to hear what was being said through the door, but he couldn't make anything out. He knocked lightly on the door and at first, nothing happened. Just as he was about to knock again, the door opened a few inches and the shaved head of the large black man appeared, the one that Ernesto had seen many times at the house in Vedado where he had met Oscar Leon before.

The large black man examined Ernesto from head to toe. Ernesto looked into his large, empty eyes and noticed that sweat was trickling down his temples. He slowly opened the door and indicated to Ernesto with his head to come inside. Ernesto cautiously stepped in, and the large black man closed the door behind him and locked it. In a swift movement he grabbed Ernesto by the shirt collar, turned him around, and roughly thrust him against the wall. Ernesto could feel his strength and brute power as he grabbed his arms and raised them to the wall and forced him to spread his legs with a few sharp painful kicks to the back of his legs. All this had taken less than a few seconds. The large black man was holding him by the scruff of the neck, and Ernesto's face was crushed against the wall. He did not dare move or say a word, and was terrified about what would happen next. The place was sinister and silent. After what seemed like a long time, he heard the shuffling of feet behind him.

"Ok, bring him to the kitchen," Ernesto recognized the irritated voice of Oscar Leon behind him and he felt almost relieved to hear it. The large black man pulled on his shirt collar and practically lifted him off his feet, forcing him to move forward. The kitchen was at the end of the corridor and there was a lit candle on a small, used table. The black man pushed him down roughly into a chair and stood threateningly behind him. The other man Ernesto had always seen at the house before was also there, the one with the brush cut and the ravaged face. He was standing behind the empty chair in front of Ernesto, arms crossed and eyes fixed directly on him. Ernesto noticed that the rancid body odor that dominated the small and stuffy kitchen seemed to come from him.

Oscar Leon came into the room and sat in the empty chair. Ernesto was relieved to see him.

"Mr. Leon...look...I'm...," Ernesto tried to speak, but he was cut off savagely by Oscar Leon.

"Shut up," he barked, his face red with rage. He was obviously very angry. Ernesto had never seen the ugly side of him before, but the expression on his face at that moment was exactly that, ugly and frightening. Ernesto's heart began to beat furiously. "Now, you listen to me very carefully, you little bastard." He wagged his undersized finger in Ernesto's face and his hand trembled slightly. "I told you specifically and on numerous occasions not to seek me out before six months had passed, did I not?"

"Yes, you did...but..."

"Shut up!" he screamed. "I did not give you permission to speak. Now, you have broken this simple rule, and you will pay dearly for this error." The little man was sweating profusely, and he leaned back in his chair a bit, his dark eyes shifting from side to side. Ernesto looked from Oscar Leon to the man behind him, and for the first time since he began his dealings with them, he was certain that his life was in imminent danger.

"Mr. Leon, I can explain, I…" he began to say.

"I said, shut up and listen." Oscar Leon slammed his tiny hand on the table forcefully, and the candle flickered and nearly fell to the floor. The large black man standing behind Ernesto slapped him hard on the back of the head. The slap surprised him, and it stung a bit. He bowed his head in resignation, not daring to look in Oscar Leon's direction.

"Now, as I was about to say before you impolitely interrupted me, you have broken the rules," his voice was a bit more normal, but the intonations were still sharp, "and there will be a price to pay for that, but, we will get to that later. Now, because I am a fair and just man, I will give you a few minutes to explain to me why you asked for this meeting and put everyone involved in this secret operation in danger. I do hope you have an excellent reason and that that reason is not the last transaction we did together, because if that is the case, I will be very, very angry with you." His voice had risen again, and he leaned forward and placed his finger under Ernesto's chin, lifting his head and looking him straight in the eyes. He raised his other hand and wagged one of his diminutive fingers within inches of his face.

"Very, very angry, do you understand?"

"Yes. I mean, no, that is not the reason I am here, Mr. Leon, and yes, I understand." Leon removed his finger from under his chin and leaned back in his chair, and Ernesto felt that this was his opportunity to try to save his life. He threw everything he had into what he had to say.

"I have no news from that person, Mr. Leon, the one

from our last transaction, but that was the agreement I had with her and that is not the reason I am here." He looked at Oscar innocently, his eyes wide open, in what he hoped would be interpreted as a gesture of sincerity. He prayed that Oscar Leon was buying his story. The diminutive man kept his gaze on him, arms crossed on his chest, and he seemed to Ernesto to be a little less stressed.

"Ok, go on," he said, his voice a little calmer than before.

"I'm really sorry I broke the rules, Mr. Leon, really sorry, and if I could start over, I would never do that again. I really regret what I did, it was a stupid thing to do and I understand why you are angry with me. It's just that I had something to ask you that's important to me, and I thought that considering how well things went between us in the past, well, what's a few months, eh?" Ernesto smiled and tried to appear relaxed and a bit dumb. He looked up at the man behind Oscar Leon and smiled sympathetically in his direction, but the other just stared at him with contempt, showing no reaction. Oscar Leon uncrossed his arms and looked at Ernesto intently.

"It was very foolish of you to have done that, you know, and very dangerous." He let his words hang in the air for a while and then he leaned forward on the table and looked directly into Ernesto's eyes. "So tell me, what is so urgent that you would take this chance?" Although he still had a stern look on his face, Ernesto sensed that some of the earlier tension had dissipated.

"It's really simple, Mr. Leon. I came because I must leave as quickly as possible. A sudden emergency has come up and beckons me, and I must leave without delay. I would like to make the arrangements for that and I am willing to pay extra for the trouble I have created by breaking the rules." Ernesto was aware that he was dealing for his life; he figured that if he didn't make an interesting offer, they would kill him and make him disappear permanently. He looked from Oscar Leon to the man behind him and hoped that they were taking the bait. Oscar Leon did not answer, and seemed to be pondering things over. "...I would really like that, Mr. Leon, if you could do that for me," he added, his eyes begging and filled with submission. Oscar Leon said nothing, just looked at him intensely with his little black eyes. Finally, after a long silence, he said,

"I see," and nodded his head gravely. "But tell me, what is this sudden emergency that you have to attend to?" Ernesto had anticipated the question and he had an answer ready for him.

"Well, you see, I have an old grandmother in Miami, Mr. Leon..." Ernesto was lying, but he thought that since Oscar Leon's mother was in Miami and he was trying to help her, his story would strike a favorable chord with him, "...and she is extremely sick and has only a few months to live. She has expressed the wish to see me, her only grandson, before she leaves us, so you understand Mr. Leon, I have to go, I have to go see her and kiss her before she... before she leaves..." Ernesto bowed his head as if overcome by emotion, and pretended to wipe some tears from his eyes. Oscar Leon looked at him and felt like laughing, he loved it when someone came up with a story as good as his own story about his sick mother in Miami. There was another prolonged silence, during which Ernesto kept his head down, and finally Oscar Leon said,

"Ok, Ernesto, I will help you to see your grandmother before she dies, even though I am not happy with you for what you did. I will help you, but I will charge you a fine of two thousand dollars for your mistake, a fine that you will pay at the same time as the usual fee." Ernesto lifted his head, his face illuminated, and he reached out across the table and put his hands on one of Oscar's own. The man behind Oscar Leon started to move in Ernesto's direction to remove his hands, but Oscar Leon lifted his other hand to indicate to the man to stop.

"Thank you, Mr. Leon, thank you for my grandmother and for being so kind and so good to me. I will never forget it, sir, never." Oscar Leon slowly removed his hand from under Ernesto's and cleared his throat.

"You remember the house, the one where we met before?"

"Yes, of course."

"Ok, good, be there in three days at the usual time and we will discuss this further." He pointed his finger in Ernesto's direction, "…and do not talk to anyone about this and do not break the rules again, do you understand?"

"Yes, I understand, Mr. Leon and I promise I won't, on all that is sacred to me I promise I won't." Ernesto started to get up, but the large hands of the black man behind him pushed him roughly back into his seat.

"Good. I hope you keep your word this time."

"Yes, I will, and I'll be there in three days, at the usual time. Thank you again, Mr. Leon, thank you, I really appreciate what you are doing for me, I really do." Ernesto extended his hand in Oscar Leon's direction as the other got up, and Oscar Leon looked at it but did not take it. Ernesto's hand just hung awkwardly in the air for a moment.

"Stay here and don't move, and do not leave this place for at least an hour, understood?"

"Yes, Mr. Leon, understood." Without another word, Oscar Leon walked out of the kitchen with the two men in tow.

When Ernesto heard the door of the apartment shut behind them, he leaned back in his chair and let out a huge sigh of relief. He was very conscious that he had come close to disappearing forever from the face of the earth as he stared at the grayish kitchen wall in front of him and observed the light of the candle dance over it. As he had been told to, he did not move a muscle or make a noise, and it was well over an hour later, only after the candle had died, that he got up and walked out. It felt good to be outside walking the dark and narrow streets of Old Havana. He inhaled the cool evening air deeply and then exhaled with force, looking up and admiring the stars in the cloudless sky, happy to still be alive.

Over the course of the next three weeks, Ernesto met with Oscar Leon three times at the house in Vedado. The atmosphere was more relaxed than the meeting they had had in Old Havana, but the same two men who had been with him then were there at every subsequent meeting, and their intimidating physical presence was an obvious message to Ernesto. He had a good idea of what they might be capable of doing on the other's command.

At each meeting there was also the inevitable lecture on the virtues and accomplishments of the Cuban revolution and on Oscar Leon's immeasurable esteem and love of *"El Commandante,"* as he sometimes reverently referred to Fidel Castro. Ernesto was so bored during this time that he played a little game in his mind, pretending that he was insulting Oscar Leon to his face and telling him that he was "a little communist bloodsucker," or "an ass-kissing, brown-nosed little rat," and so on. He loved to play that game while looking at Oscar Leon and nodding gravely at his words, as if he were genuinely interested in the seriousness and importance of what he was saying. He would smile at him and Oscar Leon would smile back, convinced that Ernesto appreciated his intelligence and insight. Still, the sessions were a form of torture for him and he couldn't wait to leave and to start looking for Yaneti.

Finally a date was set for his departure. It had been three months since Ernesto had last seen Yaneti, and he was worried sick about her. He had gotten the money he needed to pay for his fee, including the two thousand extra he had to pay as a penalty, from one of his regular clients who came to Havana every year for a holiday. The money had been wired to him by Ernesto's father's relatives in Miami. Ernesto knew that for his father to ask for help from his family in Miami had been a very difficult thing for him to do, as he had had no contact with them since they had fled Havana many years before. It was not that his father was at odds with them or had anything against them, but he was a man of principle and, as he had been a government employee all of his life, he believed that any contact with them would be inappropriate. He had therefore not seen or heard from them in years. Things had remained that way until Ernesto had asked him for his help, after which he had had no choice but to contact them. Ernesto knew that his father had stepped on his pride and his principles in order to help him, and he was grateful to him for that.

On their third meeting, Ernesto had brought the money to Oscar Leon, who told him that his departure had been set. He should be ready to leave in two days and should come to the house around eleven at night. Ernesto was glad to be set at last. His plan was to go see his parents on the morning of his departure to say goodbye, and then spend the rest of that day and evening resting and waiting in his apartment until it was time to go.

Two days later, he went to see his parents to say goodbye, and it was the most difficult moment he had ever experienced in his life. His mother was beside herself with grief and she could not contain herself or her emotions. Even his father, a taciturn and emotionless man by nature, had shed a tear when the three of them had hugged and clung to each other in the living room, all of them shaking from his mother's uncontrollable sobs. They hung onto each other for a long time, bound by their grief and their love for each other and by the very real possibility that they would never see each other again. When Ernesto finally closed the door to their apartment behind him, he wiped the tears from his face and walked away with a heavy heart, feeling that something had been taken away from him forever.

A little before eleven that evening, Ernesto got ready to leave. He was nervous and agitated, as he had not slept or eaten much in the past few days and those all-too-familiar cramps in his stomach were making him suffer again. He had been jumpy and tense all day, and could not sit still as the hours and minutes had slowly ticked by. He wasn't scared, even though he knew that the journey he was embarking on was very dangerous, but he was anxious to get going and hungry for action. The waiting was killing him. Finally, it was time to go, and he checked around the apartment one more time, shut off all the lights, and quietly slipped out.

Ernesto knocked lightly on the door to the house, the same door he had seen Yaneti enter a few months before— it seemed so long ago now. The door opened and he quickly entered. The house was completely dark, and the man who had opened the door whispered to him to go to the kitchen. He could see that some light was coming from that direction as he made his way along the darkened corridor. The small kitchen was crowded and hot, and the air was foul. A faint lamp was lit and had been placed on one of the counters. As Ernesto's eyes adjusted to the semi-darkness, he counted thirteen other people sitting or standing. There were four women and eight men, and a boy with one of the women. The boy seemed to be about eleven or twelve years old. All had worried and concerned looks on their faces. Ernesto nodded to the men, who nodded back gravely. He could see the fear in their eyes, but also the mistrust; in a society like Cuba's, everyone was potentially a snitch, or a member of the army or the police, and so everyone mistrusted everyone else. It was one of the system's most efficient control mechanisms.

He found a spot and leaned against a wall, crossing his arms and looking everyone over. He saw the trepidation that was about them and how anxious and scared they all were. He noted in particular the genuine terror on the women's faces and he realized that, in order to be there, all of them had conquered their most profound fears. He admired their courage and the hidden desires in their haggard faces, and he could sense that all of them knew that tonight was the ultimate test of their determination and their will. It filled him with awe to realize that these people had reached a point in their existence where they were willing to risk everything, even their own lives, in the hope of making a better future for themselves, and that they considered the inherent dangers of their perilous journey the price they had to pay in order to achieve their goals. They had each had the audacity to run after their dreams, no matter what the cost.

The wait was interminable, and the hours ticked by at an agonizing pace. Ernesto was getting antsy, and hoped that someone would come soon to tell them that it was time to go. The woman with the young boy got up from where she had been sitting on the floor and went to the bathroom, and when she came back, she signaled to Ernesto to come over and sit down beside her. He went over to where she was sitting with her son and squeezed in beside her. She was a woman in her mid-thirties, with long curly black hair and a bright honest face, and she smiled to Ernesto when he sat down.

"Hi," she whispered, "my name is Elizabet and this is my son Manolo." Her eyes were a glowing black, and they lit up her face when she smiled. Ernesto smiled back.

"Hi, I'm Ernesto." He whispered, too; no one had told them to whisper, but it seemed to be the thing to do because of the tension of the moment. Ernesto shook Elizabet's hand and felt a slight tremor running through her body. He could see the fear in her eyes. He placed his other hand over hers, looked into her eyes, and whispered,

"Hey, everything will be ok, Elizabet, don't worry. Everything will be fine, you will see." His voice was soft and he smiled at her and her son, who was looking his way from the corner of his eye.

"Hi, Manolo," he waved to the boy, who was looking at him sullenly. The boy didn't respond, but returned his gaze to the floor in front of him.

"Thank you," she whispered, squeezing his hand, and she pointed to her son with her eyes. "I'm trying to stay strong for him, you know."

"Yeah, I know, you're doing a good job, Elizabet, he'll be fine." He leaned over and whispered in her ear, "he's just a bit scared right now, that's all, he'll be ok, you'll see." Ernesto leaned his head sideways and smiled at Manolo, who was looking their way again. Elizabet looked at her son and bit her lips, and tears appeared at the corner of her eyes. She quickly looked away and held onto Ernesto's hand tightly.

They spent the next hour whispering to each other about their lives. Ernesto learned that Elizabet was from a small village in the eastern part of Cuba and that she had left her family and an ex-husband behind to go to America with her only son. The new man in her life was waiting for her there; he had escaped from Cuba two years before and she couldn't wait to be re-united with him. Her dream once she got to America was to make enough money to get her parents out of Cuba and to be able to give her son a chance at a better life.

Ernesto shared with her his story about Yaneti and how they had met and fallen in love; how he had wanted to leave Cuba and she had agreed to come with him; how he had sent her first because they didn't have the money for two passages.

"...and now I haven't heard from her in nearly three months and I have decided to follow in her footsteps in order to try to find her." Tears appeared at the corners of his eyes, and Elizabet put a comforting hand on his shoulder and whispered,

"You will find her Ernesto, I am sure that she is waiting somewhere for you and you will be very happy together." Ernesto looked at her and forced a smile.

"Thank you," he whispered, and he leaned his head back against the wall and stared at the ceiling, making an effort not to cry. Elizabet looked at him and took his hand and squeezed it, to let him know that she cared.

They heard noises coming from the front of the house and some agitated but hushed discussions, and then the shuffling of feet coming their way. Two men appeared in the kitchen doorway and whispered to them to come silently and in single file to the front door.

They all were lined up in the pitch-black hallway, silent and waiting, holding their breaths, hearts beating wildly and nervously anticipating whatever was to come next. One of the men opened the door cautiously, and in the pale light from the street that invaded the darkened hallway, Ernesto could see the tense faces of the people lined up near him and leaning apprehensively against the wall. The man who had opened the door extended his head outside and looked left and right, and then he indicated to the first person in line to go. One by one they were let out. Ernesto was the last one to go. When he stepped out of the doorway, he saw that everyone had been sent to a waiting mini-van that was parked on the street in front of the house.

"Do not run, walk," the man whispered to him, placing his hand on the middle of his back and lightly pushing him forward. The second Ernesto was outside, he heard the door close behind him. He did as he was told and walked briskly towards the waiting mini-van. He squeezed himself in. It was dark and stuffy inside, and all the curtains were drawn, even the one between the driver and the passengers. Someone closed the door behind him, and almost immediately the mini-van began to make its way silently and slowly up the street.

Through a small crack in the side curtains, Ernesto could see the empty streets of Havana as the mini-van moved along at a good pace. He looked fixedly outside, thinking that it would probably be a long time before he saw his beloved city of Havana again. They were making their way along a large tree-lined boulevard which was well lit and empty of people. He could see only darkness in the side streets as all the lights in the apartments were out. Most people were probably in bed, he thought, or the electricity had been cut off, as happened often in Havana. They slowed down at an intersection and he saw a police car parked on a street corner, all lights extinguished, and the silhouettes of two policemen sitting in the darkened car. He felt a sudden spasm in his chest and he took a few deep breaths, imagining himself being handcuffed and thrown into a dark and foul-smelling cell. He let out his breath slowly as the mini-van continued on its way unfettered.

They were packed close to each other in the mini-van and, as there was no air conditioning, it became hot and uncomfortable. Ernesto returned his attention to the crack in the curtains. He could see that they were leaving the city now. The mini-van picked up speed and no one spoke as they sped along, rocking slightly from side to side and bumping shoulders with each other.

Ernesto leaned back and closed his eyes, and he thought about Yaneti and how she must have felt when she had been on this journey, maybe in this very same van, frightened and far from him. He hated himself for not having gone with her; he knew now that that's what he should have done. He should have been there to comfort and to protect her. He bit his lip to prevent himself from crying and to contain his rage.

The mini-van slowed down and took a sharp turn down a rough road. After a bumpy ten-minute ride, the vehicle stopped completely. Everything was dark and silent inside the mini-van and outside. No one dared move. Everyone was nervous, and the air got hotter and stuffier by the second until it became harder and harder to breath. The curtain between the driver and the passengers finally opened a little and a hoarse voice whispered in the darkness, "don't move, it won't be long, they will come for you."

The heat in the mini-van was intolerable and the air had become practically un-breathable by the time the door was finally opened. Someone tugged on Ernesto's arm and pulled him outside, whispering to him to be silent. It felt good to be outside, and he could smell the sea nearby. Everyone was out now, standing near the mini-van, and

Ernesto saw some men approaching with flashlights. The men came right up to them, and he could see that one of them was the man with the tattoos and the ravaged face. His name, he knew, was Pedro—he had overheard Oscar Leon call him that one day at the house. There were two other men with him, and Pedro pointed to some people with his flashlight and whispered under his breath, "Follow me. The others, stay here, we'll be back for you." The authority in his tone left no doubt about who was in charge. It was the first time Ernesto had heard him speak. His voice was hoarse, and like the darkness in his eyes, it had a menacing undertone. Pedro turned and, with one of his men in tow, he led the people he had pointed to in the direction he had come from. The other man stayed behind with the remaining passengers and Ernesto recognized the large black man. His enormous silhouette was unmistakable, even in the darkness that surrounded them.

Elizabet and Manolo came up beside him and she took his hand. He could feel her trembling again, and he stroked her forearm gently and squeezed her hand. Neither of them dared speak, and the silence and the darkness about them were eerie and ominous. Each minute seemed to tick by at an unbearably slow pace.

Twenty minutes later, Ernesto saw the ray of a flashlight approaching them again. It was Pedro, but this time he was alone. He told them to follow him and to remain silent. They made their way in a single file behind him, with the large black man closing the line. As they approached the water, the smell of the sea became stronger and the air got cooler, and Ernesto's heart began to beat faster. They arrived at a makeshift dock with a large rowboat tied up to it. The man who had driven the van helped them all get in, and then he got in too and pushed them off. The large black man took the position at the oars, and they began to move stealthily on the water. It was dark out and all flashlights were extinguished, but after a few minutes Ernesto could make out the shape of a boat up ahead. Its silhouette became clearer as they approached. The sea was calm, and there wasn't even a ripple disturbing the surrounding water as the rowboat touched the boat lightly with a knock. There was a ladder hanging from the side of the craft, and everyone was quickly whisked on board. The van driver stayed in the rowboat and, when all had disembarked, he rowed silently back in the direction of the shore.

Once on board the boat, Ernesto was immediately pressed down by someone. He could not see who it was, as everything was dark and no lights were on. The hands that grabbed him were rough and strong, and the man whispered to him,

"Stay down, be silent."

He sat down on the deck with his head leaning against the side of the boat. He could feel another person beside him, and he knew by the tremors that it was Elizabet.

"Elizabet, is that you?" he whispered.

"Yes, it's me," she whispered back.

"Give me your hand." She took his hand in the darkness and he noticed that her trembling was worse than before. Ernesto did not dare speak again, as they had been told to be silent, so he stroked her hand softly, hoping that it would calm her down a bit.

The boat smelled of fish and diesel oil and Ernesto surmised that it was some kind of fishing boat. It was smaller than he had imagined, and he could distinguish in the darkness a door to a cabin going down below. A sliver of light leaked around the door's contour. A minute later, the door of the cabin opened, and he saw some men crouched around a table with a feeble light illuminating them. He saw the large black man and Pedro and three other men with them around a table, an unshaven, fat-bellied white man, a lanky mulatto, and a wiry, brown-skinned *Indio*. All were listening intently to Pedro. He was leaning forward and giving instructions to the men, but Ernesto could not make out what he was saying from where he was sitting. He barked out a final order, then pointed to the deck and extinguished the light and all the men came up on deck.

Pedro walked around the deck slowly, apparently inspecting each passenger individually, and even though Ernesto could not see his eyes through the darkness, he sensed that he was assessing them and making them understand by his presence and by his demeanor that everyone's life on the boat was in his hands. After a few minutes, he turned and made his way to a ladder which led to the second deck and to the wheel of the boat.

A minute later, the roar of the powerful motors raped the silence of the night and startled the frightened passengers. They all became nervous and fidgety, eyes darting wildly from side to side, terrified that the clamor of the motors would alert the army or the police. Ernesto felt a warm liquid seeping through his jeans from his side, and he knew right away that Elizabet or the boy had pissed themselves from fear. He did not say anything, just held onto her hand tightly and pretended that he hadn't noticed what had happened.

The crew had spread out on the boat as it moved slowly forward, all lights extinguished. The lanky mulatto went to the front of the boat, while the large black man and the fat-bellied white man stayed close to the passengers. The *Indio* climbed up the ladder and stood with his back to Pedro, who was at the wheel of the boat. He lit himself a cigarette and locked his gaze onto the passengers below.

There was no wind and it was hot on the deck below, and everyone was sweating. The fat-bellied white man's filthy body odor permeated the air with its putridity, and as it mixed with the smell of diesel oil and dead fish, some of the passengers became nauseous. Others were pinching their noses in order to block out the smell.

It was a cloudless, starless night and they maintained their slow speed for about fifteen minutes, navigating in complete darkness, moving silently and furtively towards the open ocean. Ernesto was excited that it was finally happening and at the possibility that he might actually succeed. He knew that every minute was taking him further away from Cuba and closer to freedom. His heart was beating wildly and he took in a few long deep breaths and tried to remain calm. It was quiet on the boat, and he could see the lights of the shoreline disappearing in the distance. "Goodbye Havana, goodbye Cuba," he kept repeating to himself as the lights got fainter and fainter on the horizon.

When the lights had completely disappeared, Pedro sped up the motors, and soon they were moving along at full throttle. Ernesto was glad to finally feel some cool air against his face. The crew seemed more relaxed, and the large black man went upstairs and sat beside Pedro while the fat-bellied white man went below deck and shut the door behind him, to everyone's relief. The lanky mulatto up front lit himself a cigarette and stared out at the ocean. Only the *Indio* did not move from his original position, but stood where he had been since they had left, chain-smoking and fixedly observing the passengers below.

They raced across the water at full speed for about two hours, the boat fast, the sea calm, and nothing to impede their progress. Then, suddenly, Pedro slowed the boat down and cut the motors. The passengers looked at each other, not understanding what was going on. *We cannot be there already,* Ernesto wondered as he looked about, trying to see where they were. It was pitch black out except for some extremely faint and barely visible lights on the horizon. *Could that be America?* He asked himself. He stretched his neck out in an effort to try to get a better view. The idea excited him, but for some reason he had a bad feeling about what was going on and he felt that something wasn't right. The mulatto walked back from the front of the boat and went into the cabin, and the large black man and Pedro came down from the upper deck and did the same. None of them spoke to the perplexed passengers as they passed them by, and each time the door of the cabin opened, Ernesto caught quick glimpses of some machine guns and pistols that were bunched up on the small table of the cabin. They hadn't been there before, and that augmented his suspicions that something was off.

The *Indio* was the last man to come down and to enter the cabin, and he tried to close the door behind him, but it remained ajar a few inches. From where he was on the deck, Ernesto could see inside. His whole body became tense when he saw what was going on. Through the opening in the cabin door, he saw Pedro distributing the guns to the crew and barking orders and then the men began to move. Every muscle and nerve ending in his body seized up, and without a moment's hesitation, he let go of Elizabet's hand. In a flash, he had torn off his shoes and pants, kissed the perplexed Elizabet on the forehead, and silently lifted himself overboard and slipped into the cold dark water.

Just as Ernesto began to silently swim away from the boat, Pedro and his crew exploded from the cabin with machine guns and pistols raised, pointing them at the terrified passengers and shouting at them not to move. The passengers were stunned by the swiftness of the rush and the harshness of the voices, and they only started screaming and begging when the crew began to tie them up and gag them. Elizabet screamed in terror when the large black man began to tie her and her son up. In that instant of horror, she understood why Ernesto had slipped overboard, and foresaw the dreadfulness of what was about to happen. Ernesto heard her plea for her son's life from where he was treading water; it broke his heart, and he wished there was something he could have done to help her and her son.

"Please take my son with you, please," she screamed, but the rest of her plea was muffled as a thick piece of duct tape was placed over her mouth. The large black man looked at her and put a finger over his lips to indicate silence, even though he knew she couldn't make a sound because of the tape. He smiled at her sadistically, as if he were happy with her predicament and glad to be the instrument of her demise. Elizabet was crying and shaking violently, her whole being in complete shock and stunned by the large black man's cruelty.

"Pedro, one missing," the *Indio* shouted, with one finger up in the air. He was looking in Pedro's direction and he had called him by name. Everyone knew that the *Indio* never spoke unless it was absolutely necessary and he never called Pedro by name unless the situation was serious. Pedro's eyes turned black with rage, and he rushed forward and counted the passengers, frantically looking around in all directions.

"Who let that bastard out of his sight, who?" He shouted furiously. The crew all bowed their heads and no one dared look in his direction for fear that they would be blamed for Ernesto's disappearance. All feared Pedro's wrath; he would happily kill any of them for less than this, and so none of them spoke. Two of them scurried below deck and began bringing large cement blocks and lengths of heavy chains on deck, and the other two got busy securing the chains around the cement blocks and the ankles of the hapless passengers.

Pedro turned on his heels and rushed below deck. "That shithead can't be far," he muttered under his breath, and he quickly came back on deck with a large searchlight and a machine gun in the other hand. He began to scan the water around the boat with the searchlight. "Ok, where are you, asshole, eh, where are you? Come on, show yourself, where are you gonna go, eh, you gonna swim to Miami you stupid prick?" he shouted out hysterically into the darkness. "We're in the middle of the ocean you fucking idiot, in the middle of the night, no one will find you, you will drown or the sharks will eat you, so come on, come back on the boat and be a man. You're gonna die anyway, so at least let me do it, it will be quicker and less painful, I promise." His shouting was louder and more urgent now, and he was racing around the boat frantically and sweeping the beam of light in every direction. The crew all had their heads down as the enraged Pedro ran crazily around the boat. No one knew if he was furious because they had let a passenger give them the slip or because Ernesto had deprived him of the pleasure of killing him himself. One thing was sure however: no one was going to ask him to clarify.

Ernesto was treading water at a short distance from the boat, and when he saw the searchlight combing the surface of the water, he knew that they were looking for him. He dove quickly and propelled himself deeper, forward into the dark ocean and away from the light. He dove as deep and as far away as he could and fortunately, he was a good swimmer and could stay underwater for a long time. He resurfaced after a few minutes and, looking around, he saw that he was a lot farther from the boat than before and that the searchlight was directed in the opposite direction of where he had surfaced. He treaded water silently while catching his breath, and the searchlight continued to comb the surface of the water. He could clearly hear Pedro's howling and he could tell that he was furious and in the middle of a violent fit.

After a few minutes, the searchlight was turned off and all became quiet on the boat. Ernesto could make out the silhouettes of the men on the deck standing around Pedro and, because voices carry well over water, he could partially hear what was being said. He could clearly distinguish Pedro's sadistic growl and then his demented laughter, and thirty seconds later he saw something that completely broke his heart. The large black man and the fat-bellied white man lifted a writhing, tied up passenger, while the two other men grabbed the two large cement blocks and the chain that was attached to the passenger's ankles, and they tossed them overboard at the same time. His heart jolted when he heard the body hit the water. "Oh my God," he said out loud, and he watched in shock and disbelief as Pedro and his crew tossed all the rest of the passengers overboard. He could distinctly hear Pedro's voice as the bodies were heaved overboard, and to his bewilderment, he realized that he was laughing and seemed to be enjoying himself.

"Ha, ha, this one is not very heavy, boys, ha, ha, the sharks will not be happy with us about this one, ha, ha." Ernesto recognized the small writhing silhouette of the young Manolo as Pedro and the mulatto unceremoniously tossed him overboard. The sound of the splash and the laughter of Pedro and his crew enraged him, and he hit the water with his fists, tears filling his eyes. The pain he felt at that moment was the worst pain he had ever felt in his life.

"You sick bastards, you crazy sick bastards," he hissed under his breath. The rage of an uncommon fury began to build up inside of him, and if he could have, he would have jumped back on that boat and torn Pedro's heart out with his bare hands, so fierce and so vicious was his hatred of him in that instant. And yet, he also knew that there was nothing he could do but be the unwilling witness of an abominable act, so brutally horrible and so far from his own human experience that it was beyond his ability to even comprehend it. He could not help but think that this could have happened to Yaneti, and that thought drove him crazy. In his anger of the moment, however, he refused to admit the possibility to himself, and so he pushed that thought from his mind and concentrated on the more urgent matter of getting away from Pedro and his crew. He knew that if they found him they would kill him without hesitation, for he now fully understood that what he was dealing with were ruthless psychopaths of the worst kind.

It was quiet on the boat after Pedro and his men had done their business. After a few minutes, three searchlights came on and Ernesto understood that finding him had become their new priority. The boat began to move in circles, coming slowly in the direction of where he was treading water. When the vessel was close enough, he dove, and heard the boat pass slowly above him and watched the rays of the searchlights as they crisscrossed the surface of the water. He stayed down for as long as he could, pinching his nose so as not to let out any air bubbles, and when he couldn't hold the air in his lungs any longer, he let some out and slowly came up and resurfaced. He was behind the boat now and he watched it go in larger and larger circles, farther and farther away from him. Everything was silent and the sea was calm, with no wind. Ernesto treaded water quietly and after about forty-five minutes, he heard the roar of the engines being gunned and he saw the boat make its way in the direction of the very faint lights in the distance and then disappear completely.

Ernesto was alone now and everything was eerily quiet. He was perplexed about the direction the boat had taken. Why had they gone in what seemed to be the direction of

America? Or was it? It didn't make any sense to him for a minute—but then it dawned on him. They weren't going in the direction of America. The scintillating lights on the horizon were Cuba, and that's where they were headed. They had only pretended to go in the direction of America. In reality, they had gone out a certain distance and then had circled back around towards Cuba. The reasons they did this were obvious to Ernesto: they would never have dared do their sordid business in American waters or near American waters, and they had to go far enough out to sea so that no bodies would wash up on Cuban shores.

That was not good news for Ernesto though, because that meant that he would have to swim in the opposite direction from the one they had taken. He had no idea how far he had to go, but he was certain that it was a good distance. He kept treading water for a while before committing to the direction that he would take, fully aware that he was betting his life on a hunch. The other problem he had was that he didn't know how far he was from U.S. shores and if he could even swim that far and for that long.

After a minute or two, his mind was made up, and he took off his socks and shirt and turned to look in the opposite direction that the boat had taken. There was only darkness ahead of him, and he knew it would be a very long swim—probably the swim of his life. He had never been much of a long distance swimmer, but he was strong and sure of himself, and he also understood that it was swim or sink for him.

So he began to swim, slowly and methodically, and the calm sea helped him keep a straight line. The last thing he wanted to do was to swim in circles, and he prayed that the wind wouldn't pick up and agitate the sea, making it more difficult for him to keep his direction. He paced himself, saving his energy and taking in air with deep controlled breaths. He was determined to make it. He thought about drowning a few times in those first few hours that he swam, and he thought about sharks. He knew they were out there and that they would not hesitate to attack him in his vulnerable situation if they became aware of him. But he pushed those thoughts from his mind as best he could and he pressed on. He couldn't allow fear to take control of him, because he knew that if it did, it would be game over. So he tried to keep his mind on positive things; he thought about his parents and about Yaneti, and it gave him the mental energy that he needed to keep going.

It was a long swim, a very long swim, the longest swim he had ever attempted in his life, and all through the night the jellyfish stung him and many times he thought that he wouldn't make it. When he needed to regain some strength, he would tread water for ten or fifteen minutes and take long deep breaths, and once he had regained some stamina he would keep going. As the sun began to appear over the horizon he still could not sight land, and he became concerned. He had been swimming for hours and he didn't know how long he could keep going. Even worse, he was stopping more and more often to tread water and to catch his breath, and he knew that his strength was beginning to wane.

It was during one such stop that he spotted something floating on the water about sixty or seventy feet from where he was treading water. He swam over to the object, and was astounded to discover that it was a thick beam of wood about ten feet long which had probably come off a dock somewhere in a storm and that the currents had carried out to sea. He lifted his body onto it, and it supported his weight completely. He was overjoyed, for he understood that this miracle piece of timber would save his life. For fifteen minutes, rested up while hanging onto it, and then he began to paddle with his feet and push the beam forward. There was no way that he was going to let go of that god-sent piece of wood; he figured that his paddling and the currents would eventually lead them both somewhere.

He paddled on for a few hours, and the sun got higher in the sky and hotter, and very quickly he became parched and sunburned. Sometimes he would doze off for a few seconds, but he would always shake his head and force himself to stay awake and keep paddling. At about noon he looked up and he thought he saw something on the horizon. Wondering if it was an illusion, he pushed himself up with his two hands using the beam as leverage. Then he saw it again: a shoreline. It was far away, but he was sure of what he had seen. It gave him new energy and he began to paddle faster. The shoreline slowly became more visible and nearer every time he lifted his head.

After another excruciatingly difficult few hours of paddling and pushing, when he had just about reached the limit of his strength, he finally felt land under his feet. He had been leaning his head on the beam to rest, and when he looked up, he saw a beach in front of him. He stood up hesitantly and began to make his way towards the beach, but fell after only a few steps. He had to crawl the final distance on all fours in the shallow water. He was shaking violently and every muscle in his body hurt him terribly. When he reached the beach, he fell face down in the sand and instantly passed out.

He was out for a few hours—he wasn't sure for how long, but when he came to, he was dehydrated and his lips were cracked and he felt terrible. It was late afternoon and the sun was lower in the sky. He lifted his head. His face was caked with sand, and he sat up and spit the sand out of his mouth and looked around with bewildered eyes. He slowly got up and saw that in front of him and to each side were tall apartment buildings. It was quiet; no one was around. For a few minutes he just stood there, wobbly and confused and unable to process his thoughts clearly. He had no idea where he was and he realized that all he had on was his underwear. He hesitantly put one foot forward and then another. His feet felt heavy, and every movement he made hurt him somewhere. He made his way in the direction of the nearest building and that's when he saw it—a shape that stopped him dead in his tracks, fluttering lightly in the late afternoon breeze. It was an American flag, and to Ernesto it was the most beautiful thing he had seen in his entire life. He just looked at it and smiled, and a tear rolled down one of his cheeks. He knew then that he had made it. He was in America.

PART III

LITTLE HAVANA

Little Havana, *la Pequena Habana*: Cuba in the heart of Miami; the emotional, cultural and political center of Cuban-American life and home of the famous Domino Park, the *Viernes Culturales,* the Padilla Cigar Factory, the Calle Ocho street festival, and of some of the best Cuban restaurants and fiercest anti-Castro newspapers in America. It is where the Cuban American National Foundation was born, the political arm of the "exiles," that first wave of Cuban immigrants who arrived after the Cuban revolution. Little Havana, a little bit of Cuba transplanted in America and where Cuban-Americans still gather at the landmark Versailles restaurant to eat, reminisce, and discuss the latest news or the latest rumors coming from the island and where they came to share in their common love of Cuba and their profound attachment to its culture and to its people— affection which is only equaled by their deep loathing of Fidel Castro, his brother, and their communist regime.

The "exiles" were the older generation, the hardliners and staunch anti-communists. Most of them had fled Cuba over fifty years ago, but a lot of them still dreamt of returning there one day and once again being useful to the country of their birth. As the years trickled by, though, their yearnings became more ingrained in the world of wishful thinking, and it became more and more unlikely that any of the things that they discussed would ever happen. Most of them had become American citizens, and they had homes and children and grandchildren in America. The Cuba that they left behind didn't exist anymore. Deep down they all knew this, but none of them would ever say it out loud, and so they dreamed on, making plans for the future of Cuba, unable to let go of the past and of their roots and of the hurt and the pain which wounded them so deeply in the flower of their youth.

The "exiles" were very aware that their dreams and aspirations for Cuba meant very little to their children and grandchildren. For most of the younger generation, Cuba was just a place—few of them had ever been there, and although they were sympathetic to their elders' preoccupations, Cuba for them was a curiosity, or at best, perhaps, a future business opportunity. That was it, though; they were Americans, born and raised in America, with American habits and American dreams. They envisioned their future in America and nowhere else in the world. So when talk about Cuba heated up on Sunday afternoons or at family reunions, the younger generation were indulgent with their elders, because they knew that it was a sensitive subject for them, but they participated very little in the discussions and they would fade away discreetly into the background. It was not their world being discussed; it never had been and never would.

Newly arrived immigrants like Ernesto were different,

and had not necessarily fled Cuba for political reasons like their predecessors. They were economic refugees and the path they now tread had been laid out for them by those who had come before. There was one simple rule, and that was that they had to touch American soil first. If they touched U.S. soil and had not been picked up at sea, then they were immediately granted political asylum. This was stipulated by the Cuban Adjustment Act, or the "wet feet, dry feet," policy, a law whose provisions were very favorable to Cuban immigrants, granting them immediate permanent residency, without the usual review and waiting period, and allowing them to work legally, to collect welfare or unemployment benefits, and to have access to free medical care.

Most of the new arrivals like Ernesto hated politics and had had enough of that in Cuba. They had been born and raised in a communist system, had been subjected to its redundant rhetoric and privations, and they had all witnessed first-hand what disastrous effects a lousy system could have on ordinary people's lives. Many had fled Cuba because of the failure of the communist government to deliver anything except misery and hardships. For others, it was to reunite with their long lost relatives. Mostly, though, they came at the risk of their own lives, on makeshift boats and rafts, braving storm and sea, to pursue their dreams of a better life. They were just people who wanted to get jobs, get married, have kids and live—live, not merely exist, like they had been forced to do in Cuba.

For all of the new arrivals, freedom and democracy were new experiences and an added bonus. To be able to indulge in such luxury for the first time was like breathing in their first breath of fresh air. It was confirmation that they had arrived at their destination and that from then on, their lives would be whatever they wanted them to be.

Two week after his dramatic arrival on American soil, Ernesto was sitting with his Aunt Ivette and his Uncle Jorge in the Versailles Restaurant for lunch. It had been an exciting and eventful time for him, which had begun by him being picked up by the police near the beach where he had washed up. He had been wandering about, dazed and barefoot in only his underwear, without any identification papers. Luckily for him one of the police officers spoke Spanish and had been kind to him and had given him some water and a blanket to cover himself.

He had been quickly handed over to the immigration authorities and his aunt and uncle, anticipating his imminent arrival, had hired a lawyer ahead of time in order to help them with the bureaucracy and the process. The lawyer had been checking in regularly with immigration officials about him and that lawyer was the person they had called when they realized that they had Ernesto in custody. His aunt and uncle had helped establish his identity to the satisfaction of the authorities and had gotten him released and placed in their custody pending a final decision on his status. Ernesto was happy to get out, even though he had been well treated while in custody. He had been given clean clothes and had been well fed. Most of the people he dealt with during his detention spoke Spanish, and one very sympathetic officer, whose parents were Cuban exiles themselves, even explained to him the process he was in and how it would play out. Even so, to be detained, even for a short time, had not been a pleasant experience, and he was grateful to be released.

Meeting his aunt and uncle for the first time had been an awkward moment for Ernesto. They had become very emotional when they had seen him, and had greeted him like a long-lost son, hugging and kissing him at the same time and both of them crying and clinging to him as if someone had died. Ernesto was a bit taken aback by their emotional reaction and did not know what to do or say. After all, to him, they were perfect strangers, and even though he had heard a lot about them from his parents as he was growing up, he still knew very little about them and their sudden emotional outburst made him a bit uncomfortable. He had been nice about it, though, and had held onto them tightly and smiled a lot.

What Ernesto didn't understand was that for his aunt and uncle he was more than just a nephew—he was a living reminder of Cuba, of everything that they had left behind and everything they had been torn away from so many years before. Seeing him there, standing in front of them, had brought all of that back to them and they had been overtaken by a powerful surge of pent up emotions.

Ernesto, for his part, was grateful for their presence there and that they had been willing and able to help him. He understood that it would make things a lot easier for him and he would never forget that it was their money that had financed his escape from Cuba. He knew he was in debt to them, but still he felt strange and out of place as they hung onto him almost desperately, so overcome by their feelings that neither of them was able to speak coherently for what seemed to him like a long time.

Ernesto's aunt and uncle had fled to the U.S. right after

the revolution, and both were now American citizens. They had two children, and lived in a large and comfortable home in Hialeah, a predominately Cuban-American suburb of Miami. Ernesto was very impressed by their large house, with its two garages, outdoor swimming pool, and all the modern appliances and fancy electronics. As for his cousins, his first impression of them was that they seemed more American than Cuban. Both used American-sounding names and both had adopted the language, the clothes, and the culture of the country of their birth. As for their Spanish, it didn't seem to Ernesto that they had a very good command of the language, but he kept that reflection to himself. He also noticed that they didn't seem very interested in Cuba or what was going on there; they were only ever politely curious about the island and its politics. It wasn't a subject that seemed to raise much passion with either one of them, and Ernesto found that odd at the time.

For his aunt and uncle, it was a completely different story. Nothing was more important to them than Cuba, and they wanted to hear everything Ernesto had to say about it. They would make him repeat things over and over again and they just could not get enough of his explanations and stories. They asked him constantly if he knew this person or that person, or if he had news about a cousin or an aunt. They continuously talked about their own exile from Cuba as if it had happened only yesterday; they were sincerely convinced that change would come to Cuba soon, and they hoped to have a role to play in that. They speculated constantly about what would happen after the fall of the Castro regime. It was a source of interminable discussion amongst them and all of their friends.

All of Ernesto's aunt's and uncle's friends dropped by the house to shake his hand and to welcome him to America and to listen to him tell his harrowing tale of escape from the hands of what all of them had concluded were "Castro's criminal, mercenary killers." His story had spread quickly in the Cuban-American community, and Ernesto became a mini-celebrity in his aunt and uncle's circle of friends. All of them wanted to talk to him about Cuba and about what was going on there, and whether he thought the regime would fall soon and how the people were getting by and so on and so forth. It was a repetitious barrage of questions and queries, but Ernesto was generous and patient with them, because he felt their goodness and their sincerity. Even though it appeared to him that they were completely disconnected from the reality of modern Cuban life, he did not feel it was his place to say that, and so he indulged them. He understood that these conversations and discussions were about their love of Cuba, the country of their birth and of their youth, which, even after all these years, still remained the central preoccupation of their lives. It was what united them and was the bond that held them together and made them who they were.

"So, Ernesto, you're getting used to America, things are getting easier now, eh?" Uncle Jorge tapped him on the shoulder, smiling. The restaurant was packed with lively and animated people who were engaged in discussions, smiling and laughing, and the waiters and waitresses were scurrying about with full plates of hot Cuban food. The place was brightly lit and decorated with taste. Ernesto marveled at it all, wondering if this was the way Cuba had been before, when people were free and allowed to live their lives as they wanted, when there was food for everyone and laughter and life was going on as it should, vibrant and uninterrupted.

"I feel much better, thank you, Uncle Jorge—and thanks to both of you, for everything you have done for me. I truly appreciate it," he smiled at them and leaned forward, placing his hand on his aunt's hand. She smiled back, and his uncle looked at him and beamed, obviously pleased.

"Hey, come on, Ernesto, we are your family and we are more than glad to help. Now, what do you say we order some food, eh? We need to make you strong because next week I will help you find a job. A man has to work and to earn money. It makes him feel good and here in America, it is not only possible but it is how a person lives, not like in Cuba."

"Thank you, Uncle Jorge, I appreciate it and I can't wait to start working and to earn some money. I can't be living off you two forever, now can I?" He smiled at them, but then suddenly, in a split second, his eyes turned moody and he looked down at his menu. His aunt glanced at her husband with a concerned look.

"Ernesto?" She squeezed his hand, "Ernesto?" She recognized that sudden change of disposition—she had seen it before in him, and she knew what it was about. He did not raise his head, but whispered,

"It's just that I wish Yaneti were here, you know, with me. Then, everything would be perfect." Ernesto felt a wave of emotion come over him and he desperately wanted to suppress it, but the wave was stronger than his will to beat it back and his eyes filled up with tears that he quickly wiped away with his hands. "I'm sorry," he said, his voice choked up.

His aunt leaned forward and whispered,

"It's ok, Ernesto, we understand."

His aunt and uncle had listened in silence the first time he had told them the incredible story of his narrow escape from death, and how Yaneti had used the same contact to get across as he had and that no one had heard from her since. They had bowed their heads and drawn a dire conclusion about Yaneti's fate, but had not shared their thoughts with Ernesto, hoping that he would come to the same conclusion himself.

But Ernesto was far from ready to give up on Yaneti. He remained convinced that she was still alive, and as soon as he had gotten out of detention , with the help of his uncle he had contacted her relatives in Miami. They had confirmed to him that they had not heard from her either. That had been a discouraging moment for him, but although he feared the worst, he did not let that thought dominate his mind. He persisted in believing that she had made it. He had decided that he would look for her everywhere, and that he would "turn Florida upside down" if he had to. He was convinced that like him, she had miraculously made it, but that maybe she was unable to communicate for some reason, or she had sustained some kind of head injury and couldn't remember her name or where she was from. He imagined every possible scenario and hung onto them desperately as a drowning man gasping for air. They were his salvation and what helped to keep him going and prevented him from falling completely apart.

"Well, yes," his uncle coughed dryly, breaking the awkward silence, "it would be nice if she were here, Ernesto, that's for sure. So let's hope that we hear from her soon, eh?" He was a bad liar and he looked fretfully towards his wife, who nodded her head in agreement just as their food arrived.

"Ok, let's eat up now, Ernesto," his aunt said cheerfully. "Things will work out, you'll see." He lifted his head and forced himself to smile.

"Thank you, Aunt Ivette," he whispered. They all began to eat, but the mood for the rest of the meal remained subdued and mostly silent.

As promised, Uncle Jorge helped Ernesto get a job, but he was not thrilled with his nephew's choice.

"What do you mean it's what you want to do? How can somebody want to be a dishwasher or a kitchen worker? It doesn't make sense, Ernesto, you have so much potential and there are so many other things that you could do, I mean..."

"Please, Uncle Jorge, I told you why I want to take this job. It doesn't require too many skills and it will give me time to learn English, and also, I can work shifts that will leave me some days free to search for Yaneti. You know how important that is to me." His uncle looked at him and sighed.

"Ok, Ernesto, if that's what you want." He hesitated for a moment before continuing. "But look, Ernesto, this Yaneti situation...well, I have to tell you it worries us. I mean, sooner or later you'll have to consider...well, you'll have to consider that maybe she didn't make it. I'm sorry to have to bring it up this way, but it's a real possibility and you're going to have to come to grips with that, son. You can't go on like this, Ernesto, you just can't." They were sitting alone in the large living room of his uncle's home in Hialeah, and his voice had dropped to a whisper. He had promised his wife that he would try to have this conversation with Ernesto and to try to reason with him. It had been months since Yaneti had left Cuba, there was no sign of her anywhere, and no one had heard from her. Ernesto looked at his uncle intensely, his eyes unwavering.

"I know she made it, Uncle Jorge. I can feel it here," he put his hand on his gut, "and I will find her. I swear I will." There was a fierce determination in his eyes and his uncle looked at him sadly, his drooping eyes filled with resignation.

"Ok, Ernesto, but promise me you'll think about what I just said, ok?"

"Yes, I will, I promise." His uncle nodded his head, but he knew that Ernesto didn't really mean it. He got up slowly and so did Ernesto, and he extended his arms to him and gave him a hug, patting him gently on the back.

"Ok, then, you just sit here for a bit and take it easy and I'll go make that call about the job."

"Thank you, Uncle Jorge. I really appreciate your help."

"It's ok, don't mention it. I'll be in the kitchen if you need me," he pointed towards the kitchen where his wife was busy cleaning up.

It was not a great job, but for Ernesto it was perfect. The hustle and the bustle of the kitchen, the constant clanging of dishes, the shouts of the chefs, the noise of the machines, everything kept conversations between co-workers to a minimum and he enjoyed that, it allowed him to remain in his head most of the time and to think about Yaneti and his plan to search for her. The other people who worked in the kitchen were immigrants, too. One was from Nicaragua, another from Mexico, and a third one was like him, a newly arrived Cuban, who'd been in the U.S. a little over a year. He wasn't from Havana like Ernesto, but from Santiago de Cuba at the eastern extremity of the island. His name was Alfredo and he was a well-rounded and friendly mulatto, who loved to laugh and to share his life experience with anyone who cared to listen.

"Hey Ernesto, want to go have a beer after work, I know a bar that has great Cuban music." Alfredo smiled and his large rows of impeccable white teeth shone through the steam of the machine he was leaning over. Ernesto smiled back. He liked Alfredo; he was an honest and decent person who had had it a lot rougher than Ernesto did in Cuba.

"Yeah, ok, Alfredo, but just one beer though and that's it." Alfredo looked and him and laughed. He had a deep, rich laugh, genuine and communicative. Alfredo enjoyed life for what it was, not for what it could be.

"Ha, ha, oh you're a funny one Ernesto, ha, ha, 'one-beer Ernesto' is coming with me to a bar later, ha, ha, ha." Ernesto smiled. He loved how Alfredo found even the silliest things funny. He was the best thing that had happened to him in a long time, and the closest he had allowed anyone to come to him since he had arrived in America. He had become a friend and had helped Ernesto a lot in those first few months when he was still disoriented and trying to find his bearings. Alfredo hadn't been in the U.S. very long himself, but he shared everything he had learned with his new friend, and a lot of it was useful and practical information. But besides his generosity, Ernesto enjoyed how he was always bubbly and got excited about everything and nothing, laughing at his own jokes and telling innumerable funny stories about the people he knew back in Cuba. This permitted Ernesto to be silent most of the time and to just listen and not to have to talk too much about himself or his preoccupations.

Ernesto blended in well to life in the U.S., and although it was a learning process for him, he was a quick study and he picked up on things fast. Of course the fact that he was surrounded by people of Cuban decent and living in a vibrant and organized Latino community was a big help. He felt supported, and everybody was kind and wanted to help him out, and since just about everything was done in Spanish, he felt a lot less like an outsider.

With his recently met cousins it was different, though. Even though they were supportive, he could feel that a world of difference existed between them. They had been brought up in comfort, lacking for nothing, bathing in the abundance of America and enjoying its rewards since their birth. They were first and foremost Americans and spoke mostly English, even amongst themselves. They never asked about Cuba or what he had done there—and why would they, he often asked himself. His answer would surely have been of no interest to them. As far as they were concerned, Cuba was just another backward country that needed an American handout and was in dire need of some light to be shed on it. Ernesto's presence in their home was the living proof that whatever was going on there was not very good, for sure. Of course, his cousins never said anything like that out loud to him, but he felt it in their silences and in their body language. Their attitude toward him didn't bother him as much as it had when he had first arrived, though, because now he understood how they felt and where they were coming from.

Taking on America was a big job for the senses. It was an eye opener for Ernesto, and was quite a shock for someone like him, coming from such a radically different socio-political environment. There was so much to absorb and so much to understand that it was mind-boggling at times. Everything appeared to be bigger and faster and there seemed to be no limits to what a person could do or aspire to. There were things that were inspiring and things that left him perplexed, and everything seemed to be continuously twirling about in an exhilarating cocktail of intermingling life. It was thrilling and overpowering and it was more than everything he had ever dreamed it would be. He only wished his parents could have seen what he was seeing and that Yaneti could have been there with him, to breath it all in and to feel the joy and the magic and to be touched by the excitement.

The first order of business for Ernesto as soon as he had arrived had been to perfect his English. His command of English had been very limited; he only knew a few words and expressions that he had picked up from the odd tourist in Havana. Upon receiving his very first pay check, he had immediately signed up for English courses. He worked very hard at this and was an avid student, practicing his skills with anyone who would put up with his broken and hesitant conversation, and he forced himself to watch English television and to read English newspapers. Ernesto knew that his command of the language was crucial in his search for Yaneti, and so he applied himself with great diligence to this task. His tenacity and determination were so complete that he very quickly became fluent enough to carry on a conversation, and even though he had a heavy accent and his choice of words was not always correct, he held his own.

At his aunt's suggestion, hoping it would get his mind off Yaneti, he had become a volunteer at a local church. The church sponsored a group that helped newly arrived immigrants to adapt and get settled in. There were Cubans among the new arrivals, and they were of particular interest to Ernesto. He questioned each one of them as soon as he had a chance to do so, and showed them Yaneti's picture. One of the theories he had about her disappearance was that she had never left Cuba and was being secretly held in one of Castro's jails, and he thought that maybe someone arriving from Cuba would know something about that, or recognize her from somewhere. It was a long shot, but he believed that it was something worth trying. Of course no one ever recognized her, but that did not slow Ernesto down; he remained optimistic and carried on. He was in severe denial about what had happened to her, but he was so sincere that everyone was sympathetic and willing to help.

Once a month he went to visit Yaneti's relatives in Miami, and they would call her parents in Cuba during those visits. Ernesto would tell them what he was doing in his search for her and ask them expectantly if they had heard anything on their end. Talking to them was an especially heartbreaking moment for him because he always had so little to report and he felt so guilty for having sent her out alone. He could sense that her mother blamed him for her disappearance, even though she never said it out loud. That hurt a lot, but there was nothing he could do or say to assuage her pain or his own. He could just tell her that he loved Yaneti and that he would never stop looking for her. The visits always ended in everyone crying and Ernesto leaving even more depressed than he was already.

He called his own parents once a week, and that was not much easier. His father was always his usual laconic self, and his mother would plead with him to get on with his life and to forget about Yaneti.

"Please, Ernesto, you have to forget her, something must have happened to her, no one has heard from her in months, please, my love, you have to get over this." His mother's voice was gentle and soothing and it reminded him of how she had talked to him when he was a little boy.

"I can't, Mama, I just can't," he answered, and began to weep silently. His mother started to cry too, and soon they were both sniveling over the phone.

"I love her, Mama. I love her so much and I can't live without her," he whispered through his sobs.

"Oh, my poor baby, how I wish I were there with you. I'm... I'm so sorry sweetheart," she let out a long sigh and Ernesto was too choked up to say another word. There was a long silence and then his father's deep and grave voice came on the line.

"How are you, son?" Ernesto sniffled and stiffened up a bit at the sound of his father's voice.

"I'm ok, Papa, thank you." He wiped his tears with his forearms and took a deep breath.

"Your mother and I are very worried about you, you

know?" His voice had its usual intonations of authority, but there was a touch of concern in it too.

"I know, Papa, I know. But I'm really fine, you know." Ernesto made an effort to sound reassuring. "I have my job and my volunteer work at the church, and Uncle Jorge and Aunt Ivette are very nice to me and I lack for nothing. I miss Havana, though, and I miss you two a lot, but apart from that I'm ok."

"Good, I'm glad to hear that. Your mother is right, you know, you have to let this go, son. It will consume you. You have to get on with your life; you can't go on like this. Do you understand what I'm saying?"

"Yes, Papa, I do, I understand." Ernesto didn't want to argue with his father, not in the situation they were in and he knew it was better to just agree with him. His conversations with his parents always ended on a bit of a sad note; their disagreement about the fate of Yaneti and the fact that they could not see each other weighed heavily on the three of them.

It was a somber period for Ernesto, that first year in America, and as time passed he became more moody and depressed and silent around people. He lost his appetite and became emaciated, and he walked about like a zombie. Everyone was worried about him and they all hoped that he would snap out of it soon. He did nothing that was not related to his job, his volunteer work, or his search for Yaneti. He spent many hours and many days calling government agencies and anywhere else that he thought might help him in his search for her. There wasn't a call that he wouldn't make, or a website he wouldn't check out if he believed there was a chance of gleaning some useful information about her. He was relentless in his efforts, and many nights he fell asleep in front of his computer screen.

The only thing that he really liked to do and that gave him some kind of satisfaction was his volunteer work at the church. He loved to be one of the first persons to help newly arrived immigrants and to tell them that he was an immigrant himself and that he had only been in America a few months. It was an approach that worked, and people would open up to him. A lot of them needed help to find friends or relatives, or a job, and Ernesto was more than willing to be of service. He heard some pretty extraordinary stories from the people that he met. He was inspired by their resilience and determination and was glad to be able to help and to give something back.

Nighttime was the worst time for him, when all was quiet and he was alone in his darkened basement bedroom unable to fall asleep. He would clutch Yaneti's picture in his hands, hold it against his body tightly, and pray out loud, whispering inaudibly for fear of waking up the household. Huddled like that, he would cry until sleep finally came at the end of his tears. He would fall into an agitated slumber and sometimes he would have nightmares of Yaneti being thrown overboard by Pedro and his men. He would hear them laughing sadistically and he would wake up suddenly and sit up in his bed upright, eyes wide open, frozen in fear. Then he would lower his head and put both of his hands on his temples, praying for the clamor inside of his head to stop.

One night, the nightmare was so real and so vivid that he shouted out loud. It woke up his aunt upstairs and she came to see if he was ok. She turned on the lights, came halfway down the stairs, and worriedly asked,

"Ernesto, are you alright, dear?" Ernesto looked at her bewildered, realizing that he had had another one of his nightmares and had screamed out loud.

"Yes, I'm ok, Aunt Ivette. It was just a bad dream. I'm sorry, please go back to sleep." She was not reassured. Coming down the steps the rest of the way, she went over to sit on the bed beside him. She passed her hand affectionately through his hair and whispered,

"I worry about you, you know? I wish you would get over this and move on with your life. This is not good, Ernesto, not good at all. Please promise me you will try?" He looked up at her and his eyes were filled with the crushing pain that was assailing his heart. His aunt felt sorry for him, but she also knew that there was nothing she could do for him and that his grief was a battle that he would have to win on his own.

"I'll be ok, Aunt Ivette, just go back to bed, please." His aunt looked at him and sighed, knowing she wasn't getting through to him.

"Ok, Ernesto, but try and get some sleep now, will you?" She kissed him on the forehead, then stood up and slowly made her way towards the stairs.

"Thank you, Aunt Ivette. Good night."

"Good night, Ernesto."

Once his aunt had retreated upstairs to bed, Ernesto spent the rest of the night staring at the ceiling, unable and too afraid to fall asleep again, for fear that the nightmares would return to haunt him.

A few weeks later, Ernesto was having one of his bad nights and was sitting up in bed, wide awake. He was leaning against the pillows that were propped up against the bed board and was staring blankly at the television screen. It jumped from station to station as he clicked absentmindedly on the remote control. Then something caught his eye, and he clicked on the remote to get back to the previous channel. What he saw shocked and stunned him.

There was a small child standing in the middle of a debris-strewn street, dirty and bloodied and screaming at the top of his lungs as empty-eyed, dust-covered people passed him by without taking notice. He raised the volume and listened as a distraught reporter surrounded by rubble commented on the situation. The caption at the bottom of the screen said, "Disaster in Haiti." It suddenly dawned on him that his aunt had told him about the earthquake in Haiti at dinner, but it had not registered as he had not really been listening. He had developed a dinner time technique to make sure that his aunt and uncle didn't worry too much about him. He would tell them about his day, omitting no boring details or insignificant anecdotes, and always made sure he had a cheerful disposition when he was talking to them. Once reassured on his state of mind, his aunt and uncle would often discuss things between themselves, and this allowed him time to wander off in his mind. He was in one of those semi-absent states when his aunt had told him about the earthquake in Haiti. He had nodded his head and forgotten what she'd said before she had even finished saying it. But the images he was seeing now, flashing across his television screen, really hit him hard. They were brutal and appalling, and he was astounded at the horror that had devastated Haiti. The reporter's voice was high-pitched and strained, and it was obvious by the intonations in his voice that what he was witnessing first-hand was profoundly troubling him.

"The scenes here, Brian, are unbelievable. Communication systems are down, air, land and sea transportation are impossible or, at best, extremely difficult. Some hospitals have been destroyed and a lot of them have been damaged, and the ones that are still standing have all been overrun by the incessant flow of the dying and wounded. Rescue and aid efforts are just starting to get organized, but everything is being hampered by the unimaginable level of destruction and the confusion that reigns all around us. There is no more functioning government and nobody knows who's in charge; many ministers are dead or unaccounted for and many government buildings have collapsed. Even the National Palace, the official residence of the Haitian President, is partially collapsed. There are dead bodies everywhere— some estimates put the number of dead in the hundreds of thousands—and there are many, many more injured and homeless people here tonight. The scenes around me are heart-wrenching, Brian. This is disaster on an unbelievable scale, and I can only describe the situation here as chaotic and mind-boggling." As the reporter spoke, the images of the catastrophe that had been filmed by the television crew that day were broadcast. Each more ghastly than the one before, with grisly scenes of dead and grotesquely twisted bodies piled up in the debris-covered streets, buildings collapsed everywhere, adults roaming aimlessly about in shock and children and babies unattended to and covered in dust.

Ernesto put his hand to his mouth and involuntarily let out a short, shrill cry. Tears filled his eyes and began to roll down his cheeks, blocking out his vision. He was profoundly touched. He felt deeply for the people of Haiti and for the immeasurable pain and incalculable sorrow that were upon them, and he couldn't help but think of how difficult it would be for him if a catastrophe like this happened in Havana. He wouldn't be there to see if his parents were ok and to help them if they needed him! The thought made him feel terrible and painfully aware of how powerless he would be if a situation like this one occurred.

Somehow, the realization about his parents and the images of the disaster in Haiti woke something up in him, and he felt invigorated. It was as if the air had suddenly come back into his lungs. He took in a few long, deep breaths and exhaled slowly, then jumped out of bed and began to pace about the room feverishly. His brain went into hyperactive mode and he asked and answered his own questions, sometimes mumbling and sometimes talking out loud. After a few hours of pacing and frenzied thinking, he suddenly stopped and froze in place. "Yes," he said out loud, "yes" and he hit his fist in the palm of his hand and smiled. He knew exactly what he needed to do, and that was to get involved and do something to help the victims of the earthquake. He didn't know what he was going to do, but he knew he was going to do something, and that thought acted like a balm on his soul. It felt as though something was lifting him up, and suddenly he didn't feel listless and empty like he had been feeling for the past year or so. He looked up out of the small window of his basement room as the first light of dawn came creeping through it and was filled, in that moment, with an intense feeling of purpose and a pressing sense of urgency. He was excited as he got dressed, in a hurry to tell his aunt and uncle about his decision. He would later say that it was on that night, as he paced about his room endlessly and took the decision to do something to help the people of Haiti, that Yaneti let him go.

His aunt and uncle were surprised by the over-talkative and excited Ernesto who showed up for breakfast that morning.

"It's terrible, Aunt Ivette, just terrible!" Ernesto described the horror of the images he had seen on television the night before. "Everything is destroyed, there are dead people everywhere, it's just horrible...I...," he fell silent and stared blankly into space, lost in his thoughts for a moment. His aunt looked nervously from him to her husband and put her hand on Ernesto's.

"Yes," she said softly, encouraging him to go on.

"Oh, I'm sorry, Aunt Ivette; I was thinking about... well, you know...I was thinking that this could have happened in Havana and about my parents and how I wouldn't have been around to help them if they had needed me." His aunt looked at him solemnly and squeezed his hand, and his uncle pursed his lips downwards and said gravely,

"Yes, that would have been terrible, Ernesto, absolutely terrible."

"I want to do something to help, Aunt Ivette. I need to do something to help the people of Haiti. I don't know what, maybe I could volunteer or something? What do you think, Uncle Jorge?" His uncle looked at him blankly; he had been thinking about Havana, and Ernesto's question surprised him.

"Yes, Ernesto, yes, that's a good idea," he answered absentmindedly.

"That's a very good idea, Ernesto," his aunt added with much more conviction.

"Thank you, Aunt Ivette," Ernesto looked at his aunt tenderly and smiled.

"Maybe you could go down to the Red Cross," his uncle said, snapping out of his momentary reverie. "They are the ones in charge of the relief effort here in Miami; that's what they said on television. They are the ones airlifting the supplies and the people in and out of the country and taking donations and all that. I'm sure they could use an extra volunteer." He smiled and got up from the table. "Don't move. I'll get you the address." His aunt was still holding Ernesto's hand, and she looked at him fondly.

"It is a good thing, what you want to do, Ernesto. I'm very proud of you." Her eyes were lit up and sparkling with pride and affection.

"Thank you, Aunt Ivette. I'm glad to be doing this." His uncle came back, beaming, and gave Ernesto the address of the Red Cross.

As he sat back down, Ernesto looked at them both, and a large smile broke out on his face.

"Aunt Ivette, Uncle Jorge, there is something that I need to tell you and I need to do it right away." He reached across the table and took his uncle's hand in his. "I want to thank both of you for everything that you have done for me. You have saved my life in more ways than you can ever imagine and for that, I will be grateful to both of you for the rest of my life." His aunt's eyes filled with tears, and even his uncle's eyes became watery. "Thank you," Ernesto whispered, squeezing their hands, "thank you from the bottom of my heart." His aunt got up and hugged him, and his uncle squeezed his hand and wiped a tear from the corner of his eye.

"We love you very much, you know," his aunt whispered in his ear.

"I love you too, Aunt Ivette, both of you." He looked over to his Uncle, who smiled and squeezed his hand again.

As soon as breakfast was over, Ernesto rushed out of the house and made his way down to the American Red Cross. He knew it would make him late for work, but he didn't care. "Nothing is more important than this," he kept telling himself as he stared out the city bus window.

The atmosphere at the Red Cross in Miami that morning was hectic, to say the least. The air was electrically charged and there were people running all over the place. Phones were ringing incessantly and everyone was shouting to be heard over the din. Although Ernesto had arrived early, there were already a few hundred people standing about the main reception area who, like him, had spontaneously decided to show up in order to volunteer. The two receptionists were swamped, and were trying very hard to answer everyone's questions and to explain what forms to fill out while handling the constantly ringing phones. At one point, one of the receptionists got up and shouted for silence, as the situation was getting a bit out of hand. The whole reception area had become packed with people; they were backed up through the open doors and all the way outside, where more people were arriving every minute.

"Please, people, please—be quiet for a moment!" The noise simmered down. The woman who had shouted for silence was a large black woman who had a look about her that said she meant business. Her voice was loud and authoritative, and it carried well above the crowd. "Thank you. Now, as you can see, we're very busy here this morning and we know you all want to help, but we need you to do this in an organized and orderly manner, otherwise you're just adding to the chaos. Am I being clear so far?" As she said that, the woman took off the glasses that had been hanging on the end of her nose and she scanned the crowd from left to right with a pair of large, wide-open, intense eyes. Heads nodded, and murmurs of approval rippled through the crowd. "Ok, good, now that we understand each other this is what you have to do. You will all need to fill out the forms that are over there by the far wall. We need to know who you are, what you do, any special skills that you might have, and how we can get in touch with you. Now, if any of you are doctors or nurses or have any experience in a disaster area, come up to the counter right away because we will be talking to you first. The rest of you, please be patient, we'll get to all of you eventually. Just fill out the forms, and then form a line on the other side of the room so we can get this thing started. We have more people coming down here to help us out shortly, and with your cooperation this should go smoothly. Thank you for your understanding and for your patience."

Everyone began to shuffle about, taking the forms and finding a place to fill them out. Ernesto filled out his form slowly, as his command of written English was not that good, but he got it done and then patiently waited in line. It was more than three hours before he was finally sitting in front of a Red Cross employee.

He slowly told the man his story: how he had fled Cuba and that he had not been in the U.S. for very long, but that he had a job and was learning English and that in his spare time he had been working as a volunteer helping newly arriving immigrants to adjust and to get organized. The Red Cross employee listened patiently as Ernesto spoke very slowly and deliberately articulated every word. English was not his mother tongue, and he did this because he wanted to be sure that the man understood everything that he said.

"So anyway, I am here this morning because I want to help. This disaster is just too terrible and I can't sit at home and do nothing. You understand me, yes?" He smiled, and his soft-spoken sincerity and honest face convinced the Red Cross employee that he was someone who could be trusted and could be helpful.

"Yes, Ernesto, I understand you and I think we could use someone like you. Now, just give me a day or two and I'll get back to you, ok?" A large smile broke out on Ernesto's face and he got up and extended his hand to the still-seated employee. When the man offered his hand in return, Ernesto took it and shook it vigorously.

"Thank you, sir, thank you very much; you don't know what this means to me." He held onto the man's hand a little too long, and kept shaking it and smiling. "And remember, I am available twenty-four-seven, no problem." The man gently pulled his hand from Ernesto's earnest grip and said,

"Ok Ernesto and thank you for coming in. Like I said, we'll be in touch shortly." He smiled and then turned his attention back to his computer screen. Ernesto just stood there glowing for a few seconds before he realized that maybe he should go.

"Ok, then, and thank you again, sir, thank you very much." The man just waved his hand in Ernesto's direction while keeping his eyes glued to his computer screen, so Ernesto turned around and excitedly walked out of the building. He was beaming as he walked hurriedly towards the bus stop, and for the first time in a very long time, he felt almost happy.

He was very late for work and he was concerned about what his boss Mr. Odio would say. But Mr. Odio had called his uncle when Ernesto had not showed up for work that morning, and Jorge had explained everything to him. Mr. Odio came to see Ernesto in the kitchen the minute he got in.

"It's ok, Ernesto, don't worry about anything, we'll work something out; it is a good thing, what you are doing, a very good thing." He shook Ernesto's hand and without saying another word, he made his way out of the kitchen.

The Red Cross called that very afternoon and Ernesto was told to report there the next morning at 7:30. Before leaving work for the day, he went to see Mr. Odio and arranged to take some time off. Mr. Odio graciously accepted.

Ernesto got to the Red Cross early the next morning, where he was sent to an information session with many other volunteers. They were told about the Red Cross and its work, and more specifically about the Haiti earthquake and what the Red Cross would be doing in connection with that disaster. Just before lunch, the meeting broke up and they were all sent to the administration offices to sign some papers and to take care of some other formalities.

When he got back from the administration offices he was told that he had been assigned to a group that would be working at the Red Cross's Temporary Emergency Refugee Center that had been set up in Miami to receive and treat victims of the Haitian earthquake. He was sent to a room where three other volunteers were already waiting. He introduced himself and shook everyone's hand. There was Janet, a nurse in her early sixties; a young woman of Haitian origins named Amber, who was a student and spoke some Haitian Creole; and finally Jean-Baptiste, a retiree who had been born and raised in Haiti but had immigrated to the U.S. when he was a young man. Like Ernesto, all of them had been deeply touched by the news of the earthquake and were eager and anxious to help.

"The news from Haiti is not good, you know," Jean-Baptiste said as he shook Ernesto's hand. His short, curly white hair contrasted with the blue blackness of his skin. He had large bags under his eyes and deep worry lines etched into his forehead.

"Yes I know, I saw it on the news, it's very bad," Ernesto replied gravely.

"Do you know that they are going to bury people in mass graves because of the dangers of disease and because the morgues and cemeteries are overwhelmed? Can you believe that? It's beyond comprehension. I can't even look at the news anymore, it's just too damned disturbing, all of it." Jean-Baptiste stared blankly into space, lost in his thoughts. Janet approached him and put a friendly hand on his shoulder.

"I heard that too, Jean-Baptiste, it's terrible, just simply terrible." Jean-Baptiste turned his head to look at her and she saw the profound sadness in his eyes.

"Thousands of people at the same time, thousands, they push them into mass graves with bulldozers, can you believe that?" He looked down at the floor and everyone was silent, the air charged with emotion. Janet wrapped her arm around Jean-Baptiste's shoulder in a comforting gesture and gave him a gentle squeeze. After a few moments, she asked,

"Hey, will you be ok there, Jean-Baptiste?" He raised his head and looked at her.

"Yeah, I'm ok, sweetie, thank you. But it's hard, you know, very hard." She squeezed his shoulder again and whispered,

"Yeah, I know."

Just then a woman entered the room. She was a short, sturdy woman in her early forties, who walked with a determined gait and had a warm and friendly disposition about her. She told them her name was Gail and that she was their team leader. Gail sat down with them and gave them an update about the current situation in Haiti, and handed them some information leaflets. She then went over the rules and regulations governing the actions of Red Cross volunteers. It was basically the code of conduct that they were expected to adhere to once they started coming into contact with disaster victims, and Gail made sure that they understood clearly what that was all about.

"Any questions, people?" She asked when she was done, but no one had any.

"Ok then, moving on. Now, in about four or five hours,

the first group of earthquake victims will be arriving at the Temporary Emergency Refugee Center and we will be part of the group that will be taking care of them upon their arrival. They are mostly women and children whose removal from the disaster area was a question of life and death. Now just to be clear, people, their legal status in the U.S. is not our concern; these people are all being flown here on humanitarian grounds and our job is to establish their medical situation and to attend to their needs on a case-by-case basis. We are here to welcome them and to make sure that they receive whatever it is they need in a timely fashion. Don't forget that all of them have been traumatized and what they need most right now is a friendly face to help them deal with what they have just been through. That friendly face is you. Do all of you follow me so far?" Everyone nodded their heads. "Good. Now I will pair you off, as you will be working in twos, and then give you a tour of the Center."

Ernesto was paired off with Amber and Janet with Jean-Baptiste, and then Gail walked them over to the Center and showed them around. She explained to them that the Center had only been set up in the past thirty-six hours and that everything had been organized to receive a large number of people. There were dormitories, individual rooms, kitchens, common areas, and a large modern medical clinic, with doctors and nurses at the ready. Ernesto was greatly impressed by the efficiency and the speed at which the Red Cross had gotten everything organized. At the end of the tour, Gail sat down with them in the cafeteria for a late lunch and gave them their final pep talk before going into action.

"Ok, listen up people, I just have a few more things to tell you and then you'll be as ready as you'll ever be. The most important thing to remember is that this is not very complicated and that you can all do this. Just be yourselves, be patient, show kindness and understanding, and everything will go well, you'll see. If you're not sure of something, don't be shy to ask, that's what I'm here for. Now, most of these people will have some kind of urgent need, so find out what that is and if you can, take care of it. Remember that if we all do our jobs right, things will work out fine. Also, and this is very important, don't forget that you are the face of the Red Cross and of America throughout this whole thing. That's a big responsibility, so try to live up to it, please." She paused to let the weight of her words sink in, and they all nodded their heads in agreement. "And finally, don't forget that it helps to see a friendly face, so smile a lot, people, and you'll see that it goes a long way. Do a great job and make me proud, ok?" They all smiled and answered, "Ok," in unison.

Four hours later, a supervisor came to fetch Gail and told her that it was time. She walked over to where Ernesto and the three other volunteers had been sitting around waiting and told them to follow her. They all made their way outside the building to where Gail's supervisor and seven other Red Cross employees and fourteen volunteers were waiting beside four parked buses. Everyone boarded one of the buses and they headed towards the airport, where they would be picking up a group of seventy or eighty victims of the earthquake.

The scene at the airport felt surreal to Ernesto. The news media were out in force, with their mobile units and crews and commentators and bright lights, and the haggard-eyed, blanketed victims seemed completely bewildered by all the attention they were getting. The Red Cross employees and volunteers quickly hustled everyone onto the waiting buses. All of them were obviously in a state of shock and a lot of them were bandaged up or limping. Some of them had to be helped onto the buses. Ernesto smiled and welcomed the victims warmly as they climbed into the buses; he was grateful to be where he was and doing his part so soon after the disaster.

When they arrived at the center a little while later, everyone quickly got to work. The victims were provided with food and clothing, and each adult was interviewed individually and their information and condition were duly noted. They were then assigned to a duo of volunteers to help them get settled in and adjusted to their new surroundings. Ernesto and Amber took as much time as was needed with each person they accompanied and they were very attentive to their questions and their needs. Amber translated some things for Ernesto's benefit, even though her Creole wasn't that good, and Ernesto used sign language the rest of the time, which worked out ok for him.

Ernesto understood very quickly in those first few hours that what the victims of the earthquake needed, as much as medical attention or food and clothing, was to be able to tell their story to someone. They needed to expunge the fury and the wrath of Mother Nature that had so violently interrupted their lives. He was sure that a kind listening ear was as good as a hot cup of coffee, and so with the help of Amber he encouraged everyone he met that evening to tell him their story about the disaster and about who they were and what it had done to their lives.

The stories he heard that evening were all heart-breaking and difficult to listen to, and some of them made the hairs on the back of his neck stand up straight. They were stories of demise and destruction and of loss and heartache; they stung like iodine in an open wound and they bit the ear. The words that carried them smelled of death and devastation, of wicked wounds that had been brutally and ferociously inflicted and that were so deeply rooted within the minds of those who had pronounced them, that it had fractured their core, and left gashes that would take years to cauterize, if ever at all.

Ernesto was greatly moved by what he heard that evening and he felt a deep compassion for the simple and humble people he met. He experienced their pain as if it was his own, and he desperately wanted to do everything he could to help them and to make a difference in their lives.

As he rode the bus home later that evening, Ernesto thought about the horror that the people he had met had been through and it sent chills down his spine. He was astounded by their resilience and their capacity to still have faith in the human experience. He believed there was a reason why his path and theirs had crossed, and he was certain that it wasn't just randomness, or fortuitous circumstances, or fate or something equally elusive; he felt its importance and its inherent potency vibrating at the center of his being.

He was excited the next morning when he entered the Center. His first day as a volunteer had been an incredibly rich and humbling experience for him. To have been in contact with people who had suffered so much and had absolutely nothing in the world but the clothes on their backs had made him acutely aware of his own privileged situation. That first day had changed him, and he felt that he had received something from his experience, something that he did not quite understand and that he wouldn't have been able to describe had he been asked to. Whatever it was, he had the distinct impression that it was somehow helping him to become whole again.

EAST L.A.

East L.A., or Eastside as the locals called it, is a city
within a city, capital of "Mex-America," with a population
of over two million people, where smog alerts and thick,
slow-moving traffic are a fact of everyday life and where
Mexican Americans and immigrants, legal and illegal, mix
in an incessant whirlpool of swirling humanity. East L.A.,
with its low-rise industrial buildings of concrete and stucco,
its chain-linked fences and steel bar doors, its barbed wire
and auto shops, its empty strip malls and bustling taco
trucks, its swap marts and *Banda* music, East L.A., home of
the Chicano gangs and the Latino Walk of Fame and
Mariachi Plaza and Tecate beer and pink tequila. East L.A.,
sitting in the heart of Los Angeles, sanctuary city, where
immigrants are safe and out of harm's way, for a moment
or forever, its protective arms reaching out into the warm
California sun, inviting and generous, its soul rich and
strong, its heart warm and vibrant and echoing with the
love of its residents, who for generations had made it their
haven and their home away from home.

Maria was sitting at the kitchen table with her Aunt
Fabiola, an untouched cup of coffee in front of her. She
was still wearing her pajamas even though it was nearly
noon. Her eyes were glazed over and she was staring

blankly in front of her. She was still in shock from her terrifying experience in the desert, and she kept reliving it constantly in her mind. Nothing in her life had prepared her for the horror she had witnessed, and no matter how hard she tried she just could not get those awful images out of her head. It had been a week since she had arrived at her Uncle Marcelo and Aunt Fabiola's house in East L.A. and all she had done was to mope about the house, refusing to go out or to get dressed. Mostly she just stayed in bed, curled up against a pillow and feeling absolutely miserable about everything. She was a mess; her eyes were sunken in her head and her hair was disheveled and she spent her days and nights crying her heart out. The pain was always there—it would not go away or leave her alone for a second—and there was the fear too, the fear of everything and of nothing, pure and mean, an omnipresent dread which stayed with her constantly and gnawed at her soul, rendering her immobile and freezing up her body and her brain with its paralyzing power.

Every time she thought of Teresa lying on the desert floor, with a hole in her forehead and blood gushing out of her wound, she would start to sob uncontrollably. She would have done anything to have been able to be with Teresa's children and to hold them in her arms and tell them what a wonderful person their mother had been. She desperately wished that there was something she could do for them, anything that would help to ease their pain or make their suffering more bearable, but she didn't even know Teresa's surname or how to get in touch with anyone in her family, or if they even knew that she was dead. That thought devastated her even more.

She had called her parents the very first day that she arrived in L.A. They were greatly relieved that she had made it to safety and that she was under the protective roof of Marcelo and Fabiola. They had been very worried about her, and Maria was happy to talk to them and glad to know that all her family was fine. Her heart sank, however, when they told her that they had not heard from Eduardo, and her next call had been to his parents. His mother told her that she had had no news from him, either, and Maria could hear the grave concern in her voice over the phone. Alicia Olmeda made her promise to call her the minute she found anything out and after many reassurances and a few shared tears, Maria hung up and sat down on a chair nearby, her forehead creased with worry lines. She had a very bad feeling about the situation and deep down, she knew that something was terribly wrong.

"Please, Maria, please." Her aunt reached out across the table in her direction and put her hand on Maria's. Her hands were strong and muscular and her fingers were short and thick with skin that was rough at the extremities. They were the hands of tireless labor and of countless sacrifice.

Fabiola was a short, stocky woman, strong and sturdy and well-planted on her feet. She was a profoundly religious person and deeply attached to her Mexican roots, even though she had been born in America. Her parents had come to the U.S. during the Second World War to find work, and they had stayed after the war was over. Like countless Mexicans before them, they had settled in East L.A. Fabiola met Marcelo a short time after he crossed into the U.S. illegally from Mexico. They were both twenty at the time and were married a few months later. They had been together ever since, and with their five children and fourteen grandchildren they formed a very close-knit family. All of their lives, Fabiola and Marcelo worked very hard to make ends meet, doing the jobs that Americans didn't want to do in order to provide for their family and to pay for the humble house that they had bought in East L.A. Both worked in domestic services and had made a good life for themselves in the U.S., leading exemplary lives. Fabiola bent slightly forward in her chair in order to make eye contact with Maria.

"Maria, please, you must snap out of this, you are young and you have your whole life in front of you. You must stop doing this to yourself." She spoke softly, still holding Maria's hand in hers. Maria looked up and forced herself to smile. Just looking at her aunt's face, full of love and goodness, brought tears to her eyes.

"I'm so miserable, Aunt Fabiola. I don't know what to do. I think about Teresa and about the horrible way that she died and about her children and it hurts me here," she put her other hand on her chest to indicate her heart, "plus, I don't know what happened to Eduardo or where he is or if he needs me. I don't know what to do next, I just don't know…I…," she stopped mid-sentence and tears slowly rolled down her cheeks. Her aunt pulled Maria towards her. Taking her trembling body into the folds of her robust arms, she placed her niece's head against her chest, rocking her gently. Maria's tears turned into sobs, as the pain and the ache stored up inside of her built up once again and overflowed.

"Now, now, it's ok, *mi Amor*, everything will be ok, you will see. Things will get better, there, there, shhh, hush now." She continued to rock Maria quietly in her arms, staring straight ahead. She looked out the window, past the luxuriant trees and multicolored flowers that illuminated her small backyard and up to the cloudless, azure, California sky, silently imploring the God that she believed in to make her niece better. She prayed with her eyes open, even though she knew that hurt and heartache were only temporary passengers within the confines of one's heart, that life was a mysterious continuum of joy and pain, and that compassion and love were the only balms that were needed to cure her niece's heart. She had faith that God would help her, in this her time of need, but she was also gravely concerned as she continued to rock her gently and pass the wisps of her hair through her thick and nimble fingers, kissing her affectionately on the top of the head and whispering sweet endearments, into the creases of her ear.

After two weeks, Maria finally snapped out of her semi-catatonic state. She was still fragile, but in good enough spirits to finally step out of her aunt and uncle's house for the first time. Walking out and about East L.A. made her feel a bit like she was in Mexico again, and it lifted her spirits and it gave her some much needed energy and vigor.

Her aunt and uncle still lived in East L.A. even though all of their children and grandchildren lived in the newer Mexican-American suburbs that had sprung up around the city. Fabiola and Marcelo had staunchly refused to move to the suburbs over the years and had remained faithful to their beloved Eastside community. It was where they had met and had fallen in love, where they had lived all of their lives, and where they had raised their children; it was out of the question for either one of them to even think about living anywhere else.

"There is nowhere else in the world I'd want to live," her aunt told Maria one morning over breakfast. "Those fancy suburbs are not for me, no thank you," she scoffed. "You see, Maria, here we are part of a community, we stick together and we help each other out. We have everything we need right here. You'll see—you'll like it too." Apart from her dislike for the suburbs, Aunt Fabiola's other big complaint was that her children and grandchildren were more American than Mexican. She worried that they were losing their Mexican roots and the culture of their ancestors. It was a source of grave concern for her.

"I'm worried about that, you know, Maria, I want them to know the land and the customs of my parents and grandparents. It would be a shame if all of that was lost to them. Don't you think?"

"Yes, I do, Aunt Fabiola, it would be a terrible shame for sure." Maria sympathized with her aunt's preoccupations but her thoughts were elsewhere. They were with Eduardo, the love of her life, "the one," as her mother had said. "Where are you, my love, where?" She kept repeating to herself in her mind, over and over again.

Maria had decided to stay in L.A. until she found Eduardo or until she found out what had happened to him, and so the first order of business for her was to find work, any work that would permit her to earn her keep and to stay in America. She didn't really care what the job was, so long as it paid her some money and left her some time to search for Eduardo. She was convinced that this was where she had to start looking for him and she was determined to turn the city, and all of California, upside down if she had to, in order to find him.

With the help of her uncle she got a job as a maid in a large hotel; the work was boring and tedious, but it was work. The manager was a good friend of her Uncle's and he had not asked too many questions before hiring her. Most employers didn't hire undocumented immigrants because of the Audits of Employment—the check-ups immigration authorities did on companies that they suspected of hiring illegal immigrants—but thanks to her uncle, Maria had a job. Although she was grateful for that, she was unhappy of having to live with the stigma of being an illegal immigrant. It bothered her immensely to be labeled that way, as well as being reduced to doing such menial and demeaning tasks. It was, however, a great lesson in humility for her, and she learned first-hand what her compatriots had to be willing to do in order to feed their families and to make a life for themselves in the U.S.A.

The first few months Maria spent in East L.A. went by very quickly. Her aunt and uncle were of invaluable assistance to her and she greatly appreciated their help and support. Because she was educated, articulate, and spoke a little English, she integrated very quickly into the American way of life. Of course, the fact that she had landed in the largest and healthiest Mexican-American community in the country made things a lot easier for her. She kept abreast of events in Mexico via the internet and spoke to her parents once a week on Skype. Whenever she mentioned Eduardo to them, however, the communication became awkward, and Maria could feel their discomfort. When she told them that she was convinced that he was still alive and that she had started to look for him, their uneasiness became conspicuous. Even if the image on her laptop was not very clear, Maria could see how her mother would become silent and look away, and she could feel her father's nervousness when he coughed and changed the subject. She understood their apprehensions and their silences and she knew what they meant, so she talked about Eduardo less and less with them, even though deep within her bosom and buried within the secret confines of her heart, her will to find him was unbroken and unbreakable. He was with her in everything that she did and in every thought that she had. She could not, and would not, entertain the possibility of his demise, because she knew that if she did that, life would have no more meaning. So she held her head up high and carried on bravely, ignoring the knot in her gut, convincing herself of the improbable, and believing in the impossible. It was that mindset that allowed her to continue on, and not to falter or fall into the abyss of depression, despair, or something worse.

Before she had started working, her Aunt Fabiola had brought Maria to the Mexican Consulate to get a *Matricula Consular*, an identity card which established that she was a Mexican citizen living outside of Mexico. Even though Maria had her Mexican passport, her aunt insisted that she get the card anyway.

"This does not mean that you can work legally in the U.S., Maria, it only establishes who you are and that you are living here. The card will come in handy, you will see, but never forget that you are an illegal immigrant and that you have to be extremely careful at all times and not get into any trouble or attract any attention to yourself. Do you understand what I'm saying?" Her aunt was looking at her sternly, and Maria managed a half smile.

"Yes Aunt Fabiola, I do. I'll be very careful, I promise."

"Ok, good, now come on, let's go home." Fabiola took Maria's hand gently and slowly led her away, as if she were a small child.

Maria learned a lot about the reality of being of Mexican origin in America those first few months that she was in L.A. She learned that, for a lot of Americans, it didn't really matter if a person was there legally or illegally, or was even a third- or fourth-generation American; for them, they were all Mexicans, and some of them felt that they had no right to be there. Even though not one single person had ever said it out loud to her, Maria could feel it in their condescending and patronizing attitudes and in the way they looked at her, or didn't look at her, or acted like she didn't exist.

Americans, she learned, had a love/hate relationship with Mexicans and Mexican immigration. Although they craved the cheap labor for their businesses or for their homes, they didn't want to have to assume the social costs inherent to those decisions and would have loved it if their cheap and efficient employees just disappeared back to Mexico once their day's work was done. But of course that was impossible, and therefore, an uneasy co-habitation had developed between the two communities over the course of the many generations that Mexican immigration had flourished. It was a co-habitation which hid many shocking and troubling facts, and Maria was astonished to find out the things that she did.

She learned that illegal immigrants were systematically

denied drivers' licenses, social insurance numbers, education, and even basic medical services, even though human decency and fundamental fairness required that they be provided with these things. Everyone knew that no one was willing to work harder or for less money than a desperate, illegal Mexican immigrant, and some Americans were milking that for all it was worth, allowing illegal immigrants to pay taxes and into social security, while treating them as nonexistent citizens. It was clear to her that, because of the large cultural and linguistic barriers that existed between the two communities, a very subtle form of discrimination had taken root that was imbedded into the very fabric of American society. This realization shocked her and hurt her profoundly. She was even more astounded when she learned that the U.S. was building a wall over a thousand miles long along the Mexican–American border in order to prevent Mexicans from crossing into the U.S. To her, it was as if the American authorities considered Mexicans to be some kind of infestation that needed to be kept at bay. She couldn't believe the hypocrisy and crassness of the American politicians who had devised such a policy. She felt that it was adding insult to injury and the more she learned about how Mexicans and Mexican immigrants were treated, the angrier she got. Her blood boiled and the social activist in her genes rose to the surface. She became inflamed with the subject, and for the first time in a long time, the color came back in her cheeks. It was only her status as an illegal immigrant that put a damper on her desire for action. Whenever her mind overflowed with the injustices and things she wanted to decry, she would use her aunt as a sounding board, allowing her to verbalize her ideas and crystallize her thoughts and assuage the mounting frustration and resentment that was building up inside of her.

"Don't you see, Aunt Fabiola, it's just not right! Illegal immigrants have lower incomes than legal immigrants and native-born Americans, and that's just not fair. They are financial refugees, and they are being exploited! They have no voice and no power and they need to be defended and protected. For the love of God, Aunt Fabiola, this country still calls immigrants *aliens*, as if we were from outer space or something. Can you believe that?" Her aunt sighed and nodded her head gravely. She did not have opinions about such matters. Her husband was the one who had the opinions in their household; she either agreed with him or pretended to agree. That was how she had always managed things and she wasn't going to let her hotheaded niece change that. The only thing she was glad about was that Maria's urge for social justice seemed to be keeping her mind off Eduardo. She was thankful for that. She stopped what she was doing and turned towards Maria, pointing a scolding finger in her direction.

"Maria, please, you have to stop it with all of this! These ideas will bring you only trouble—you worry me. You should be grateful to be here and to have a job and a future. Some things are better to be left alone, and plus, it is not your place to say these things." Both of them were at the kitchen counter preparing the evening meal, and Maria lowered her head for a second, but it quickly came back up. She wasn't going to give up the fight that easily.

"I understand, Aunt Fabiola," Maria said softly and in a more conciliatory tone, "but don't you see that all these people, these illegal immigrants, all of them, they are all good hard-working people who send money home to provide for their families, or for their children or elderly parents? That is what Mexicans are made of, Aunt Fabiola, of love and hard work, and they are good honest people and they need our help and our support." Her aunt turned in her direction and smiled.

"You're right about that, Maria, you know, they are good, honest people, the salt of the earth. God will always have a special place for them by his side. What you have to do for them is pray, and please, please, let God do the rest." Her aunt turned around and resumed what she had been doing, and Maria grimaced and nodded her head to show that she understood, even though she did not believe that God would be of much help in this matter. She also knew when it was time to drop a subject with her Aunt Fabiola, so she reluctantly got back to her chores and said nothing more.

The more Maria read and found out about the treatment of illegal immigrants, the more annoyed she got. It became her *cause célèbre*, and so she did what she had always done when faced with injustice: she got involved. She decided that she would make a difference and would find ways to make things change. She became involved with "United We Dream," a large network of young illegal immigrants who fought for the rights and integration of all illegal immigrants. She also volunteered in a community organization that helped arriving immigrants, and all of her spare time was devoted to her volunteer work. In the process of doing this volunteering, she re-discovered her old self. Once again she was active and verbal, engaged and engaging. She even smiled a lot and seemed almost happy. Her aunt and uncle were relieved to see that her spirits were uplifted and that she was concentrating on something other than Eduardo, and they were happy to see her take an interest in life again, even though they found her intensity and forcefulness a little bit irritating at times.

Unbeknownst to them and to Maria's parents, Maria had not given up on Eduardo; she had just stopped sharing her thoughts about him with them. She was, however, as determined as ever to search for him and to find him. She used the internet and social media extensively in her search, posting his photo and description with her phone number everywhere. She also spent many hours on the phone with all the agencies that she thought he might have been in contact with, and she even checked hospitals and morgues regularly. She used her work at the community center to help her in her search, showing Eduardo's picture to every new immigrant who walked in and especially those who had crossed the desert on foot.

"Have you seen this person?" She would ask, eyes wide open, forever hopeful of a positive answer, "look carefully, his name is Eduardo Olmeda." All she ever got were shaking heads and blank expressions, but she remained hopeful, and she would smile and thank profusely, whomever she had been talking to.

Maria loved her volunteer work at the center and she loved the people that she was there to help. She was genuinely interested in them, and she always engaged with them about their lives and their families. Her upbeat attitude suffused everything that she did, and her enthusiasm was infectious. Everyone liked her because she seemed to really care. Her warmth and sincerity caused people to quickly open up to her, especially because she told them from the get-go that she was an illegal immigrant too and that they had nothing to fear from her.

But behind her cheerfulness and her helpful demeanor, and behind the bravado and the valiant smiles, hopelessness was slowly creeping into her heart and making its way home. The worst time for her was nighttime, when her aunt and uncle had gone to bed and she couldn't fall asleep. She would sit upright in her bed, rocking herself gently with a pillow pressed against her chest, and the tears would always be there, her ever-faithful companion. Sometimes, after having wept herself out, sleep would come, and sometimes it would not. When she did sleep, she would often have nightmares about Eduardo and she would wake up startled, in a cold sweat, with her heart racing. It would take her hours to get back to sleep and most of the time she just couldn't, so she would curl up on her side and the tears would come again. Some nights she became delusional, lost between the murky worlds of wakefulness and sleep, and she became convinced that Death was nearby and that she could feel its presence in the room there with her and she would feel relieved that it had finally come to deliver her of her melancholy. She would smile at Death as it lurked in the darkest recesses of her room; beckoning it forward with a gesture of the hand and she would hold her breath and wait expectantly for the moment when it would strike. It never did, though, and in those moments she would feel cheated, abandoned even by Death, until she realized that it had all been an illusion and that only her forlornness was there with her and would remain with her, throughout the night.

Then an event occurred thousands of miles away, an event that would change Maria's life forever. She did not hear about this event on the news or in the papers, as she rarely watched television and never read print journalism. She found out when she showed up at the community center. It was her day off from her job and, as was her habit, she always did a double shift at the center on those days. When she walked in that morning she felt that something was different—the place was eerily quiet and she saw that all the volunteers were standing with their eyes glued to a television set that was hung up in one of the corners of the main room. Maria walked slowly over to where her fellow volunteers were standing. They were watching some breaking news story, and she could see the words "Live Coverage" in bright red at the bottom of the screen.

"What's going on?" she asked to no one in particular. One of the female volunteers, a retired school teacher named Clara, turned slightly around in her direction and said,

"It's Haiti, there's been a terrible earthquake. Many people are dead, they say maybe hundreds of thousands." Maria saw that Clara's face was ashen and somber, and when she looked up at the screen, what she saw needed no explanation. It was horror incarnate. She put her hand to her mouth when she saw a child of not more than four or five years old standing half-naked, blood trickling down the side of his head, covered in dirt, teetering in the middle of a debris-strewn street and screaming at the top of his lungs, while zombie-eyed people passed him by without taking notice of him. All around him were crushed buildings, mountains of rubble, dust and destruction. It was utter chaos. Tears came to Maria's eyes and her heart went out to that child. If she could have been there, she would have scooped him up in her arms and rushed him to safety. No one spoke as the heartbreaking and almost unbearable images of the horror in Haiti continued to flash across the television screen.

"Oh my God, of all places on earth," Maria thought. She knew that Port-au-Prince, Haiti, was the worst place for a massive earthquake to hit. She had always been interested in earthquakes, as Mexico City was prone to such events, and she had read extensively on the subject. She remembered that most of the houses of Port-au-Prince were sitting on unstable hillsides and built of ramshackle materials. That, along with Haiti's chronic poverty, could only exacerbate the disaster. The group around her began to break up and to go back to taking care of the community center's business, many shaking their heads in disbelief.

The silence in the center was unusual that morning, and people talked in hushed voices. It was as if they were afraid that if they raised their voices, that it might send one of those barely-standing and fragile buildings in Port-au-Prince crashing to the ground. Once in a while, someone would get up and walk over to the television set to check out the latest news, and then return to their seat with a grave expression on their face. As citizens of Los Angeles, they all knew the high probability of a large earthquake hitting California, and the one in Haiti resonated strongly with them as they thought of their families and of their loved ones. Many of them wondered apprehensively when the "big one" would hit them.

The television stayed on for the rest of the afternoon and all through the evening, and Maria spent the whole day in a daze. She felt enormous empathy for the people of Haiti, whom God seemed to have chosen to inflict disaster after disaster upon. When her work was finished that evening she remained at the center for a while, eyes glued to the television, unable to rip herself away from the images of horror and devastation. Finally, she made her way home, but her heart was heavy and she felt terrible about what had happened. She realized on her way home that, for the first time in a very long time, she had gone for more than ten consecutive hours without thinking about Eduardo; she didn't know how to feel about that.

Maria stayed up late that night checking out the latest developments in Haiti online, and she found out that the American Red Cross would be a major player in the rescue and relief effort. She made up her mind then and there that she was going to get involved, and that the best thing for her to do was to head down to the Red Cross in the morning and to sign up.

She got up early the next day, and after a quick breakfast made her way to the American Red Cross. The catastrophe in Haiti had set something off inside of her, and it had also brought something back, something that had been missing. It was driving her forward and forcing her to act.

The response she got at the Red Cross was not the one she had expected. They were only taking volunteers to work the phones and to raise money, and that was not what she had in mind. She wanted to go to Haiti and to be directly involved with the relief effort; more than anything in the world, she wanted to be with the *people* of Haiti, in this, their time of greatest need. The Red Cross made it pretty clear to her that that would not happen in the near future, at least not through them. She was told that getting on and off the island was extremely difficult, if not impossible, and that the situation was chaotic and disorganized. Nobody knew who was in charge, and the only people going in and out for the moment were medical and military personnel who were attending to the search-and-rescue mission or to the urgent needs of the survivors and the wounded on the ground. Maria was very disappointed by what she heard, and she grudgingly made her way towards the exit.

Just before she left the building, she noticed a small group of young people who were gathered round in a circle in the lobby, engaged in an animated discussion. She approached them and listened in, and found out that all of them had also shown up that morning to volunteer to go to Haiti to help out, and that they had received the same answer as she had. They were disheartened and discussing what to do next. One of the girls was telling the group that Miami was the place to go to for anyone who wanted to get into Haiti.

"It's the staging ground for all the rescue and relief efforts. The only planes that get in and out of Haiti do so from there. I hear that there's also some people who are getting in through the Dominican Republic by land now as well."

A light came on in Maria's head when she heard that, and she broke off from the group and hurriedly left the building. Her mind was made up—she knew exactly what she was going to do. She rushed home and quickly grabbed her passport, filled a backpack with a few things, and booked a flight to Miami online for that very afternoon. She called her aunt at work and told her where she was going and why.

"Maria, no, it's very dangerous down there. Please don't do this; why don't you just volunteer in L.A. and do things around here to help?"

"I've tried that, Aunt Fabiola, but it didn't work out. Look, I don't have time to discuss this with you right now, so please just trust me and promise me you won't worry too much, ok?"

"But Maria, what about your job? How will you get back into the U.S.? You don't have any papers, you know. Have you thought about that?"

"Yes, I have, and I'm sorry about the job and the papers will be a problem, I know. But I don't care about all that at the moment. I just need to do this, and that's the only thing that I'm sure of right now." Her aunt fell silent, obviously displeased with what she was hearing.

"Please, Aunt Fabiola, this is important to me. I'm a big girl, you know—don't forget that I crossed the desert on foot, so believe me, this doesn't scare me one little bit."

Her aunt tried hard to get her to change her mind, but it was to no avail; Maria's mind was made up, she was going, and there was nothing anyone could do to stop her. Finally, her aunt relented, resigning herself to the fact that her niece was going to do what she was going to do, with or without her blessing.

"Ok, Maria, you do what you have to do. But promise

me you'll be careful and that you'll call me every day."

"Yes, of course I will, I promise. Thank you for everything, Aunt Fabiola. I love you very much, you know. You and Uncle Marcelo have been very good to me, and I really appreciate everything that you've done for me." Maria's eyes filled up with tears but she fought them back. She didn't want it to appear as if she were flinching.

"I love you too, Maria, and I will pray for you and light some candles at the church for you on Sunday. Goodbye *mi Amor*, I have to get back to work now."

"Yes, goodbye, Aunt Fabiola, and thank you again."

Maria felt a pinch in her heart when she hung up. Her aunt was such a good person and she hated so much to disappoint her, but she couldn't allow herself the luxury of brooding on the subject for very long. She was beyond that, and plus, she had a plane to catch.

Before leaving, she fired off a long email to her parents explaining everything and telling them that she loved them and that she would call them from Miami, and then she grabbed her bag and flew out the door in the direction of LAX.

She was both thrilled and worried as she stared out the window of the bus that was taking her to the airport. There was an unusual tingling in her gut. She was glad to be trying to do something that would make a difference in people's lives, people who desperately needed help, but at the same time she was worried about the uncertainties that were inherent to her journey. She also felt that she was leaving something behind, and that maybe that something was Eduardo.

MIAMI

Maria's mind wandered as she looked out the airplane window on their final approach to Miami International Airport. She had learned that, as the entry point for travelers and merchandise coming from all over South America and the Caribbean, Miami was sometimes called "the capital of Latin America." She pondered on some of the other things she had found out about the city while surfing the net in the waiting lounge at LAX. To her surprise, she had discovered that it was a woman who had been instrumental in the conception of Miami. The woman's name was Julia Tuttle, and she had been a local citrus grower and a rich Cleveland native who became known as "the mother of Miami." She had been given that name for helping to bring the railroad to Miami in the late 1800's. At the time, Miami was nothing more than a swampy outpost with a population of approximately 300 people. Helping to bring the railroad there was a big deal. Maria smiled when she thought about Julia Tuttle, imagining her to have been quite an extraordinary woman, for sure.

The most interesting thing she had found out about Miami was that over 50% of its residents were immigrants. Nearly 70% of them were Hispanic or of Latino origins, and Spanish was the first language of more than 60% of the population. She liked that about Miami and she smiled when she thought about it. She was confident that she would feel quite at home in Miami, even though she had no intention of spending any amount of time there. Her goal was to get to Haiti as quickly as possible, even though she knew that, as an illegal immigrant, she would be automatically denied re-entry into the U.S. and be deported back to Mexico. It was, however, a price that she was willing to pay in order to do what she believed was the right thing to do.

After they landed, Maria took a bus downtown and made her way straight to the American Red Cross. She had decided to start with them, even after the experience she had had at their offices in L.A. She was a strong-minded and determined person and she didn't believe in the concept of 'no' as an answer.

The place was crowded and chaotic when she got there, but she waited patiently in line for over an hour in order to get all the required forms. She filled out the forms, and after another two hours of waiting, she finally got to speak to someone. She didn't like what she heard; it was a repetition of what she been told in L.A., and although she insisted that it was important that she get to Haiti right away, the answer she got was the same.

"It's impossible to get into Haiti by air right now, unless you are with the U.S. military or are part of a medical emergency team. I'm really sorry, dear, but that's how it is." The person who was very patiently and gently delivering this message to Maria was a small and sinewy woman of a certain age. She had short snow-white hair and could have been Maria's grandmother.

"The last thing they need down there right now, sweetheart, are well-intentioned people like you walking about wanting to help, but who in reality are just adding to the burden because they have to be provided with security and given a place to sleep and meals and so on." Maria looked at her in dejection. She had expected being told something like that, but hearing it was a major disappointment. The elderly woman looked Maria in the eyes. She felt sorry for her because she had come all the way from Los Angeles to help out. She leaned forward over the counter and put her hand on Maria's. Her skin was wrinkled and covered in brown spots and seemed almost transparent to Maria, but she had a warm and gentle touch.

"Look, here's something you could do. You could call the Christian Charities. I heard that some of them are moving volunteers through the Dominican Republic to help with their orphanages in Haiti. It's a long shot, but it's worth a try. I can give you a list if you want." Maria's eyes lit up a bit, and she nodded her head.

"Yes, thank you, I'd appreciate that."

The woman returned to her desk and came back to the counter holding a sheet of paper which she handed over to Maria.

"Here you go."

Maria forced herself to smile. "Thank you," she managed to say.

"You're more than welcome, dear." The woman gave her an encouraging smile and Maria turned and started to walk away, but then she revised her plan and returned to the counter.

"I'm sorry to bother you, Mrs... I'm sorry, I didn't get your name?"

"I'm Mrs. Douglas, but you can call me Ilene."

"Ok, pleased to meet you Mrs. Douglas—I mean Ilene—oh, and I'm Maria, by the way."

"Pleased to meet you, too, Maria."

"I just have another quick question, if you don't mind?"

"No, not at all, what can I do for you?"

"Would you happen to know where I could rent a room close by? You know, something not too expensive."

"Yes, as a matter of fact I do. Here, let me give you the address, it's a very well-kept place and cheap, and within walking distance of this office." She quickly jotted the information down on a piece of paper and handed it to Maria.

"Thank you, you're very kind and I'm sorry if I'm a little grumpy. It's just that everything has been very frustrating and I'm a bit tired, I guess."

"I understand, dear, you just go on and rest up now. I'm sure you'll feel better tomorrow."

Mrs. Douglas watched Maria walk sullenly away, shoulders drooping, and she was disappointed for her. She had learned over the years how fragile the enthusiasm of youth could be, and she didn't want to be responsible for even one young person being turned off of lending a helping hand, and so she called out to Maria.

"Hey Miss... Maria." Maria turned around. "Come back here a minute, will you please?" Maria walked back to the counter.

"Look, you seem like a really nice person, and I don't know why, but I trust you. So, here's what I can do for you.

Come back to see me tomorrow morning at 7:30 sharp, and maybe—I repeat, maybe—I will be able to get you involved in something here in Miami. I know, I know, it's not Haiti, but they're airlifting more and more victims from the earthquake here and they'll need extra people at the Temporary Emergency Refugee Center. If I can get you in there, well, at least you'll be able to help people right away. You know, while you wait to get into Haiti. What do you say?"

A smile broke out on Maria's face.

"Oh yes, I would like that very much, thank you, thank you so very much!" The perspective of working with disaster victims first hand in Miami was not how Maria had envisioned she would get involved, but it was something that she definitely wanted to do.

"Ok then, I'll see you tomorrow at 7:30—and don't be late."

"No, I won't, I promise." Maria thanked her profusely one more time and then briskly made her way towards the exit.

She spent the rest of the day in her small rented room, updating her Facebook page and e-mailing and texting friends and family about where she was and what she was about to get involved in. Then she called and sent e-mails to every single charity on the list that Mrs. Douglas at the Red Cross had given her.

She was up early the next day, and after a light breakfast she headed for the Red Cross offices. There were already many people massed in front of the reception area when she got there. Most of them wanted to volunteer or had volunteered already and were waiting for instructions, but there were also people who wanted to donate clothes, money and anything else that they thought the victims of the earthquake might need. There were also many Haitians who were desperately seeking news about their relatives and loved ones in Haiti. Communications were very difficult with the island, and they all hoped that the Red Cross, because of its resources and because it had people on the ground, would be able to help them.

Maria made her way through the mass of people and spotted Mrs. Douglas sitting at her desk. She got up and came up to the counter when she saw Maria approaching.

"Hi," she said, smiling, "I see you've had a good night's sleep."

"Yes, I did, thank you."

"Ok, good. I'm glad to hear that."

"So," Maria looked at her with expectant eyes, "what's the news?" Mrs. Douglas looked around, then leaned forward in her direction and lowered her voice as if she were going to share a secret with her.

"Ok, look, this is what I can do for you, and only because I have faith in you, Maria, and I trust that you are a good and honest person. I will bend the rules a little and send you directly to volunteer orientation and briefing." Maria looked at her and had difficulty hiding her excitement. "Now, when you get there, they'll explain everything you need to know about the Red Cross: what it does here in Miami and in Haiti, and what is expected of you as a volunteer." She lowered her voice even more. "Now, I am told that there are quite a few planes arriving today and that they will need extra volunteers at the Temporary Emergency Refugee Center. It will be really busy down there, and who knows, maybe you'll be one of those volunteers?" She gave Maria a complicit wink, and Maria smiled and nodded her head enthusiastically.

"Oh wow, that would be great, thank you."

"Now, I'm not guaranteeing anything, Maria, but you must promise me that you'll do your best no matter what and that you won't let me down. I'm sticking my neck out for you here."

"Oh yes, I promise, and thank you again! This means so much to me, and I swear I won't let you down Mrs. Douglas. I'll be the best volunteer you've ever had."

"Ok, good, I'm glad to hear that. Now let me get you some temporary identification, and then I'll explain to you where you have to go." Mrs. Douglas returned to her desk and came back with a pass and some information booklets.

"Here you are. This will get you into the volunteer orientation session, and these you need to read."

"Thank you, thank you so very much," Maria felt like crying all of a sudden, but she swallowed hard and kept her composure.

"You're welcome, dear. Now, what you have to do is take the elevator over there past the security station and go to the fourth floor. Once you're there, just follow the indications. You got that?"

"Yes, I got it, and thank you again—you've really made my day!"

Mrs. Douglas smiled; she was touched by Maria's youthful sincerity. "You're welcome, dear. Now, you run along and do good by me, ok?"

"Yes, I promise I will." Maria turned and quickly made her way towards the elevator.

She learned a lot at the volunteer orientation and briefing session and she met a lot of nice people who had also volunteered. The Red Cross personnel were terrific and dedicated, and Maria was very happy to be there and to be part of a group of such fine people. Before they broke off for lunch, they were informed that their services would be needed at the Temporary Emergency Refugee Center that afternoon, as a large flow of earthquake victims was expected later that day.

Maria was assigned to a small intervention group, and everyone was paired off with someone who spoke Creole. She was paired with Alexandre, a young American of Haitian origins who was studying to be a dentist. He told her that he spoke only a little Creole and that he had only been to Haiti twice with his parents when he was very young, but that he didn't remember it much.

"Everything I know about the island, I've learned from my parents," Alexandre told her as they sat down for lunch in the cafeteria. "They are deeply attached to their country of origin and they have many brothers and sisters and aunts and uncles still living there. They are very worried about them right now, and the fact that I have volunteered to help out here makes them feel a little better."

"Yeah, it must be very hard for them, I can understand that." They were both silent, and Maria reflected on the people who had family in Haiti and were without news of them, and how awful that must be.

"Well, for me, it's just that I felt I had to do something, you know? I mean, I flew from L.A. to be here and I'm trying to get into Haiti. Being in Miami to help isn't my first choice, but I can at least make a difference here right away."

"I'm sure you will, Maria, and thank you for that, that's a very kind and selfless thing for you to do."

Maria blushed. "Oh, come on, I'm just doing my part, that's all. And believe me, I need to do this, I really do." Alexandre looked at her and nodded.

"Maybe you do, but you're here and you're really doing it, and that's all that matters."

Maria had only been at the Temporary Emergency Refugee Center a few hours when she saw him for the first time. He was in the cafeteria kneeling in front of a child, a young girl of maybe four or five years old. When Maria passed them by with Alexandre, the little girl looked up and smiled at her, and the first thing she noticed were her eyes. They were a unique combination of green and yellow and contrasted vividly with the shiny blackness of her skin. She was very pretty, in a mysterious and unique kind of way that was fascinating to behold, and Maria smiled back at her. That's when he lifted his head, stood up, and looked in her direction—and when their eyes locked into each other, she felt a shudder run through her body. Everything slowed down, and time seemed to stand still. Their gazes were only locked together for a second or two, but it felt to her in those few seconds as if he could see right through her. Alexandre excused himself and walked off to talk to someone he had seen across the room, but Maria was oblivious to him. Her eyes remained fixed on those of the stranger.

They smiled timidly at each other and she noticed that he was a tall and good-looking man, elegant and refined. His hair was thick and black and neatly combed back, his face was square and well-defined, and he had a flawless chin with a deep dimple in the middle of it. He wore a new beige guayabera shirt and freshly pressed black trousers. His smile exposed two rows of immaculately white teeth and his face emanated wholesomeness and sincerity. She was instantaneously struck by him. There was something about him which had profoundly disturbed her in those first few seconds of eye contact, and she sensed warmth and vulnerability and softness in his demeanor. She felt uplifted and light and giddy and giggly, and all those things at the same time. It was the weirdest feeling she had ever experienced. Her legs felt slightly unsteady and she just could not, for the life of her, unlock her eyes from his unwavering gaze. Without realizing it, she had stopped walking, and was standing a few feet from where he was. The storm that was brewing up inside of her was so strong that she felt like laughing or crying, she wasn't sure which, and she realized that it was silly, but there was nothing she could do about it. She would later tell Ernesto that that was the moment she had fallen in love with him. Everything had happened in that first eye contact; it had been that fast and that instantaneous.

"Hi," he said, and his voice was soft and gentle. It felt like a caress and sounded a bit like an apology.

"Hi," she answered, her voice almost inaudible. She was nervous and excited and couldn't understand the emotions that were running through her body.

"My name is Ernesto, Ernesto Rodriguez, and this is Eternelle," he said in his broken English, as he extended a hand in her direction. Maria took a step forward and took his hand in hers, feeling the softness of his skin.

"Maria Torres," she replied, and they shook hands timidly. He held onto her hand for a few seconds too long, and she realized that he was nervous, too. She disengaged her hand from his and knelt down to face the little girl, as much to say hi to the child as to unlock her eyes from his troubling gaze.

"Hi Eternelle, I'm Maria." The little girl smiled shyly and she took Ernesto's hand in a protective gesture and leaned up against his leg.

"She's a bit shy, but don't worry, she'll come around."

"God, she's beautiful! And those eyes, they are incredible." The little girl looked at her timidly from the corner of her eye and pushed harder against Ernesto's leg.

"Her mother is gone for an interview and I'm keeping an eye on her while she's gone."

"That's very nice of you," Maria was still kneeling in front of Eternelle, "and how about making her smile? Can you do that?"

"Yes I can, I have a trick, want to see?"

"Yeah sure, I'd love to." Maria looked up at him and smiled.

Ernesto picked Eternelle up and sat her on a chair. Then he knelt down beside Maria and pulled out the small bag of candies that he had brought with him that morning. He opened the bag slowly, and Eternelle's eyes opened wide when he offered it to her.

"*Bonbon*," he said. A large smile broke out on the little girl's face and she took the bag and began fishing into it. Maria was impressed by how delicate he was with the child. Ernesto turned towards her.

"*Bonbon* means candy in French... you know," he said

awkwardly. Maria looked at him and smiled.

"Oh really, so you speak French, then?" Maria had slightly regained her aplomb and was teasing him a bit.

"No, it's actually the only French word I know. I learned it only yesterday," Ernesto answered timidly, blushing.

"Oh, I see," Maria felt his shyness and didn't insist. She returned her attention to Eternelle. She took one of her small fingers in her hand and kissed it, and the little girl smiled at her with her cheeks bulging from the candy she had stuffed into her mouth.

Ernesto took quick side glances at Maria, observing her discreetly, and her proximity made the faint and delicate smell of her body cream enter his nostrils. It threw every neuron of his brain into overdrive and it was the hardest thing in the world not to stare at her. He was mesmerized by her, with her waist-long raven hair, luminous black eyes, and tall, slender silhouette, and he realized that he hadn't been this disturbed by a woman in a very long time. He could feel his heart beating madly against his chest and he had to breathe in deeply in order to stay calm. He bit his lower lip as he searched desperately for what to say next. He gently pulled a chair up and said,

"Please Maria, won't you sit down and join us for a few minutes? We could use the company." Maria was relieved; there was nothing she wanted to do more than to stay exactly where she was.

"Ok, but just for a little while," she said, and sat in the chair that he had pulled up for her. She smiled and waved to Eternelle in a friendly and exaggerated way.

"Do you know any Creole?" He asked.

"No, I'm afraid I don't."

"Well, she only understands Creole and a little bit of French, but what you can do is smile at her and say nice things to her in Spanish. You speak Spanish, right?"

"Yes, of course, I'm from Mexico."

"Ok, well, just remember that she doesn't understand Spanish, but she can feel it, she knows if it's something nice that you're saying to her."

"Really?"

"Yes, really."

"Ok, let me try. *Hola, hola, mi Amor.* " Maria had leaned forward and was speaking in a small voice, and a large smile broke out on Eternelle's face.

"You see, she likes you."

"How do you know?"

"I can tell."

"Really?"

"Yes, really."

Maria smiled and turned towards Ernesto, and asked,

"So, what else do you know?" He took a deep breath and said without a second of hesitation,

"I know that you are very beautiful and I am very intrigued by you."

"You are?"

"Yes, I am." Maria didn't respond. She turned in Eternelle's direction, and after a few seconds she asked,

"So, how long have you been a volunteer?"

"It's my second day. And you?"

"Today's my first day. I just got here yesterday afternoon."

"Oh yeah, really, from where?"

"Los Angeles."

"Wow, that's quite a distance."

"Yeah, I'm trying to get to Haiti, that's what I really want to do, to get down there and help. But it's impossible to get into the country right now and when I got here, they offered me work here as a volunteer for a while, at least until I can get a flight to the island."

"I see. It's a big mess down there right now, you know, and dangerous. You'll have to be careful." Ernesto's heart had involuntarily lurched at the thought of Maria disappearing from his life as quickly as she had appeared.

"Oh, I'll be ok, no worries," Maria shrugged her shoulders in a gesture which indicated that she wasn't intimidated by the situation.

"You're pretty brave to want to do that, you know?"

"Not really. To tell you the truth, I'm scared big time, but they need as much help as they can get down there right now."

"Yeah, I know, it's a terrible thing that happened." Ernesto stared blankly into space for a moment.

"Yes, it is. So tell me, the little one, what's the story with her?" Maria pointed with her head towards Eternelle and she saw a darkness enter Ernesto's eyes.

"It's not a pretty story to tell, Maria," he patted Eternelle affectionately on the head and smiled at her, "maybe some other time, ok?" He spoke gently as he turned to look in her direction.

"Yeah, sure, some other time, then." Eternelle had stopped chewing and was looking straight at them. It was as if she understood that they had been talking about her.

"Thank you, Maria, thank you for caring and for asking

about her. She's been through a lot, you know."

"Yeah, I know. They all have, haven't they?"

"Yes, they have." They were silent for a moment, and then Eternelle's mother walked up to where they were standing and picked up the little girl in her arms. Maria turned towards Ernesto.

"I have to go now."

"Yes, of course," was all he could say as he racked his brain for a pretext to see her again. Maria got up and kissed Eternelle on the cheeks and the little girl squealed with delight. Then she turned towards Ernesto and asked,

"Hey, want to have a coffee later, when you're done?" The words just spontaneously came out of her mouth. It was not in her habit to be so forward with someone she barely knew, and she was shocked to have even said that.

"Yes I would like that very much." A large smile broke out on Ernesto's face, and he blushed again. That made her smile.

"Good, so let's meet here at the end of the shift and then decide where to go?"

"Yeah, sure, that would be great."

"Ok, I'll see you in a bit, then." She extended her hand to him and they shook hands a little clumsily, and then she turned and walked quickly towards Alexandre who was standing across the room talking to some other volunteers. As she moved away, she wondered if Ernesto had noticed how crimson her face had suddenly turned.

Ernesto just stood there for a few moments, gawking and watching Maria walk away. He still had a large smile on his face, and when he turned towards Eternelle and her mother he noticed that the woman was smiling. It was the first time that he had seen her smile. She was bobbing her head up and down and was looking at him with a complicit twinkle in her eyes. Ernesto smiled at her bashfully and patted Eternelle's head affectionately as he passed them by on his way to attend to his duties.

Ernesto tried hard to concentrate on his volunteer work for the rest of the day, but he couldn't stop thinking about Maria or get her image out of his mind. A few times he even closed his eyes for a few seconds and tried to visualize her. The hours ticked by too slowly for him, and his excitement grew with every passing minute. He desperately wanted to make a good impression on her, and he had to keep telling himself to calm down. The last thing he wanted to do was to spook her, but the emotions that had turned his heart upside down that afternoon were stronger than anything that his mind could come up with to try to quell them.

They met in the cafeteria at the end of their shift and agreed to go to a coffee shop that was only a few blocks away from the Center. Maria told him that she had to go to the administration offices first because of some paper work that she had to fill out and that she would join him as soon as she was done.

Forty-five minutes later, Ernesto was sitting at a corner table of the nearly empty coffee shop, sipping his second espresso and watching the door expectantly. Maria hadn't arrived yet and he kept looking at his watch incessantly and tapping his foot anxiously on the floor. The place was quiet at this hour, the lighting was subdued, and some jazz music was playing. He let out a silent sigh of relief when he finally saw her walk through the door and stood up and smiled at her as she approached.

"Hi, I'm sorry it took so long, but there were a lot of people at administration and things are pretty hectic down there right now." Her face was flushed and her long, silky hair swayed from side to side as she put her bag and phone down.

"No problem, I was just sitting here enjoying my coffee," Ernesto said as he pulled a chair up for her. "Can I get you something, coffee, water?"

"A bottle of water would be nice, thanks," Maria pushed her hair aside, hoping that her nervousness didn't show too much. She had wondered all day about her forthrightness with him and if what she had felt when she had met him at the Center had all been an illusion of some sort. But now that she was in his presence again, she knew that it wasn't. She had felt it the instant she walked in the door. Ernesto came back with a bottle of water and he sat down in front of her.

"So, Maria, are you enjoying the work at the Center?"

"Yes. A lot! I think that Haitians are simply amazing, considering everything that they've been through."

"Yes, they are." There was an uncomfortable silence as often happens at first encounters and Maria gently asked,

"So Ernesto, want to tell me a bit about you and your family? I mean, if you don't mind me asking, of course." His eyes became somber. As all men, he hated talking about himself, at least about the parts that she wanted to hear.

"No, I don't mind, but there's really not that much to tell, you know."

"Oh, I'm sure there is. Come on, you first and then I'll

tell you a little bit about me." She smiled and he relaxed a bit.

"Ok, sure, why not?"

And so they exchanged life stories and talked about their families and school and the problems and joys of everyday life, but neither one of them talked about anything too personal or how and why they had ended up in Miami. They were cautiously feeling each other out, like two chess players, but the conversation flowed well despite that and time passed quickly, as time often does when people enjoy each other's company.

"So, Maria, tell me more about Mexico. I would love to go there someday. I've heard many good things about it and that it's very beautiful." Maria took a sip of water and thought about what she was going to say. Mexico was her favorite subject and she was very passionate about all things Mexican. She leaned forward in her chair and looked him directly in the eyes and there was a passion in them that he had not seen before.

"I would love to, Ernesto, but I must warn you, I feel very deeply about my country and its people and sometimes I get carried away, so please don't be disturbed if I get too excited, ok?" Ernesto smiled.

"Ok, I won't, I promise."

"Very well, then, so yes, Ernesto, Mexico is very beautiful. As a matter of fact it's incredibly beautiful, and diverse and rich in so many ways, and I love my country and it means more to me than anything in the world. But unfortunately, it's also corrupt to the core, infested with violent drug lords, disorganized, unable to get anything right and in dire need of so many, many things that it breaks my heart just to think about it. You know, Ernesto, there are so many things wrong with Mexico that it would take a day just to write up the list and I'm afraid that it would be a very long list." She had become serious as she spoke and had raised her voice a bit more than she would have liked to, but her passion for Mexico and its people was not something that she knew how to, or wanted to, control.

Ernesto was slightly taken aback by her tone and was uncomfortable with her outspokenness in public. Freedom of speech was a new concept for him, having been raised in a totalitarian state where it was wiser and much safer to say nothing at all, especially about anything political. Maria noticed that he seemed slightly taken aback by what she had said and that his demeanor had changed.

"I'm sorry, Ernesto, I didn't mean to be harsh, but it kind of came out that way, I guess?"

"It's ok, don't worry about it, it's just that I'm not used to hearing someone be so openly critical in public. You know in Cuba, we don't do that. I mean, it wouldn't be tolerated, and a person could be put in jail for that. Anyway, I can't say you hadn't warned me; you are indeed very passionate about Mexico, and I like that, it makes me want to go there even more." He smiled and so did she.

"Oh yeah, even after what I told you, you'd still want to go there?"

"Yes, of course. I mean, you're from there, right, so it can't be that bad, now, can it?" He looked at her mischievously and Maria blushed. "Anyway, Maria, I'm sure it can't be worse than Cuba. I mean, you do have individual freedoms and you're allowed to own things and to travel and you have a free press and there are choices that you can make about how and where you want to live and how to organize your life. Believe me, that's a lot more than any ordinary Cuban can do. In Cuba, you don't decide anything; *everything* is decided for you, even the food that you eat. There are no individual freedoms, only collective ones, and I don't think it's a situation that you would like very much. I mean, I've never been to Mexico, but I'm sure that Cubans have it a lot worse than Mexicans do, I really do." He spoke deliberately slowly, as was his manner, and used his hands a lot when expressing himself, to stress the point he was making.

She looked at him and smiled. She liked how careful and delicate he was with her and she was beginning to see what had struck her about him. There was something new and naive about him, something that was refreshing and thrilling to behold and also something pure and rare, and it felt to her like he had come from another era, from a kinder and gentler time, a time when genuine sentiments and proper manners held the upper hand. She felt that those sentiments resided within him and she liked that about him.

"You're right, Ernesto, I am too hard on Mexico and I know nothing about Cuba, and I'm sure that life is not easy there." Her tone was more conciliatory. "But you see, Mexico is the land of my ancestors and where my roots are, and I love it with all my heart, so sometimes I get impatient and angry about how things are there." Maria paused for a moment and then added softly, "it is also my home and where my family lives, and I miss them so much and I wish I were with them now, but..." she broke off, unable to finish her sentence, and she looked away for a moment and held back the tears that she felt were close. Ernesto felt the shift in mood.

"I understand, Maria, I miss Cuba, too, and my family, a lot," he whispered. "It's hard in that way."

"Yes, it is, isn't it?" They fell silent for a moment and Maria looked around the now empty coffee shop.

"Maybe it's time for us to get out of here, what do you say?"

"Yeah, I guess so. But hey, it's been really nice talking to you and I hope that we can do this again sometime soon." She turned to look at him and smiled.

"Yes, it was, and I would like that very much too."

After that first evening at the coffee shop, Ernesto and Maria met there every day after they were done at the Center, and they talked for hours, sometimes until the man who cleaned the coffee shop politely asked them to leave. Their conversations were always animated and lively and full of complicity and laughter, and their friendship grew in leaps and bounds.

On the third evening after they had met, the conversation had turned personal. Maria had realized that neither one of them had mentioned if they were involved with someone or had someone waiting for them at home. Both had briefly mentioned boys and girls they had known at school, but neither of them had talked about a serious relationship, or any other kind of relationship, and because of her growing interest in Ernesto, Maria had decided that it was time to bring it up.

"So Ernesto, I don't want to be nosy or indiscreet, but I am curious about something. I mean, you're a good-looking man and I see no ring on your finger, so if you don't mind me asking, is there someone in your life? I mean, do you have a girlfriend, or someone special in Cuba?" The question seemed to catch him off guard and she saw something pass through his eyes. It was a somber flash that only lasted a fraction of a second, but she was sure that she saw it and she had the feeling that she had troubled him.

"No Maria, I don't. I mean, I used to, but I don't anymore." He was tense and his disposition had changed. He bowed his head and stared at the floor.

"And you, do you have someone?" He asked with his head still down.

Maria hadn't expected that he would throw back the question at her so quickly, and she froze up. It was an uncomfortable moment and she hated herself for having brought up the subject.

"No, me neither," she answered hesitantly. "Hey look Ernesto; I'm sorry I brought this up, ok. It's none of my business, really, and I have no right to ask you about your private life. I'm sorry, ok?"

"Yes, ok, no problem," he answered, but he sounded a bit distant and he kept his head down. Maria leaned her head down too and tried to make eye contact with him.

"Still friends?" She whispered, and he looked up at her and smiled.

"Yes, of course, still friends."

"Ok good; I'm glad." They remained silent for a moment, but the unease between them had been created and Maria knew that things could never be the same again. They would have to go the distance on this conversation, no matter how difficult that proved to be, so, she decided to open up first and to tell him everything.

"Ok, look Ernesto, and again, I'm sorry I brought this up, but I have and I think that we have to talk about this, so I'll start first, ok?" He didn't answer and she continued. "Now, do you want to know the reason why I'm here in the U.S.? I mean the real reason I'm here?" The question hung in the air for a moment and he lifted his head and looked at her, perplexed.

"Yes, of course."

"Ok, but I need you to understand that this is a very difficult subject for me to talk about and that I have never done this before, I mean to discuss this with another person, any person who is not from my family. It will be the first time, so please bear with me." Ernesto acquiesced by nodding his head and Maria closed her eyes for a second or two and took in a few long, deep breaths and bit her lower lip. Ernesto could see that she was having a hard time dealing with whatever it was she had on her mind. He leaned forward and placed one of his hands on hers and patted it gently, encouraging her to go on, and he noticed when he touched her that a slight tremor was running through her body.

"Maria," he whispered, "whatever it is that you want to say, it'll be ok; don't be afraid, you can trust me." She opened her eyes and looked at him, and he was surprised by the melancholy that had invaded them and how barely audible her voice was when she began to speak.

"Ok, but please don't interrupt me, I really need to tell you all of this." She took another long, deep breath and began. "Well, when I was in my first year at university I met a young man from Veracruz City. His name was Eduardo Olmeda." She swallowed hard and her eyes became moist. Pronouncing Eduardo's name out loud made her want to cry badly, but she pushed back the tears and bravely continued. "Anyway, he was very handsome and warm, and everything that I wasn't looking for," she smiled when she said that. "You see, I'd made a ridiculous promise to myself that there would be no boyfriends while I was at university, and it was such a stupid promise to make, because the second I met Eduardo, that promise went out the window. He was so perfect and brilliant and everything that I wanted in a man. Anyway, to make a long story short, we fell in love, madly and hopelessly in love and we just couldn't get enough of each other and it was the best time of my life. I had never been so happy and so excited to be alive." She choked up and the tears came again, but she did not hold them back this time and they began to trickle down her cheeks.

"Well, anyway, he was a dreamer, you see, an intellectual with no practical notions about anything. I mean he didn't even know how to take a battery out of his phone. He was hopeless." She smiled, thinking about Eduardo's fecklessness. "Anyway, he became disillusioned about life in Mexico and the prospect of earning a decent living there as a writer and a journalist. It was not an easy choice, for sure. So one day, out of the blue, he and his friends came up with the idea of crossing into the U.S., illegally of course, and heading for Los Angeles. He had a vague plan about making it big there and he was convinced that very quickly he would be able to send for me. Of course, I was violently opposed to the whole idea. For me it was a betrayal of Mexico and of our life there. I didn't want him to go and I fought him bitterly about it and as hard as I could, but he went anyway. And....," she paused and swallowed back the lump that had come up into her throat, "...and a lot of time has passed since then, and no one ever heard from him or his friends again." She had whispered the last part of her sentence, and her voice was cracked and charged with emotion.

There was a long silence, and then she recounted the interminable weeks of anguish as she waited in Mexico City for news of him, and her decision to follow in his footsteps in the hope of picking up his trail and finding him or finding out what had happened to him, and her nightmarish trek across the desert and how difficult that had been, and the horrible death of her friend Teresa and how she had been constrained to leave her there on the desert floor where she had fallen, and how it hurt her to know that she had not been able to attend to her, or to give her a proper burial, because she had had to run for her own life. She lowered her head and began to cry softly and whispered,

"Every time I think about her children and especially the youngest one, Roberto, who will never see or know his mother, it breaks my heart and I have trouble breathing so much it hurts."

She wiped the tears from her cheeks and finished her story by telling him how miserable she had been in L.A. and about her desperate and futile search for Eduardo and how she had hoped that by some miracle he was still alive, but that she had finally concluded that it was time that she stopped deluding herself and had accepted the fact that he was never coming back.

"That is why I came to Miami, Ernesto," she managed

to say through her sniffles, "I want to help, of course, you know, because of the earthquake and all that, but I also hoped that it would help me forget him somehow, and forget that he is gone and that he is never coming back." She raised her head to look at him and was surprised to see that his face was contorted in pain and that tears were running freely down his cheeks.

"Ernesto, I'm sorry, I didn't mean to disturb you like this with my story and to burden you with all of this. If I had known it would trouble you so much, I would have…"

Ernesto put a trembling finger to her lips. "Shhhh…, no Maria, it is not just you or your story. Please… please, just listen."

He wiped his tears with the back of his hand and looked directly into her eyes. "I want to tell you, Maria…I want to tell you the real reason why I am here in Miami." His voice had a tremor in it and she could tell that he was doing everything he could to control his emotions. He moved his body forward and took one of her hands in his, and she noticed that he was trembling.

"My story resembles yours in many ways, in many, many ways. I too fell in love when I was young, with a girl called Yaneti, and we were very close and sure that we would be together for the rest of our lives. We were crazily in love and we believed that nothing or no one could ever come between us. But I had this idea, this fixation that I needed to get out of Cuba, because it is a land without opportunities, and my plan was to flee to the U.S. and to make a life for myself and Yaneti there. I was obsessed with this idea and I convinced her to be a part of my plan. Anyway, the only way to leave Cuba is by sea, on small boats, and it is very dangerous and it costs a lot of money. So I found some people, smugglers, who bring people across, and they were very bad people, but I didn't know that at the time. I had only enough money for one passage and I convinced Yaneti to go first. She was scared to death to go and didn't want to leave without me, but I convinced her and she did it, because she loved me and trusted me. Anyway, that night that she left to get on that boat was the last time I saw her alive. I waited for months to hear from her, but she never arrived in Miami and no one has seen or heard from her since." He fell silent for a few seconds and turned his head sideways, staring into space, and then turned back towards Maria and continued.

"And exactly like you, Maria, I took the decision to travel by the same route that she had taken in the hopes of finding her or finding out what happened to her. I went to the same people whom I had dealt with before and I convinced them to take me across too, for even more money than I had given them for Yaneti. How could I have been so stupid, so naïve? Those rotten bastards," he hissed, curling one of his hands into a fist, and turned his head sideways again, his face twisted in anger. "Excuse my language, Maria, it's just that..."

"It's ok, Ernesto, please, just continue."

And so with great difficulty he told her the last part of his story. He kept getting choked up and had to stop often in order to be able to express himself clearly. He told her of his harrowing escape from Havana in the middle of the night in a crowded and airless van, and of Elizabet and her son, and of the frightening boat ride across pitch black waters and his split second decision to dive into the water in order to save his life when he realized what they were going to do with them. The worst was when he told her of witnessing the crew methodically heaving the bound and gagged passengers overboard while they were still alive. That sent chills down Maria's spine and tears pouring down her face, and she was amazed when he told her of how he had swum for hours to near exhaustion and then, by pure luck, had come across a piece of floating debris that had ended up saving his life.

"We had a dream, you know, a dream of starting a new life here in Miami, and to have a house and a family and to be happy. That's all that we wanted. Was it too much to ask for?" He whispered as he looked at Maria with tear-filled eyes, and she shook her head and said,

"No, Ernesto, no, it wasn't."

"You know, I couldn't accept for a long time that she was gone, but now I know, I know that she is gone forever and that it's my fault. I will never forgive myself, Maria, never." Ernesto fell silent, and he lowered his head and put a trembling hand over his mouth and the tears flowed freely down his face.

Maria leaned down so that her face was only inches from his and she took his chin in her hand and lifted his head gently.

"Listen to me, Ernesto, it's not your fault, ok, you wanted a better life for her, just like Eduardo did for me. You did nothing wrong, Ernesto; you loved her and you tried to make her life better, that's all." He lifted his head slightly and looked into her eyes.

"Thank you, Maria, thank you for listening and for understanding. This is the first time that I've told this story to anyone, you know." She was still holding his chin in her hand and they were inches apart. She wiped his tears tenderly with her other hand.

"And thank you for sharing your story with me, Ernesto, and for listening to mine. They are now ours to keep and to cherish, aren't they?"

"Yes," he whispered, "yes, they are." She put her forehead on his and they stayed that way for a while, in silence, heads together as if in prayer. Each was profoundly disturbed by the other's story and astonished by the similarities of their trajectories and the randomness of their encounter.

They saw a lot of each other over the course of the following week, but neither of them mentioned that encounter again; it had been too poignant and too painful a moment for both of them. They both felt its presence when they were together, though, and they both knew that they would be forever connected by it.

That week was a busy and hectic one at the Center and their volunteer work took up most of their time and energy, but as the days passed Maria felt more like her old self. She was bubbly and supercharged and overflowing with thoughts and ideas that she wanted to discuss and to share. Her resurging vitality showed in the radiance that emanated from her face and from the light that scintillated in her eyes, and it had a lot to do with her growing friendship and attraction to Ernesto.

The same was true for Ernesto. Ever since he had met Maria, thoughts of her filled every second of his waking hours, and his mind was filled with images of her mimics and of her smile and he could hear her voice in his head. He had a permanent anticipatory tingle in his gut that could only be calmed by the sight of her, or by being with her, even for a few stolen moments.

"I'm telling you, I've learned a lot about the situation of Latino immigrants in the U.S. since I've been here." Maria was particularly fired up one evening. They were sitting having a coffee after work in what they now called "their coffee shop," and Maria, the unrelenting and passionate activist that she was, was on fire. She always spoke in rapid bursts and was in a hurry to share her knowledge or opinions about the subjects which were close to her heart. Ever since she had worked with arriving immigrants in L.A., the situation of illegal Latino immigrants in the U.S. was of particular interest to her. Ernesto was in awe at her capacity to bite into a subject like a dog on a bone. He had learned very quickly that once something was "in her jaws," she didn't let go easy. He sat silently sipping his coffee, eyes smiling and mesmerized by her energy and fervor.

"Did you know that there are eleven to twelve million illegal immigrants in the U.S.?" As was her habit, Maria did not wait for his answer. "And that fifty-six per cent of them are from Mexico and twenty-two per cent from Latin America. Seventy-eight per cent of illegal immigrants are Latinos—now that's a big number, Ernesto." Ernesto nodded his head gravely. "Well, I've learned that most illegal immigrants pay into social security, and yet they have limited or no access to public services! Now, that is not fair, Ernesto, and something has to be done about that. People have to know about this." Maria took a sip of water and Ernesto leaned forward in his chair and cleared his throat.

"You are right, Maria—but don't forget that this country opened its arms to us and helped us and sheltered us, and it has given us the opportunity to make a better life for ourselves. That is what all immigrants want, isn't it, to make a better life for themselves and for their families? Isn't that why we all come here?"

"Yes, of course, but don't forget that this country opened its arms to *you*, Ernesto, because you are Cuban and that Americans have a thing for Cuba. It's like a love/hate thing, but still, it's a thing. They also have a thing for Mexicans, but believe me, it's a much more unfair thing when it comes to us."

"You don't really believe that, now, do you?"

"Well, yes and no. It is partially true. Now, don't get me wrong, there are a lot of wonderful and generous people in this country who have been very kind to me and I am thankful for that, but there are also some very callous people, who don't like Mexicans, and whether we were born here or not and whether we are here legally or illegally makes no difference to them. For them we are all Mexicans, and that's just the way things are, Ernesto. It's a reality that I, as a Mexican immigrant, have to live with and accept. Also, don't forget that I, as an illegal immigrant, have had a very different experience here than you. I mean, you were welcomed here with open arms and you can live and work here in all legality, and that is extraordinary, Ernesto, and I am happy for you for that. But what about us, Ernesto? What about those people who are not welcome here but who have come here anyway, by their own means, in search of a better life, and who only want to feed their families and to contribute to society, and who sometimes end up being abused and exploited by unscrupulous people, and who the system turns its back on? They are people too, Ernesto, people that deserve to be helped as much as anybody else."

"Yes, Maria, you are right, but these people, they chose to come here and to take their risks with whatever they found. You can't blame the U.S. for their decisions, Maria. You can't blame the U.S. for everything." Ernesto's eyes had become darker, and Maria could see that he was becoming a little irritated. She continued cautiously, speaking slowly and enunciating her words carefully.

"Of course not, Ernesto, and that's not what I'm saying, nor am I saying that things are as bad here as in Mexico, or Cuba, or some other Latin American country. All I'm saying is that some things need to get better, especially when it comes to the treatment of illegal immigrants, who, as I have already told you, are mostly Mexicans. And you know how I feel about Mexicans," she smiled at him, in an effort to ease the tension that she felt had built up inside him.

"Yes, I do, Maria," he smiled too, "and since I've met you, I am also a great fan of Mexicans and I have a special place in my heart for them."

"Thank you, Ernesto, it's very sweet of you to say that and just so you know, I feel the same way about Cubans. I mean, now that I have met you, of course." She had a mischievous twinkle in her eyes when she said that, and after having paused for a second, she decided to press the subject a little bit more.

"Ok, look, Ernesto, let me just say one last thing about

this and then I'll change the subject, I promise, ok?" She didn't wait for him to answer. "Let me give you an example of something that is very unfair. Now, there are over three million minor children living in this country who are U.S. citizens because they were born here, and all of these children have a least one illegal parent. Now, did you know that the mothers or fathers of these children could be deported because of their illegal status? Well, that's a fact, Ernesto, these families could be split up and we are talking of *children* here, of school-age children or younger, who did nothing wrong and did not ask to be born here or anywhere. That is not right, Ernesto, and it shouldn't be."

Ernesto looked at her with admiration; he was proud of her uprightness and decency and of her sense of justice and determination.

"Yes, Maria, you're right, that is cruel and unjust and it shouldn't be, and something should be done about that. But on the other side of things, look at where we are: free to do as we wish and to talk like this. That is something that I would never have been able to do in Cuba, Maria, never. I would have been thrown in jail or shot. Here, at least, you can live like a normal human being, and of course there are things that need to be made better. There are always things that need to be made better, but situations are always more complicated than they appear to be and are not always what they seem." A smile broke out on her face; she loved the way he always tried to be sensitive to her feelings, while at the same time trying to give her a different perspective on things.

"Thank you for listening, Ernesto, it means a lot to me, and I'm sorry to bore you with my stories of immigrants and politics and all that."

"You're not boring, Maria; I like it when you speak your mind. That is how you are and I want you to be yourself. I'm ok with that, and it makes me feel good here." He pointed to his heart and she smiled.

"Thank you. It's just that things take forever to change and it's so frustrating."

"But things do change, Maria, because of people like you, people who always think of others before themselves. I'm glad someone like you exists and cares so much." Maria blushed and lowered her eyes.

"Thank you, Ernesto, thank you for saying that and for being so nice to me," she said softly. "I know I can be a lot to handle sometimes and I appreciate it."

"You're welcome. To tell you the truth, I really enjoy listening to you." She looked up at him. "I mean, you're interesting and passionate and you really care about things, and to me, it's like…well, it's like listening to music, in a way."

"Ha, ha," Maria burst out laughing. "Oh, come on, Ernesto, that's such a *cliché*."

"No, Maria, I mean it. I really do. I enjoy listening to you that much." The sincerity in his voice and in his unwavering gaze stopped her laughter, and she cocked her head and looked at him with a semi-curious, semi-mischievous expression on her face.

"Really?" she asked, her tone slightly playful.

"Yes, really," he replied resolutely.

The following morning, Maria got a call from one of the Christian organizations that she had contacted the first day she had arrived in Miami. The woman who called her told her that they would be sending a small group of volunteers by land through the Dominican Republic to an orphanage that the organization owned and operated in Port-au-Prince, and she wanted Maria to come down to their offices the following Monday for an interview. She told Maria that the orphanage had been partially destroyed by the earthquake but was still functional and was overflowing with new arrivals, and that they were considering her as a potential candidate. She had insisted a lot about how bad the situation was down there and she wanted to be sure that Maria was aware of the dramatic and dangerous situation she would be getting into. Maria had answered that she was fully aware of the situation, and agreed to be at their office the following Monday at nine a.m.

Maria was troubled by the call, and surprised that she had agreed to go to the interview without really thinking things out. The second she got off the phone she began to pace about her tiny room nervously, and she walked the eight or ten paces from the small window to the far wall for over an hour. Her head was spinning and she was tormented about what she should do. She kept telling herself that getting to Haiti to help was the main reason why she had come to Miami. But that was before—before she had met Ernesto.

Later that morning, Ernesto and Maria were sitting in the cafeteria at the Center during a break, and Ernesto was fidgety and couldn't stay in place. There was a reason for his restlessness. The previous evening, he had decided that he would invite Maria out to dinner in order to tell her how he felt about her. He considered that he just couldn't ignore his feelings for her any longer, and that he had to speak up.

He was concerned, though, that maybe she wasn't ready to be in a relationship and that all she wanted to be was friends, and that asking her out to dinner would confuse things between them. He was also uncertain if she felt the same way about him as he did about her.

Maria was telling him about a Haitian that she had met that morning when he clumsily cut her off mid-sentence.

"Maria, look, I'm sorry to interrupt... but there's something...there's something I want to ask you." She stopped talking and looked at him inquisitively.

"Yes, Ernesto?"

"Well...well, I'd like to invite you out to dinner," his words just hung there for a second or two, and then he hesitantly continued, "you know, like, in a restaurant... a nice restaurant, I mean. Do you think...do you think that you would you like that?" He immediately knew that his request had fallen a bit flat and he looked away embarrassed, afraid to cross eyes with her, but when he turned his head back in her direction, he saw that her eyes were lit up and that she was smiling. She reached out across the table and put her hand on his.

"Of course I would, Ernesto, I would like that very much!" She squeezed his hand lightly.

"Really?"

"Yes, really."

"Wow, that's great!" A large smile broke out on his face, and he had trouble hiding his relief.

"Would tonight be too soon?"

"No, tonight would be fine."

"Great, I could pick you up around seven, would that be ok?"

"Yes, seven's good." Ernesto was elated and beaming with satisfaction.

His uncle lent him his car for the occasion, and he reserved a table for them in a small, cozy restaurant in Little Havana that he knew.

"It is where you're Aunt Ivette and I would go for romantic dinners when I was courting her," he told Ernesto enthusiastically. "It's a great place, you'll see, very intimate and the food is terrific." Ernesto blushed as his pleased aunt and uncle walked him to the door. He knew their hearts were filled with hope for him and that his aunt probably prayed for him every day in the hope that he would find someone to fill the void left by the absence of Yaneti.

"So, when will we get to meet this Maria? You can't hide her from us forever, you know," his aunt asked excitedly.

"Oh, hush now, Ivette, let the poor boy be. Come on, now, off you go and enjoy yourself." His uncle gave him a gentle push out the door. "You don't want to be late, now, do you?"

"No, of course not," Ernesto peered over his uncle's shoulder at his aunt. "You will meet her soon, Aunt Ivette, I promise. You'll like her, I'm sure." He flashed a large smile at her and she blew him a kiss over her husband's shoulder. Ernesto waved to them both as he made his way to the parked car in the driveway and then drove off to pick up Maria.

It was a small restaurant, cozy and quiet. Each table was covered by a freshly pressed white table cloth and there was a lit candle on each one. The lighting was subdued and some soft music was playing in the background. The decoration was simple but in good taste, and the whole place exuded intimacy and romanticism. The smiling and polite owner, an older gentleman, and his friendly salt-and-pepper-haired wife greeted them at the door and directed them to a small table near the back of the restaurant. There were two other couples in the restaurant and they were both sitting closer to the large street-side windows in the front of the restaurant and away from Ernesto and Maria.

Ernesto quickly stepped over to Maria's side of the table and pulled her chair out for her. She was wearing a white satin blouse and her favorite black leggings and black ballerina shoes and the silver bracelet and ring that her grandmother had given her on her fifteenth birthday. Her hair was freshly washed and bouncy, her eyes scintillated in the flickering candlelight, and she emanated freshness and splendor. Ernesto went to sit in front of her and his face was glowing as he looked in her direction. He was unable to take his eyes off of her and his heart was racing and thumping madly against his chest. He adjusted his stiff, freshly pressed shirt collar, which he wore thanks to his aunt's good care. She had overseen everything that he had put on and she had made sure that he wore a clean pair of black pants and that his black shoes were impeccably polished. Ernesto was tense but he was also calm, because his mind was made up about what he was going to say to Maria that evening.

The smiling owner came over to their table to personally take care of them as he had promised Uncle Jorge he would do when he had called earlier to make the reservation. It was a task that he acquitted with elegance and professionalism, and after having doted on them and profusely inquired a few times if everything was all right, he ran off to place their order and fetch their wine.

Things were a bit awkward between them at first, as it was the first time that they had sat down in a restaurant and formally shared a meal together. The ambiance and the cozy atmosphere of the restaurant worked its magic, however, and things soon became more relaxed. Time flew by, and neither of them ate much, but the wine was good and it flowed freely and it made their faces glow in the candlelight as it raced through their bodies and did what wine does and has done for young couples standing together on the precipice of love for hundreds of years, opening the doors of intimacy, helping to break the barriers of timidity, and allowing life in all its magnificence to take its flight.

There was a break in the conversation and Ernesto leaned forward to reach across the table and gently put his hand on Maria's. She didn't remove her hand from under his, and she looked at him intensely, her eyes dark and brilliant and his warm hand on hers causing her heartbeat to accelerate suddenly.

"Maria." Ernesto's voice was a little hoarse and he coughed to clear it. The strong emotions that had been building up inside of him for the past few days were rising to the surface. "Well, Maria, there's something I want to ask you and something I need to tell you."

"Yes, Ernesto?" She squeezed his hand gently to encourage him on.

"Well, first of all, my question, and please, do not be taken aback by it." He paused and then asked. "Do you believe in love at first sight?" She smiled and there was a touch of complicity in her eyes.

"Yes, Ernesto, I do," she said softly, and her eyes watered up as he put his other hand on hers.

"So do I, Maria, and that is why I need to tell you what I am going to say and again, please to not be taken aback." He paused for a second. "Well, the truth of the matter is that I've been in love with you since the very first second I set eyes on you, and it was so instantaneous that I thought my heart would explode right then and there. And tonight—well, tonight I had to tell you, because I can't hold back what I'm feeling any longer. I love you, Maria Torres, I love you like I never thought I would be able to love again." Maria squeezed his hand and a tear rolled down her cheek. "I hesitated a lot, you know, because of…, well, you know why, because of…," he stopped, as if to pronounce Yaneti's name was too painful a thing for him to do. "Because of Yaneti," he finally managed to say, and his eyes became watery too and he couldn't continue. They looked at each other with tear-filled eyes, both of them caught up in their own storm of overflowing and conflicting emotions.

"I love you too, Ernesto Rodriguez," she whispered, "and I also have loved you since the first moment I set eyes on you. I love you so much that it hurts here," she pointed to her heart, "and I'm so scared, you know," tears were pouring down her cheeks now, "of falling in love and of being hurt again, like with…like with Eduardo. I couldn't survive something like that again, Ernesto, I just couldn't."

"I know Maria, and believe me; I'm as scared as you are right now." She wiped her cheeks with the back of her hands and smiled, and Ernesto leaned over the table and pulled her gently towards him, and their lips touched lightly for an instant.

"Aren't we silly, sitting here saying we love each other and crying like babies the whole time?" Maria asked as she did a quick spin around to see if anyone in the restaurant was looking their way, but the restaurant had emptied out and they were the only two customers left.

"Yes, we are, but I'm so happy right now that I feel like screaming at the top of my lungs and shouting to the world that I love you." Ernesto raised one of her hands to his lips and kissed it.

"Thank you, Ernesto, thank you for having come into my life," she whispered, and their lips met one more time and they lingered that way for a moment. Maria looked at him and his eyes were closed, and he seemed transported to another world. Then he opened his eyes and looked into hers and he saw in her eyes what he felt in his heart.

"And thank you for having come into mine," he whispered, and they stayed that way a while, holding hands and smiling and basking in the warmth of their newly declared love.

A few minutes later, Ernesto asked for the check, and they got up to leave. The smiling owner with his wife by his side accompanied them to the door and wished them goodnight. On the sidewalk, Maria took Ernesto's hands in hers, and he was excited by the feel of her hand as they slowly made their way towards the parking lot in the back of the restaurant.

It was a perfect Miami evening. A warm sensual breeze was drifting about and the sky was clear and overflowing with stars and there seemed to be a unique benevolence and gentleness in the air that was enveloping them and carrying them with it. They felt light and happy and ecstatically alive.

They arrived in the parking lot and Ernesto walked over to the passenger side of the car to open the door for her. When he turned around she was standing in front of him, only inches away, and looking directly into his eyes. No words needed to be said as he put his arms around her waist and gently pulled her towards him. He slowly lowered his head, and she wrapped her arms around his neck, and when their lips met it was nuclear fusion and spontaneous combustion at the same time. They devoured each other's lips until the blaze of their embrace became contagious and every cell of their bodies was ignited and flared up in a fiery outburst as they became one for the first time. They could feel each other's ardor as it travelled on their skin and the passion of their kiss was powerful and potent and all the pent up yearning which had been building up inside them, was finally released. They kissed for a long time, there in the quiet and darkened parking lot, unwilling to let go, hanging onto each other, and there was no force in the world which could have pulled them apart.

When they finally disengaged, Maria put her hands on his face and kissed him on the cheeks and on the forehead, and he kissed her behind the ears and on the neck she shivered when he did that.

"I love you," she whispered in his ear, "oh, God, I love you," and he kissed her neck again and then lifted her slightly off the ground and began to spin her around slowly. He was a little taller than she was, and strong, and it felt to him like she was weightless. He spun her around and around, laughing, and she squealed with delight.

"I love you!" he shouted, "I love you, Maria Torres." He stopped spinning her and set her down, and they just stood there for a moment, eyes locked into each other and breathing in each other's essence, oblivious to the rest of the world.

They drove in silence in the direction of Maria's place, holding hands all the way, and occasionally Ernesto would turn and take a quick look in her direction and she would look at him and smile. When he arrived in front of her building she took his hand and kissed it and looked at him tenderly.

"Come in, my love," she whispered, and Ernesto was surprised by the invitation.

"Are you sure about this, Maria, I mean, it's ok if you..."

She put a finger to his lips before he could finish his sentence. "Ernesto, I have never been as sure of something in my life as I am about this." Her gaze was steady and unflinching and he leaned in her direction and kissed her lightly, and then turned the engine off and got out of the car. He went over to her side and opened the door for her, extending his hand to help her out. Then he pulled her towards him, holding her gently by the waist and pressing her against him, their lips only inches apart. She pecked him on the lips, and pulled on his hand, and led him inside.

That night, their first together, the gods of love descended upon them and anointed them with their grace. Neither of them got much sleep, and they gave themselves to each other with the tenderness and the intensity of unconditional love. Whispering over and over again in each other's ears their love for each other, there, in the confines of her tiny rented room with only the lights of the city in the background entering through a small window, they celebrated the marriage of their hearts and of their souls and they loved themselves to the end of love, until finally, at the break of dawn, they fell asleep, exhausted and content, empty of love and full of love and blessed by a wonderful fatigue and an unquantifiable bliss.

The next morning they made love again, and lingered for a few hours in bed intertwined in each other's arms.

"I have to go soon." Ernesto was lying on his back with his eyes closed, and Maria's head was comfortably tucked into his shoulder. She had an arm wrapped around his chest and was snuggled up against him.

"Ummm…" she moaned lazily, "in five minutes, ok?"

"Ok, but not much longer. I have to bring the car back to my uncle, and my aunt will be worried about me. She does worry about me, you know." He opened his eyes and kissed the back of her head, and Maria smiled and kissed his chest.

"She does, eh," she replied, a bit sarcastically.

"Yes, she does." He looked at her and grinned, amused by what she was implying.

"I just wish we could stay like this all day." Her voice was raspy and still laden with sleep.

"So would I."

"Want to have a coffee? They make a great one just around the corner."

"Yes, I'd love that." He tickled her and she jumped and squealed with delight.

"Hey, stop that, I like to wake up slowly." She kissed his chest again and ran her hand along his shoulder and looked up at him.

"Do you still love me this morning?" She asked, kissing her finger and pressing it lightly on his lips.

"Yes, I do, I love you more this morning than yesterday, if that is even possible." She lifted her head so as to be level with his and pecked his lips.

"Good, because I love you that much, too." He looked at her and smiled.

"You're wonderful, you know?"

"And so are you," she whispered, and they kissed again.

He gently pulled backed and asked, "And now can we go have that coffee?"

"Yes, my love. Come on, let's go."

Maria was fully awake now, and she disengaged herself from his arms and got up. She grabbed a t-shirt that was on the floor and pulled it on, and then began to rummage through her bag for something else to wear. Ernesto sat up in the bed and looked at her, admiring her as she bent over semi-naked, her long black hair swaying from side to side as she tossed things around in her bag. He was mesmerized by her beauty and couldn't get over how lucky he was to have found her. He smiled to himself and chuckled, and slowly got out of bed and got dressed.

They sipped their coffee only inches apart, smiling and silent. Deep down, Maria was troubled, though: she hadn't told Ernesto about the appointment she had the following Monday and she felt bad about that. She kept suppressing the urge to tell him. The night before had definitely shaken her resolve to go ahead with her plan.

Ernesto smiled at her, unaware of the turmoil that was going on in her mind. He gulped down his last drop of coffee, got up and bent down to kiss her.

"I really have to go now, Maria. I'll see you later, ok?" They had been given a day off from the Center and they had agreed to meet at the end of the afternoon and to spend the rest of the day and the evening together.

"Ok, I'll see you later. I love you," she said, her eyes bright and full of light.

"I love you more," he answered, kissed her again, and was off.

As he drove back to his aunt and uncle's house, Ernesto sang every Cuban song that came on the radio at the top of his lungs, and he waved and smiled to everyone that he passed. Some people were surprised, and looked at him like he had lost his mind, and others waved back smiling and were amused. Ernesto was happy like he had not been in a very long time and he was pleased to share his joy with the world.

Maria sat for a while in the coffee shop after he was gone, going over the events of the past twenty-four hours in her mind. She cried a bit, not because she was sad, but because she was so happy, and she chuckled a few times and even laughed out loud once and her whole body tingled with the constant flow of love that was running through it. She thought again about the commitment she had made to herself about going to Haiti and she knew now that she wasn't going to that interview the following Monday, her new-found love for Ernesto had changed everything.

Later that morning, Ernesto was sitting at the kitchen table with his aunt having a coffee and telling her excitedly about his evening with Maria.

"She is really wonderful, Aunt Ivette, and I can't wait for you to meet her. I know you'll like her." His aunt sighed profoundly; everything he had been telling her brought back memories of her youth and how wonderful it was to be young and in love.

"I'm so glad for you, Ernesto. She seems like such a nice girl."

"Yes, she is, Aunt Ivette," he said, as thoughts of Maria filled his mind. His aunt smiled and patted his hand affectionately.

"Now, Ernesto, I know you're excited about Maria and all that, but did you forget what day it is today?" He looked at her with a puzzled look on his face.

"Did I forget someone's birthday?"

"No, you didn't, but today is an anniversary, Ernesto, and a very important one." His face was blank, and he obviously had no idea what she was talking about.

"Well, one year ago today you washed up on the Florida shore. It's been one year, Ernesto." His looked at her with wide open eyes and a surprised expression on his face.

"Wow," was all he managed to say.

"You'd forgotten, eh?"

"Yes, I had, Aunt Ivette, I'd completely forgotten. I'm...," he stopped in the middle of what he was saying and stared blankly into space.

"Ernesto?" His aunt looked at him, worried that he was having some kind of a relapse, but he quickly snapped out of his momentary absence and looked at her and smiled.

"Aunt Ivette, you're the best, and I love you. Thank you so very much, so very, very much." He abruptly got up and kissed her profusely on the cheeks.

"You're welcome, dear," his flustered aunt answered, "I hope I didn't trouble you too much by reminding you of this?"

"No, you didn't, Aunt Ivette, but there is something that I need to do and I need to do it right away. I'll explain to you later, ok?" Before she could say another word, he was gone.

"What's the big rush?" his baffled aunt shouted out after him, but he was already out of ear's reach.

Ernesto took a quick shower and shaved hastily. He put on a pair of clean white jeans and an open collar white cotton shirt and then ran downstairs to see his uncle, who agreed to let him have the car again when he told him what he was off to do.

It was about five o'clock by the time he got to Maria's place, and he ran up the stairs to her room and knocked on the door, hiding the large bouquet of flowers he had bought for her behind his back. She opened the door and was surprised to see him.

"Hey, you're early, aren't you?"

"Yes, I am, a little." He pulled the flowers from behind his back and at the sight of them, her face lit up.

"Oh my God, they're gorgeous." She took the flowers and smelled them, obviously pleased.

"Thank you," she smiled and kissed him. "That was very thoughtful of you. I'm not ready yet, though; you'll have to give me a bit of time." She turned to go inside and he followed her into the room. Maria looked around for something to put the flowers in, and Ernesto realized for the first time how small the room was, with its double bed that took up most of the space and the tiny window which let in a little bit of light and the very narrow space between the bed and the wall that led to the cramped bathroom. There was barely enough room to put a bag or a suitcase down, but when he looked at Maria, humming and arranging the flowers in a small plastic garbage can that she had transformed into a makeshift flower vase for the occasion, the size of the room became unimportant, because all he could see was her and how beautiful and extraordinary she was. He went up to stand behind her and put his arms around her and kissed the back of her head.

"I love you, you know." Maria turned around and smiled.

"I love you too," she answered, and they kissed and she passed her hands through his hair and he pressed his body tightly against hers. Maria slowly pulled back from the kiss and smiled at him.

"I need to get ready now, don't I?"

"Yes, you do." He was still holding her by the waist, and she pecked his lips, then disengaged herself and slipped by him, picking up her bag from the floor and throwing it on the bed.

"So, where are we going?" She asked as she rummaged through her bag with her back to him.

"I can't say. It's a surprise."

She turned and looked at him with an inquiring expression on her face.

"A surprise?"

"Yes. I want to show you something."

"Oh yeah, what?"

"I can't say; like I said, it's a surprise."

"Well, that sounds a bit mysterious." She looked at him inquisitively, trying to read his face for a clue, but there was none.

"Look, Ernesto, if you want me to be ready, I'm going to need at least ten to fifteen minutes," she said as she resumed looking through her bag.

"Oh, ok," he answered, understanding that she wanted him to leave the room. "I'll head downstairs then and wait for you in the car," he said as he turned towards the door.

"Thank you for the flowers," she shouted over her shoulder as he walked out and closed the door behind him.

She came down ten minutes later wearing a white chiffon summer dress that she had hastily bought that afternoon and some gold-colored Roman style sandals that laced half way up her calf. The dress had thin shoulder straps and was open at the back, and the fabric was light and fluid and a touch transparent. It swayed sensuously when she walked. Her hair was tied up in a bundle and her face and eyes glowed and radiated from the new-found happiness that now resided inside her heart. She got into the car and Ernesto looked at her and smiled.

"Wow, you're so beautiful. I'm the luckiest man in the world, you know." She smiled, pleased with the compliment.

"Thank you. Now will you tell me where we are going?"

"No, not yet, but you'll find out very shortly." He started the car.

"This is all very secretive, you know."

"Yes, I know, but just be patient my love; you'll see, it'll all be fine."

"Ok, but this better be good," she added playfully.

"It will be. I promise."

It was a magnificent Miami day and the late afternoon sun was still strong, enveloping everything in its warm embrace, as the two young lovers got on their way, occasionally turning in each other's direction to exchange a complicit smile or to mimic the lyrics of a song that was playing on the radio. The warm air rushed through the open windows of the car, caressing their faces with its balmy touch as they raced along the waterways heading south, passing some massive Banyan trees that were swaying lazily in the gentle Florida breeze. They drove for nearly an hour before Ernesto finally turned off the highway in the direction of the ocean and parked. Maria looked at him inquisitively as they exited the car. He had become unusually silent as the drive had progressed and she was dying to know what all the mystery was about. He had a serious expression on his face and he said nothing as he took her hand and led her towards a stretch of beach.

When they reached the edge of the beach, Ernesto stopped and began taking off his shoes and socks.

"Please take off your sandals, Maria." She did as he asked, and when she was done they walked hand in hand and barefoot in the direction of the ocean. The beach was deserted. When they got to the water's edge, Ernesto stopped and looked out to the open sea. The water was calm and it was a beautiful day, idyllic and serene, and the sun had already started to descend on its slow trajectory towards the hidden side of the horizon. Ernesto stared at the water intently and remained silent for what seemed to Maria like a long time. Although she didn't understand what was going on, she sensed that something important was happening, and she remained respectfully silent.

"This is the place, Maria," he whispered. She turned towards him and it suddenly dawned on her where they were.

"Ernesto," she gasped incredulously, "oh my God." She put a hand over her mouth and looked at him in complete shock.

"This is where I came ashore, Maria; this is the exact spot. It was one year ago today that I swam up onto this beach. It seems so long ago now." There was a tremor in his voice when he said that, and he stared out to sea, squinting, as if he were searching for something on the horizon. She lifted his hand and kissed it tenderly, fully aware of the emotions that his presence there must be stirring up inside of him.

"It wasn't that long ago, you know, Ernesto," she said softly, "it's just that you've come a long way since then and you're a different person now."

"Yes, I guess I am." He turned towards her and looked her in the eyes.

"You know, Maria," he paused and took her other hand, "there is a reason why I wanted to come here today and it's not only because it's the anniversary of my arriving here." He paused again, "…and I know that what I'm about to ask you is going to sound crazy, but," he hesitated for a second before continuing, "…but it's something that I very much want to do and I want to do today and right here and on this spot." She looked at him perplexed as he fished into his pocket and retrieved a small red velvet pouch, and she noticed that his hand was trembling slightly. Her eyes became round with astonishment when she realized what she thought he was about to do, and she raised one of her hands and placed it in front of her mouth.

"Oh my God," she exclaimed.

He got down on one knee and opened the pouch, retrieving a small diamond ring from it, and then fumbled with the pouch and dropped it in the sand in his nervousness. He looked up and took Maria's hand and held up the small diamond ring in her direction.

"Oh my God, Ernesto." Her eyes filled up with tears. "Oh my God," she repeated, and there was a tremor in her voice and her lips trembled slightly.

"Maria Torres, I know this is very sudden and that we have only know each other a very short time, but will you marry me?" She looked at him in complete shock, tears pouring down her face. He was looking lovingly at her and her heart went out to him, but he had rendered her momentarily speechless with his surprise request and she was unable to utter a sound.

"Maria, will you marry me?" he repeated. "Will you marry me and be my wife?" There was a tinge of concern in his voice.

Maria fell to her knees in the wet sand. She was trembling and her lips were quivering, and she looked at him with tear-filled eyes and she smiled, and Ernesto knew what her answer would be and his heart soared. He felt in that instant that her smile was the most beautiful thing he had seen in his whole life.

"Oh yes, oh my God, yes, I want to marry you, Ernesto Rodriguez. I want to marry you more than anything in the world." A huge smile broke out on his face and he gently slipped the ring on her shaking finger. His eyes filled up with tears too, and he pulled her towards him and held her in his arms.

"I love you," he whispered in her ear.

"I love you, too," she answered. "Oh God, I love you." They kissed, and it was a long and passionate kiss, and the salt of their tears mixed with the sweetness of their bliss and the tenderness of their love lingered on their lips. They came apart and leaned their foreheads against each other and stayed that way for a moment, with the gentle rhythm of the wavelets lapping against their limbs and breaking the sanctity of the moment with their irreverent pitter-patter.

"Are you sure about this, Ernesto?" She whispered.

"Yes, Maria, more than sure. You are the person I want to spend the rest of my life with, as well as the next one."

She smiled. "You're crazy, you know."

"Yes, I know, I'm crazy about you." He smiled and helped her get up, and they stood facing each other.

"I didn't expect this, you know. You have made me very happy just now, more than I have ever been in all my life. I shall never forget this moment."

"And neither will I, Maria."

She looked out to the tranquil ocean, and the ruby light of the sun reflected in her eyes and illuminated them and they glistened like drops of dew in the early morning sunlight. Her face was lit up and ablaze with the glow of contentment and with the promise of fulfillment.

"It's so beautiful here," she said softly, "and this moment is so perfect, and you, and everything—I don't know what to say, Ernesto, I'm speechless."

"Sometimes there is nothing more to say, Maria," he said softly. "All I know is that this day and this place will always have a very special meaning for us now." She turned towards him and there was a radiant smile on her face.

"Yes it will, Ernesto and for the rest of our lives."

"Yes, my love, for the rest of our lives."

THE END

ABOUT THE AUTHOR

Ian Tremblay works in the entertainment business and is an avid world traveller and fishing aficionado. He studied English Literature and has self-published three other books, *Tales of Inhumanity and Retribution, Tales of Duplicity and Discontent and The Illegal and the Refugee - An American Love Story.*

Some of the individual stories of his first two books are in the process of being made available on all digital platforms.

Aisha - A Tale of Retribution, is the first, and is a story about poverty and opulence, beauty and misogyny, abuse and revenge, and of an unexpected form of triumph. If you wish to find out more about the author go to his website **www.iantremblay.com**

www.ingramcontent.com/pod-product-compliance
Lightning Source LLC
Chambersburg PA
CBHW071450170626
46811CB00007B/2532

* 9 7 8 0 9 9 3 6 3 0 7 0 5 *